Please return / renew by date shown.
You can renew it at:
norlink.norfolk.gov.uk
or by telephone: 0344 800 8006
Please have your library card & PIN ready

2 9 JAN 2011

NORFOLK LIBRARY
AND INFORMATION SERVICE

GET ME
OUT OF HERE

Also by Henry Sutton

HENRY
SUTTON

GET ME OUT OF HERE

Harvill Secker
LONDON

Published by Harvill Secker 2010

2 4 6 8 10 9 7 5 3 1

Copyright © Henry Sutton 2010

Henry Sutton has asserted his right under the Copyright, Designs and Patents Act 1988 to be identified as the author of this work

In *Get Me Out of Here* Matt Freeman expresses some highly subjective views about a variety of well-known brands and shops. These are purely a product of his imagination and state of mind and are in no way shared or endorsed by the author or publisher. This is a work of fiction

First published in Great Britain in 2010 by
HARVILL SECKER
Random House, 20 Vauxhall Bridge Road
London SW1V 2SA

www.rbooks.co.uk

Addresses for companies within The Random House Group Limited can be found at: www.randomhouse.co.uk/offices.htm

The Random House Group Limited Reg. No. 954009

A CIP catalogue record for this book is available from the British Library

ISBN 9781846552847

The Random House Group Limited supports The Forest Stewardship Council (FSC), the leading international forest certification organisation. All our titles that are printed on Greenpeace approved FSC certified paper carry the FSC logo. Our paper procurement policy can be found at www.rbooks.co.uk/environment

Mixed Sources
Product group from well-managed forests and other controlled sources
www.fsc.org Cert no. TT-COC-2139
© 1996 Forest Stewardship Council

Typeset by Palimpsest Book Production Limited, Grangemouth, Stirlingshire

Printed and bound in Great Britain by
CPI Mackays, Chatham ME5 8TD

To Rachel

Great ideology creates great times.

Kim Jong-il

ONE

Irrational Exuberance

I knew what was coming next. Jesus Christ, how I knew.

'Well, sir, I'm afraid there's nothing more I can do. It's company policy. We can replace them, or give you another model, but we can't give you a refund.'

'Why do you think I want a refund?'

'Because you are not happy with the product, sir,' she said.

'Dead right. They cost me nearly £500 and they are utterly useless. This is the third time I've been back here in three months, because they've broken, again and again. It's not my fault. It must be a design fault, at the very least.'

'As I said, sir, we're willing to put in polycarbonate lenses. These are much stronger.'

'Why didn't you do that in the first place? Or the time after that? Besides, when I initially bought them you told me you'd fit them with the toughest lenses known to man. I said I needed a strong, reliable pair of glasses, I do a lot of travelling, often to extreme and dangerous places. I can't just pop into Canary Wharf every ten minutes. Do you think they have a David Clulow in Kabul, or in Baghdad, or in fucking Pyongyang? How often have I had to come back here already? This is wasting a huge amount of my time, and money. You've got no idea how busy I am.'

'I'm very sorry.'

She was quite pretty – darkish, long, straight hair tied back, with a good figure, neatly tucked into a rather demure, patterned blouse and tight black trousers. A uniform of sorts or she was still under strict parental guidance. Perhaps there was a devout spouse. Already? I wanted to shake some sense into her, if not life – before it was too late. 'I just haven't got time for this. I want a refund. Now.'

'I can have another word with the regional manager.'

'Fine. Speak to whoever you have to. But I want a refund.'

As she walked back over to the phone, I continued to search the fiddly, hopelessly fragile display racks for a pair that might do instead. I picked up frames by Oliver Peoples, Alain Mikli, Prada, Tom Ford, Philippe Starck – I hated Philippe Starck, out of principle, anyone who tried that hard to make a statement – Giorgio Armani and Paul Smith. Oh dear, what'd happened to poor old Paul Smith of late – too successful? Resting on his laurels? Simply relying on past performance? Didn't I know how that scenario could develop.

I had seen all these frames before of course and the only ones that I thought might be OK, by Tom Ford – now there was a brand on the make – were far too similar to the pair I was currently wearing. What I wanted was a pair like the ones that had just broken the third time and destroyed my trust. These were by Lindberg – Danish, titanium, hypoallergenic, weighing just 2.5 grams or something ludicrous. I needed them as a second pair, a spare pair, to the pair I was wearing now, which I thought of as a more fashionable pair. These were Oliver Peoples – plastic, tortoiseshell effect, with neat silver bits at the tips of the arms. They weren't very comfortable, especially in hot weather, because they made my nose sweaty and slid about even more than usual. And they were virtually impossible to wear playing tennis, or doing anything remotely physical, because they didn't just steam up and slide about but could fall off too. So I'd plumped for the Lindberg rimless, which probably were the most expensive pair of glasses in the shop, but fuck it, with their special, hypoallergenic silicon nose and ear pads, creating an almost perfect fit, at least a secure fit, I wondered how I could go wrong. As usual I wanted the best. Pay the most and look what you got – rotten lenses, or a crappy frame that cracked perfectly good lenses.

I couldn't fly off somewhere, and who knew where that might be, comfortable in the knowledge that I could rely on those rimless. I always travelled with two pairs of glasses in case a pair broke. Obviously my Oliver Peoples were going to be hopelessly inadequate as an all-round pair. I wouldn't even be able to have a gentle knockabout.

She eventually came back, this demure babe, with the bland smile. 'As compensation, the manager says he'll fix your glasses with the polycarbonate lenses, obviously at no extra charge and we'll give you another pair of glasses, complete with lenses, for free.'

'Right.' I wasn't expecting this.

'We're very sorry, but is that acceptable?'

'I guess so.' What could I say? I didn't want yet another pair of glasses. I had drawers full of them at home. But I wasn't so keen on the pair I was wearing, my supposedly fashionable pair, and not just because they weren't so practical. The tortoiseshell effect was actually more solid brown than tortoiseshell – clearly not enough attention had been paid in the production – and too dark for my pale complexion and however much I had them adjusted they were still slightly wonky set against my eyebrows. I hated that, how they sat there on the slant. And I didn't think they were the best-made pair of glasses I'd ever had by any stretch, whether they were Oliver Peoples and supposedly made in Japan or not. The plastic composition seemed too soft and they sort of squeaked oddly when I bent them however lightly, plus the hinges were certainly nothing special, let alone built to last. I was a stickler for detail. And quality.

Also I wasn't at all sure about the Lindberg rimless pair either – the ones apparently they were going properly to fix at last. They were just a bit too angular, a bit too Danish. They made me look like a fucking architect – one of those architects who wore crisp white, collarless shirts done up to the very top button. And whenever I had occasionally popped them on I couldn't stop taking them off again and fiddling with the special silicon nose pads. One pad wasn't quite in line, despite the fact that the glasses looked straight enough on, and so I didn't trust this pad, this arrangement not to get worse, when I was God knows where. At least I was overly aware of the problem, of being caught out, but obviously it made me feel even more uneasy and insecure about the glasses in general.

Oh, they were far from perfect. And who the hell was Lindberg anyway? Sounded more like a footballer than an architect. Frankly I was pleased when they broke this morning. I desperately wanted something different. More specifically I needed a refund so I could buy a pair I'd already spotted in Roger Pope, in New Cavendish Street, while I was in that part of town on business the other day. How I loved Marylebone. The money, the discretion.

These were by Lindberg too, but they were a titanium and plastic, or rather acetate mix, from a line they didn't seem to stock in David Clulow, and much more like my trendy Oliver Peoples pair. They looked fat and stylish enough, but appeared to have the practical and comfort factors I craved also. I could travel with these and play tennis with them, and go to meetings and for drinks and openings and dinners and parties. I could probably fuck in them. In short I felt I could happily live with them and very quickly I couldn't get them out of my head and became more and more convinced that they were exactly what I wanted, and not the Lindberg rimless pair I'd already and rather rashly purchased, from a high-street chain in a mall too, which was why, when I was fiddling with them this morning, I possibly bent an arm back with more force than was strictly necessary. Though the lens did snap very easily. It could have happened when I was away, or at a meeting, or playing tennis. Who knows when and who knows at what inconvenience.

However, the poor young sales assistant and her regional manager, not to mention David Clulow, whoever he was – and I wasn't even going to waste time and effort referring to him obviously and crassly as Clueless except I couldn't now get that word out of my mind – had ruined that plan. Suddenly I not only had to choose another pair, from a selection I'd already pored over for really quite a long time that morning and countless times before, but would have to wait days, if not weeks before I got the rimless pair back with their supposedly indestructible polycarbonate lenses. However, I was certain that I could break them. Indeed I knew I would break them, if I was not suddenly overcome with a newfound passion for them, and couldn't find a remotely decent free pair right now, and still fancied having those plastic and titanium glasses from Roger Pope. Now there was a fine name, devoid of blatant soccer overtones and not easily lending itself to cheap amendment – more than suitable for an upmarket opticians.

Wondering what sort of bra she was wearing under that horribly frumpy top, if indeed she was wearing a bra and was not sporting some elaborately entwined religious cloth, I said, 'I'm only agreeing to this on the condition that if they break again I get an instant refund, regardless of whether you give me a free pair or not.'

She smiled and nodded but didn't verbally confirm any such thing. What could I do? I eventually chose another pair – I didn't even want to think about them until I had to pick them up, which wouldn't be until at least Monday, though apparently that would be a week sooner than I could expect the Lindberg rimless to be ready. Those fucking polycarbonate lenses had to be specially ordered from somewhere or other and because of the severity of my astigmatism they weren't a standard order anyway, which was only going to add to the delay.

Due to the severity of my astigmatism I'd always stuck with glasses and hadn't switched to contacts, which I was sure would have saved considerable time and effort, not to mention a huge amount of money over the years. I'd heard that you could now get contact lenses for my prescription, but they were hard ones, or weekly ones or whatever, and could I be bothered with all the cleaning paraphernalia that they would entail? No. Especially as I did so much travelling, to all these out of the way and underdeveloped places, and I knew that if you were prone to eye infections contact lenses only exacerbated the problem. Bobbie was always having eye infections and resorting to wearing her truly hideous glasses, which she'd had for years and were falling to bits too. But she hung on to them because she insisted that she was really a contact-lens wearer, the glasses were only for emergencies or first thing in the morning, even though she spent most of her fucking life in them. What would I do if I were in Kazakhstan, or say in Sierra Leone and developed an eye infection? Would I get decent medical attention out there? Not likely. Some secondary infection would probably develop and before I knew it I'd be blind, or worse. I could just imagine some particularly nasty bacteria working its way from my eye socket to my brain – it wasn't so very far. Even if I was in New York or Tokyo it could prove to be a major problem, certainly a very expensive one. Did I have adequate medical insurance? Did anyone?

Plus I'd grown quite fond of wearing glasses. Being bald – well not bald exactly but thinning, prematurely, and chronically to be honest, and shaved what hair I did have to a number one – I'd found that glasses gave my face structure and depth. And colour. They suited me, especially the heavier, plastic frames, as long as they weren't too heavy or dark. I really didn't know why I'd bought the rimless. Well I did, because they were supposedly the best on the market, the lightest and strongest etcetera, etcetera, but I probably always knew they would never work out. What a complete waste of time, again, and money, unless I got the refund. But if I got the refund I'd definitely buy the other pair from Roger Pope. Though I'd probably buy those anyway – who could resist that outlet? I didn't like to think about how many pairs of glasses I'd then have, even though I'd only recently mangled and binned a couple of old pairs to make more space for the bloody Lindberg rimless. I couldn't stand clutter, or having a home full of unnecessary items. Everything had to be perfectly wearable or usable, utterly reliable and of course of the very highest quality. And stylish.

Leaving David Clulow and stepping straight into the heaving mass of Canary Wharf at lunchtime, or to be specific where the east and the west malls met at Cabot Place – the shockingly bright, subterranean commercial epicentre – was almost the last straw. I was not in the mood for it, which was why I somehow found myself wandering around Gap, escaping the crowd. I tried on three pairs of trousers I knew I didn't like and knew wouldn't fit, because Gap trousers never fitted me. Part of me always thought I'd find a bargain in a chain like Gap – what was the point in spending £180 on a pair of trousers from Paul Smith or Margaret Howell, say, which frankly weren't always the best made in the world, when you could buy a pair of cords from Gap for £30? Until in the dressing room. Aside from the fact that none of the trousers remotely fitted me, and I'm an easy size, a simple 32 32, or maybe more like a 32 33, the colours were all slightly odd – why couldn't they make a chocolate brown a chocolate brown, instead of some browny purple colour, or a dark grey a dark grey without any hint of blue? – plus they were made by Gap, or rather teams of sparely paid South East Asians, or Eastern Europeans, or North Africans, or Mexicans. Whoever, but certainly not by experienced, gentlemen's tailors.

I wasn't going to be seen dead in a pair of Gap trousers, but I was increasingly coming round to the idea of not being financially squeezed by more exclusive designer brands, such as, and I suddenly couldn't get them out of my head, Paul Smith or Margaret Howell, and was valiantly trying to stick up for places like Gap, especially in these fiscally restrained times. I wasn't a boutique snob. But the quality was simply not there, not that places like Paul Smith or Margaret Howell were as good as they once were. Nothing was.

Bobbie rang as I was stepping back onto the concourse. How I hated that concourse. It wasn't just the luminous artificial light, the cheap marble flooring, the ubiquitous second-rate stores, the overweight office workers shuffling from outlet to outlet while stuffing their faces with foul-smelling Wotsits – why did everyone have to snack all the time, mostly the obese? No, it certainly wasn't just the density of the crowd, nor the unimaginative decor. It was the stink of hollow money. There was nothing remotely discreet. Or particularly real. This, all this, amid a growing global recession. Give me muted Marylebone any day. Or

Mayfair. I could take wealth, even extreme wealth, if it had a bit of class, and beauty.

'Hi,' she said, 'just wondering what you are up to.'

'I'm really busy. This is not a good time. I've had a terrible morning. One meeting after another. And now I'm late for a lunch. Really late. With a complete jerk as well.'

'Oh, honey, I'm sorry.'

'It's OK. Look, I'm sorry for sounding stressed. It's just this new business plan is getting to me. It's so bloody complicated, and crucial. But once it's over, things will be a lot easier.'

'How about I come round and cook you supper? I'll call in at M&S on the way. Or we could get a takeaway. Or go out, but the TV's quite good, and I wouldn't mind having an early night and just chilling.'

I thought of my apartment, suddenly remembering what had happened there yesterday. 'I can come to you.'

'Really?'

'Yeah, it's fine. I'll need to get out by then. You should see what I've got to do at my desk this afternoon, after this fucking lunch. So many people want to be in on this venture. I should be grateful in this climate. But I'm completely snowed under.' I removed my phone from my ear and wiped my forehead with my sleeve. As usual the mall was bringing me out in a cold, air-conditioned sweat. 'I'm the victim of my own success,' I said, clamping the thing to my head again and sighing.

'I'm sorry, honey.'

I wished she wouldn't say that.

'I'll make everything all right.'

'Yeah.' I pushed the end call button, and stomped over to Waitrose.

What a day. It felt like the end of the world, not a mild, early evening in November. But I had to keep reminding myself that comfort, or at least Bobbie, still awaited. However, I wasn't there yet, and I knew that the slightest thing would set me off. I simply didn't need any more hassle. But of course I wasn't able to determine how smoothly things went from now on. What I increasingly hated about London, perhaps what I'd always hated, was how the smallest, most inconsequential things could suddenly flare up. And I wasn't thinking of the weather, but how so many seemingly mundane, pathetic little events and incidents – not to mention the more elaborate goings-on and out-and-out threats and catastrophes in the making – could so easily conspire against you. It was virtually impossible to get around, to simply exist in this town without being fucked about by somebody, either through incompetence or maliciousness. Because obviously it wasn't just the machinery failing – gadgets, systems, signals screwing up, endlessly – but the idiots behind it. Not to mention activists and terrorists, and petty bureaucrats from Health and Safety adding to the mayhem. What exactly, I wondered time and time again, were Londoners so fucking proud of? Putting up with it all? Perseverance? To be a Londoner. Big deal.

Of course I was going to drive, though I hated driving, especially at night, what with my astigmatism and love of fine wines – and fear of marauding gangs – but the offside rear tyre was flat. It shouldn't have been flat – a relatively new tyre, a top of the range Michelin, with an eco tread designed to save the planet. I didn't remember kerbing the car the last time I'd driven the thing, not that I was particularly car proud or attentive and cautious when it came to manoeuvring in tight spots. There were many other things to be concerned about, in this environment, if you ever wanted to get anywhere. On closer inspection the tyre actually looked slashed, or rather stabbed. Who the hell would do that?

Surprised with how calmly I was taking it, given all that had recently happened, though it was only my despised vehicle, a brand and defunct model so embarrassing I'd often contemplated mutilating, I began walking to Moorgate Tube as I was parked vaguely in that direction, and I needed to get on the Northern Line. At least I thought it would be quicker in the long run than going back to Barbican Tube.

It wasn't – Moorgate was shut, apparently due to a body under a train. Not a Northern Line train, but a Hammersmith & City, which must have taken some suicidal planning, or a particularly opportunistic pusher, given the reliability of that line. Still, was it necessary to shut the station? It had recently happened, so I was eventually informed, or rather so I overheard, which might have explained the numbers of police and paramedics, and the few London Transport officials. Though frankly they didn't seem to be doing much, except chatting amongst themselves at the half-shuttered entrance. The thin crowd of resigned commuters and passers-by was slowly dispersing.

I could have walked on to Bank, but I was more than aware it was getting late and I hated the Tube at the best of times, plus it was beginning to drizzle. I was pleased for an excuse to take a taxi though not at all happy at the prospect of paying some outrageous fare. Amazingly a cab materialised just as I was thinking I wouldn't be able to find one, given the weather and the problem at Moorgate and who knew what else, so I hastily climbed in, ignoring the stench of sweat and cheap perfume – who had just been in here, and doing what? – sat back and watched the rest of the City crawl by. Rain smudged the windows and the streetlights stretched into long, bleary lines. Finally crossing the Thames, the windows steamed up completely.

According to *London Tonight*, we were in the middle of a particularly mild and muggy spell. It was meant to be late autumn, but didn't feel like it. It felt like it always did. Cocooned in the back of the fetid cab, I sent a text. *Car fucked. Tube fucked. Body on the line! In smelly cab. But stuck in traffic. There shortly? x.* I knew I wouldn't be but at least the cabbie wasn't trying to talk to me. He was listening to Radio 5 Live, loudly. It was Arsenal versus Luton, a Carling Cup game. I hoped Luton won, but not enough to want to listen.

There was little point asking him to turn it down, judging from past experience, so I tried to ignore the tiresome racket – sports commentators, honestly – as south London snarled up. He was taking a very odd route – we were passing the vast council blocks of Loughborough Junction, or maybe we were just off the South Lambeth Road, in deepest Stockwell – but I didn't say anything. I must have been more exhausted than I imagined.

It cost me £29.80 to get to Bobbie's. Out on the sodden pavement I handed him £30 through the window, properly noticing his amazing gut. How he'd managed to drive his cab, especially on such a circuitous route, I had no idea. He appeared to have been poured behind the wheel. I told him to keep the change. Why Bobbie, or indeed anyone, would choose to live in this far corner of Clapham I had no idea. It was almost Wandsworth. Perhaps it was. Bobbie always referred to it as Battersea Rise, or just the Rise. As far as I was concerned it certainly wasn't Battersea. Battersea was miles closer in.

As usual I'd got the cab to drop me a street or so away from her place. I never liked to reveal my exact destination to anyone, especially cab drivers, however fat and obviously incapable of pursuit on foot. It was still drizzling and horribly mild and passing the rows of compact terraces, curtained for the night, I couldn't help thinking that it wasn't that easy to shut yourself off from the world and enjoy an evening at home with your loved ones. Plenty had told me as much.

Bobbie had a maisonette on the top two floors of a small

Victorian house, which should never have been turned into flats. Nothing fitted properly, everything was flimsy and the sound insulation, particularly on the first floor, was virtually non-existent. I still didn't have my own set of keys and her buzzer wasn't working so I had to call her on the mobile to tell her I was finally here.

She took ages to answer. 'Matt, where the hell have you been?' I could hear the TV in the background.

'Didn't you get my text?'

'Yeah, but that was ages ago.'

'I've had the most terrible fucking journey. You wouldn't believe it.' I was waiting for her to say 'I'm sorry, honey', but she didn't. 'Aren't you going to let me in?' Eventually the first-floor sitting-room window opened, Bobbie appeared, waved briefly, and dropped me the keys. I failed to catch them, and had to root around in the dirt by the overflowing wheelie bins to find them. The bins stank of fish. What sort of refuse collection service did they have in Wandsworth anyway? I guessed that that was what you got for not paying any council tax. Served them right. Though at least Bobbie didn't live in Lambeth, where, as I knew all too well, residents didn't only have to pay record council tax, but had to put up with even worse public services, and crime. I'd found myself living in Lambeth once – albeit briefly. I was mugged twice, at knifepoint. Sometimes I wished they'd managed to stab me in the heart, at the very least between the ribs, rupturing my lungs. They seemed so much more accurate nowadays.

Having dropped me the keys Bobbie must have rushed back to the TV not bothering to unlock the door to her flat as she normally did. However, standing in that dismal first-floor corridor, I remembered that I hadn't bothered to bring any wine. She took ages again to haul her arse off the sofa and to walk the few small steps to the door. It might have been a maisonette but her flat was tiny. Fortunately her flat-mate was in America.

'Hi,' she said, barely glancing at me before rushing back to the sofa and *I'm A Celebrity . . . Get Me Out Of Here!*

I walked over to the walk-in kitchen. A saucepan with a few clearly drying parcels of Sainsbury's Taste the Difference Slow-cooked Pumpkin Ravioli sat on the dirty hob. She'd been eating the pumpkin ravioli solidly for months.

'I'm sorry, honey,' she shouted, not taking her eyes off the TV, 'I couldn't wait, I was starving. You don't mind do you?'

'Is there any wine?'

'Gabriella's probably got some. Try her cupboard. We can replace it.'

We never did. I bent down and looked in Gabriella's cupboard. It was stuffed with grimy tins and packets and jars and right at the back was a bottle of wine. An Australian Chardonnay, probably my least favourite wine of all time, but there was nothing else and even though it was above room temperature, because it had been stuck next to a central heating pipe, I unscrewed the top. 'Want some?'

'No, I'm fine, thanks.'

Lucky you. I poured myself a large glass, forked a couple of the cold, stiff ravioli into my mouth and walked over to the sofa. Bobbie was almost prone, taking up the whole length. 'Do you want me to sit on the floor?' The pasta was disgusting. Bobbie didn't answer. To take the Taste the Difference taste away I took a huge glug of wine. It was the sickliest, warmest Chardonnay I'd ever had the misfortune of having to drink and I just knew it was going to give me a terrible headache. She eventually budged up a bit and I sat down, wondering when she was going to make everything all right. I couldn't watch the TV so I watched her watching it.

She kept smiling and chortling quietly and saying, 'Urrgh', and 'Gross', and 'I can't stand that woman', and 'Why would anyone want to do that?', and 'Urrgh no, they've really gone too far this year', and 'I love him, I'm going to vote for him. Look at his chest. Fit or what?'

If she hadn't been so exceptionally pretty I'd have left by now. She was simply gorgeous, even when she was engrossed in some tired reality TV show. She was still wearing her work clothes – a tight dark skirt and thin, baby blue polo neck, with patterned, light pink tights. She went for bright colour co-ordinations, said it was in this season – and she would have known – but for someone who was so careful about her appearance she was remarkably careless about her clothes. She never hung them up properly, choosing instead to leave them where they fell. The bathroom floor was awash with them, along with dirty, damp towels. I had no idea how she managed to look so smart and not remotely crumpled, or skanky.

She had straight, thick dark brown hair, dyed a little darker than it was naturally and cut into a severe, lopsided bob. She had greeny blue eyes and pale skin and usually wore dark red lipstick, but it had rubbed off, possibly when she'd toyed with her ravioli, or more likely long before that when she was sipping one of her endless mochas. Certainly she had not bothered to replace it for my benefit. I started to stroke her leg. She had long legs and thin ankles and long flat feet. Her feet were her worst feature – look hard enough and obviously you'll find faults – but I never paid them as much attention as she did. Compared to my previous girlfriends she was in a different league.

My fingers were stroking her right calf, and working their way to the back of her knee and up the inside of her thigh. Her short, tight skirt was no hindrance at all, because her legs were slightly parted and her skirt was riding high – she was always so very casual with her limbs, her poise. It was hard to tell when she was being suggestive or lazy. Maybe

15

she could have been a model, which was what she told anyone who was interested, despite her feet – or perhaps because of them – and this was what I was thinking about, generously, given that I was shoved into the far corner of the sofa with a glass of warm Chardonnay in one hand. With my other hand I was reaching for the hot patch right between her legs. I didn't give a shit about Ant and Dec and didn't think she should either. I was suddenly feeling very randy. Funny how a crap day can do that.

'Matt, I'm watching TV.' She pushed my hand away and made an attempt to close her legs tight and pull them up into her. This was new. Normally she'd let me caress her whether she was interested or not.

'What's up with you?'

'You.' She hadn't taken her eyes off the TV.

'What have I done wrong?'

'Where do I begin?' She glanced at me, briefly. 'You turn up here two hours late, pissed and start groping me.'

'What do you mean pissed? I'm not pissed.'

'You reek of alcohol.'

'I had a glass of wine with lunch, that's it. It would have been rude not to. You should have seen how much this guy drank. Business still revolves around being social and accommodating, however much you might loathe whoever you're meeting, which also means occasionally having to drink when you really don't want to – the sort of people-orientated business I'm involved in anyway.'

'I'm glad you're working with such conscientious, sober people.'

How could she say this, given her professional role? But she never saw reason. 'I would have been here hours ago, but it's not my fault my car had been vandalised and someone jumped in front of the Tube, and then the bloody cab driver went some completely ludicrous route.'

'You could have directed him. You usually do.'

'It was raining so as usual the traffic was horrendous. Plus you should have seen how fat this guy was, he could barely turn the wheel. I didn't think it was appropriate to make it any more uncomfortable for him.'

'That's very decent of you.'

'As it was it cost me a fortune. For what? I don't know why I've bothered to come over.'

'Neither do I.'

I leapt up and stepped over to the kitchenette and refilled my glass. 'Bobbie, I've had an extremely stressful day.' I knew I should have left right then. But something pulled me back.

'And I haven't?'

'I doubt it somehow.' She claimed she worked in fashion PR, organising events. As far as I could tell all she had to do was sit around looking good, send the odd email, aside, of course, from attend endless parties and functions, where she invariably drank too much cheap bubbly before making a fool of herself. How glad I was that the fashion industry wasn't exactly crawling with alpha males. But maybe I was wrong.

'You only ever think you're the one who's worked off their feet. That really pisses me off, Matt. With you it's always "me, me, me". "Oh, I'm so busy, you wouldn't understand. Poor me. It's not my fault but his fault or her fault or the weather's fault." Pathetic. It's always someone else's fault. And you never ever think about anyone apart from yourself. Unless you're after something. You're nothing but a leech.'

'A leech?' Where had she got that idea? Oh, Ant and Dec and yet another ridiculous task. I wasn't going to inform her that actually leeches had numerous beneficial uses, especially when it came to bloodletting. What was the point?

'Why do you watch that shit?'

'It's my TV, I'll watch what I want.'

'I thought it was Gabriella's TV. I didn't think you had a TV.'

'Don't be an arsehole.'

I didn't know what had got into Bobbie. I had never known her to be so aggressive. 'Perhaps we should start the evening again.' I took a slurp of wine, and immediately wished I hadn't. 'Hello Bobbie, how are you? Good day at the office? Lovely to see you.' I walked back to her, bent down and kissed her on her lovely pale cheek. She was trying to ignore me so I kissed her on the lips, but she wasn't reciprocating. Not in the least. Ant and Dec had her full attention. 'Thanks for cooking me supper, it would have been delicious, I'm sure, had someone not slashed my tyre and then someone else not decided to jump in front of the Tube – unless, it occurred to me, it was the same person – 'and it had not been raining and my cab driver not so hugely fat and incompetent. My fault, as if. I tried my best to get here as quickly as possible. I really did, just as you tried your best to cook me a great meal.' Had I gone too far? 'I was defeated, simple as that, by this fucking city.'

Leaning back in the sofa, but making sure I didn't get too close – I didn't want her to get the wrong idea again – I realised how exhausted I was. It was like being hit by a tidal wave of jet lag. I wanted comforting. 'Bobbie, I'm sorry. I'm shattered. I've had a truly terrible day. You think I had some boozy lunch with this potential business partner, well it wasn't like that at all. It was hell. Trying to impress and persuade a complete idiot. And who got landed with the bill? Plus you want to know what happened first? This morning? My new glasses broke. Can you believe it? Things just went from bad to worse.'

'Which ones?' She was still glued to the TV, but my mentioning an accessory had attracted some attention.

'You know, my rimless ones. Those supposedly indestructible, titanium Lindberg glasses.' I proceeded to tell her the
whole saga.

'So you get a new pair for being a pain in the butt?' she
said, that stupid, chirpy signature music of *I'm A Celebrity*
. . . playing in the background. It was over at last, at least
for another night.

'The trouble those things have caused me, that was the
least they could do.'

'I thought you didn't like them anyway.'

'That's not the point.'

'I like the ones you've got on. I never saw what was wrong
with those.'

Finally I had her full attention. She was facing me, legs
akimbo, the outline of her knickers just visible in the crotch
of her tights. In the early days we used to have sex on the
sofa. We'd be watching TV, or she would anyway, and
suddenly we'd start kissing and cuddling and the next thing
I'd be ripping off her underwear, with the sofa not exactly
providing the right sort of support in the right places – it
was an ancient Habitat model – but she was young and
athletic and just as keen as I was. Amazingly Gabriella never
caught us at it, but the people downstairs once banged on
their ceiling. We weren't sure whether that was because we
had the TV up so loud, or whether our lovemaking was rever-
berating around the house. Also, those were the days when
Bobbie put on something of a performance when she came.
She barely made a squeak nowadays. 'That's just as well,' I
said, crossly, 'because the pair they're giving me are almost
identical.'

'Yeah? That's a shame. You should have gone for a bigger,
more obvious pair. I know the ones you are wearing now are
big compared with some of your others, but big, retro big is
really in. You know how sunglasses have got so much bigger,

well glasses glasses are going the same way, finally. It's part of the whole nerdy geek thing. Geek is cool.'

If anyone would know, I supposed, it would be Bobbie. But I couldn't believe this. I'd just spent all morning in David Clulow trying to rectify a mistake, only to be told, and by my very significant other, that I'd made a further mistake by not ordering a pair of nerdy, geeky outsized frames. I wasn't sure I'd even seen any in the store. 'I don't want to look like a fucking geek.' I leapt up, again.

'Fine, look like a middle-aged loser.'

This was obviously a very sore point. As far as Bobbie knew I was thirty-three. She was definitely twenty-four. Of course I was fortunate to be with someone so young and beautiful. But she wasn't the brightest girlfriend I'd ever had and I definitely wasn't exactly a loser. I'd had a good position in a global corporation and now ran my own business. OK, it was a start-up, but I was getting somewhere with it, in troubled times too. I had a mid-century modern flat in the Barbican, near the Barbican anyway. I had a wide circle of interesting and successful friends. I had no dependants, no complicated ties. I was not a loser. As my mother might once have said, I was quite a catch. 'What's wrong with you tonight?'

'Nothing.' She got off the sofa and rushed upstairs, slamming the bathroom door behind her.

I didn't follow immediately but went back to the kitchenette and refilled my glass. I'd reached the end of the bottle already and knew there wouldn't be anymore. I sunk the wine and threw the glass into the sink. I didn't mean for it to break but it did. Who knew how cheaply it had been manufactured and from which crappy outlet it had been purchased? I doubted it had even borne the IKEA stamp of quality. It hadn't been made to last. Nothing was anymore.

I looked at the photos and takeaway menus stuck to the fridge with a collection of faded and dusty fridge magnets.

I had never understood the appeal of fridge magnets, and it baffled me as to where people bought them. Most of these were trying to be mini items of food such as burgers or hot dogs or bananas or slices of pizza and failing abysmally, as those things always did, while the other magnets were meant to be items of clothes, which were designed to be stuck in some humorous order on either a male or female master outline. Except neither Bobbie nor Gabriella had bothered to do this so I tried to dress the man as a woman and the woman as a man but bits kept falling off, along with the pieces of paper and photos and fliers they had originally been supporting. I kicked the lot under the bottom of the fridge and headed upstairs. The bathroom door was locked and pressing my ear to the sticky surface I could hear running water and sobbing. I rattled the handle but it wouldn't give.

'Bobbie, let me in.' She didn't answer. 'Bobbie, come on, let me in.' I rattled the handle some more and banged on the door also. I could have pushed the door in if I'd wanted. The door and the frame were not original, having been poorly flung up when the house had been converted into flats. 'For God's sake, what's the matter?'

'You,' she shouted.

'Me? What have I done?'

'I can't take it anymore.' She could barely get the words out.

'What? I don't understand.'

'You. I can't take you anymore. You're impossible. You're too much.' She was sounding clearer, more confident, more sure of herself, more certain. 'I want you to go away. I don't want to see you again. I've had enough.'

'Wait a minute. Just wait a minute. What the hell are you saying?' I was banging on the door with some force now. Maybe it wasn't so flimsy.

'Go, Matt. It's over. I don't want to see you anymore.'

'Just because I bought the wrong pair of glasses?' Suddenly nothing made sense. I was being dumped because I wore the wrong fucking spectacles?

'What is the matter with you?'

'What is the matter with me? What is wrong with you more like. Let me in.'

'Matt, I don't want to see you again. It's over. Leave me alone.' She was shouting again.

'Why are you having a bath?' The water was still running. She never had baths at night. She washed in the mornings, if at all. Then it hit me. 'You've been seeing someone else, haven't you? I'd understand, I would Bobbie, but just tell me. I need to know the truth.' She wanted to wash all traces of him off her before I'd worked out what had been going on for myself, courtesy of his sweat and semen and stray pubic hair and who knows what else she might have picked up – crabs, lice, genital warts, herpes, chlamydia, AIDS? Except I'd rumbled her. She must have seen him at lunchtime, which was why she had called me, when I was at Canary Wharf. She was checking where I was. Checking I was well out of her way. Because she rarely called me during the day. Where the hell had she gone with this guy? Quickly back to his place? Did he live in west London, near her offices? Some Notting Hill type – I could just picture him. The skinny jeans, the trench coat, the hat, the cash. Or central London? Was he a West End boy? A City boy, God forbid? He couldn't have lived more centrally than I did. No one did.

'Of course I haven't been seeing anyone. Apart from work and you breathing down my neck every five minutes, when would I have time to do that?' She was clearly watching what she said. She must have realised that she had to be extremely careful. One slip and I'd have extra proof. It was almost proof enough, her talking like this.

'Right, so now you're suddenly rushed off your feet at work. You're always telling me you don't have enough to do.' I shouldn't have gone to Canary Wharf at all today, and gone to Notting Hill instead. That's what I often did at lunchtimes or early evenings. Not always to meet Bobbie but to be in the vicinity in case she had a free moment, or in case I accidentally bumped into her. Those fucking glasses. David Clulow was going to pay for this. I hadn't finished with them by any means. 'Open the door, Bobbie, let's talk about this properly, face to face. We're both grown-ups.'

'You're not.' She was shouting again. 'You're the most immature man I've ever met. You're a complete child.'

'So one minute I'm a middle-aged loser and the next I'm a kid.' I left the dingy corridor with its horrible woodchip wallpaper, painted magnolia years ago, and the worn, fawn carpet and stomped into Bobbie's bedroom. It was at the back of the house, and the quietest bit of the flat, bearing the original configuration of walls, and least prone to neighbour noise. Still the floorboards shook as I went over to her chest of drawers. I opened the top drawer, her underwear drawer, and started throwing the contents onto the bed. I didn't know what I was looking for but was sure I would know it when I saw it. I recognised all the underwear and the tights and loose socks and hairbands and scraps of paper and old receipts. What a mess. It wasn't of course the first time I'd had a good look in there. I slammed the drawer shut and started going through the drawer below. This was her T-shirt and jumper drawer and it didn't take me long to find nothing of note in there either.

'What are you doing, Matt? Get out of my bedroom. I can hear you.' Bobbie was shouting from the bathroom.

If she wasn't going to have the decency to unlock the door and confront me face to face, especially given what she had done – oh, the betrayal – I wasn't going to stop what I was doing. She was hiding something in her room all right. I looked under the bed and flung open her wardrobe and pulled her dresses off the rack and chucked them on the bed too, some came with their hangers and some came without. And some came free with a faint ripping noise. How absurdly delicate were these things? How weakly constructed? And considering how much they must have cost, even with the hefty discounts Bobbie got – because supposedly she was in the fashion business. What a joke.

She had so many pairs of shoes and most were almost identical. Manolo Blahnik, Jimmy Choo, Prada, Christian Louboutin, it made little difference what luxury brand. I'd never quite realised. She might have thought I had many similar pairs of spectacles but what about her shoes? I threw them around the room, some landing in that horrible corridor. What's more, I couldn't understand how she could spend so much money on shoes, even if she got them at hugely discounted prices, and not give a shit about the state of her accommodation. Even a paint job would have made a difference. One shoe smashed into her bedroom window, but the drawn curtain probably stopped it from cracking the glass. I had an incredible urge to damage not just her stuff but the place as well. What a shit hole.

Finally, at the back of the bottom of the wardrobe, I found what I was looking for – a shoebox, an Agent Provocateur shoebox of all things, stuffed with letters and photos and other highly incriminating mementoes. I couldn't believe I hadn't found this before. She must have recently moved it from somewhere else. Why? To add more stuff?

'I've got it,' I shouted. 'You liar. You coward. Try and get out of this one.'

'What are you talking about? You've got what?' Her voice, though muffled, betrayed clear anxiety.

'Your little cache of love notes and photos, etcetera, etcetera.'

'You've got what?'

'All your secrets, hidden in the Agent Provocateur shoebox.' I didn't even know Agent Provocateur did shoes. How out of touch was I? 'Not exactly a coincidence they're in there, is it? Who bought those for you? Your lover? What is he, one of those foot fetishists? Into high heels, is he? Into pain, is he? Does he make you walk all over him?' Like you walk all over me, I thought.

She was out of the bathroom and grabbing for the box before I knew what was happening.

'Let go. It's private,' she screamed.

'I bet it is.'

'It's nothing to do with you. Get off it.'

She was still fully dressed, despite having been running that bath, and frantically cleansing herself, or whatever it was she was doing in there, and with one hand I managed to grab a chunk of her baby blue polo neck and pull her away from me and the box. However, she instantly fought back and was pulling at my jumper, which happened to be a relatively new, black V-neck Smedley. I could feel her nails catching on the fine, merino wool. She certainly knew how to fight dirty.

'Get off it, Matt. It's private.'

'So you keep saying. What have you got to hide?'

'Nothing. It's all from ages ago. It's not really about me anyway. You wouldn't understand.' She was crying hysterically. 'Give it back, give it back now.'

'No. You don't have secrets from me.' I had the lid off and was trying to read what I could but it was almost impossible with her still pulling and scratching me and fighting for the box. She wasn't going to get it. 'I can't believe you betrayed me in this way. How could you?'

'I haven't,' she wailed. 'What are you talking about? I haven't betrayed you. I haven't been seeing anyone else. If only. You're insane. Give me back my things. You don't understand how important they are.'

'Oh yes I do.' She wouldn't stop fighting so I found myself pushing her further against the wall, to try simply to contain her wild limbs and nails and teeth, and to stop her from being so hysterical. I had to let go of the box but managed to stop everything spilling out as it dropped to the floor with a thud. There was so much material in there. I kicked it further away.

'Get off me, Matt, you're hurting me.'

I wasn't hurting her but containing her.

'Get off, you're scaring me. I can't breathe.'

I just wanted her to calm down and be reasonable and to tell me, face to face, that she had betrayed me. We could have worked something out. But I had to get her to be still first. It was taking so much force. For someone so slight she was no weakling. She caught my glasses with her chin somehow, hard. They went spinning, hitting the chest of drawers and landing in the corner, by her wicker bedroom bin, which was overflowing as usual with soiled cotton-wool balls and empty make-up tubes and compacts, and used condom wrappers for all I knew — I wondered what brand he favoured, what particular product line. Elite? Fetherlite? Sensation? Comfort XL? One arm of my glasses was looking weirdly bent. I couldn't see whether she'd cracked a lens. Obviously I still wasn't applying enough pressure. 'Now look what you've done. You've broken my glasses.'

'I can't breathe,' she struggled to say yet again.

I couldn't breathe. I was the one who was gasping for breath. I was the one who had had the air knocked out of me. I was the one who was choking and puce and bulgy-eyed, with everything drifting in and out of focus. It was all too much. I hadn't been expecting this. Not after the day I'd had. David Clulow, the failed meeting, my slashed tyre, the body on the line, the rain, the traffic, the price of the cab, Battersea Rise, cold pumpkin ravioli, warm Chardonnay, Ant and Dec, Bobbie's affair with a foot fetishist. The fucking fashion industry.

She had only made everything so much worse, when she was meant to have made it so much better. Her polo neck, my hands hooked around it. It wasn't my fault there was no give in the cheap, man-made material. Another branded rip-off. She should have stuck to John Smedley, like me. And what a lurid colour. Did I care whether bright colours were in this season? Colours to be matched and mismatched. Or geeky glasses? Last season, this season, next season, they were all the same to me. It was always drizzly. It was always muggy. Nothing ever worked properly. Nothing lasted. Everything broke.

TWO

Escalated Asset Values

Iraq, Iran, Afghanistan, Zimbabwe, North Korea, all still out of control in their various ways, and with no one, from the so-called international community, able to do very much, despite all the talk, the rhetoric, the money, and the arms. The good intentions. How I hated that concept. How hollow those intentions always were, and how self-serving and egotistical were the people leading the calls. The radio had set me off, the *Today* programme, for once not talking about the economy, but international security and the continued threat from terrorism and rogue states. It should have been called the *Yesterday* programme. I couldn't believe we were still concerning ourselves with these issues, these places. Did anything ever really change, for the better?

And, frankly, what about America, Britain, Russia, China, Israel? The bigger the power, the bigger the arsenal, if you asked me, the more to bully with, and abuse. Tragically the weak would always be punished. Africa, especially, would forever be on its knees, with or without the good intentions. Sierra Leone, Nigeria, even Kenya nowadays, let alone Ethiopia, Sudan, Somalia, Malawi, the Democratic Republic of Congo. Democratic? Ha. A vague memory of a terrible disco song popped into my head – the line 'in Zaire' overlaid with bongo drums. Renaming, like refinancing, could only get you so far. Just how many stable, truly civilised, let alone fiscally sound nations were there, not just in Africa, but in the world? No one ever acted in time, or with enough intelligence. Or force.

How easy it was to contemplate poverty, famine, disease, torture, death on an unimaginable scale. And this was so much of the world today, a world I knew and travelled incessantly. I struggled to think of anywhere remotely pleasant. As for London, it offered little relief from the suffering. Lying in bed, my mind drifted far and wide, settling for a while on the former Soviet satellites of Latvia, Ukraine, Georgia. Why, I couldn't help thinking, was I always drawn to deprivation, corruption, instability? When surely I should have been searching for a simple place to lie low, a sunny safe haven. Not another dreary police state, in all but name.

Maybe I wasn't ready for calm, to lose myself in some quiet outpost in, say, South America. I still had ambition. And I didn't think I was sleazy enough, or certainly ready to explore my baser self, like so many Western males had before me, in South East Asia. I was going to forget Thailand, the Philippines, Vietnam and Cambodia. For now. I was feeling strangely robust, both physically and mentally. Despite recent events, or perhaps because of certain incidents – all the tragedy and the suffering, precipitated, I could see it so clearly, by the failure of infrastructure and monetary regulations, of society, of civilisation – I was feeling, in a way, immortal.

Evan Davis was now talking about how fat the British had become, according to a new survey. I hated fat people. There didn't seem any justification, however medically fanciful. Someone was blathering about the fat gene – what an extraordinary notion from supposedly a learned fellow. Fat flesh, those folds and dimples, that cellulite, the overhangs and spare tyres, simply made my stomach turn, which was why, thinking back to my patchy global tour and that earlier report on the programme, I put two and two together and arrived, once more, at North Korea. Weren't the people of North Korea perpetually on the verge of starvation? There would be no fatties there.

The location was good, stuffed out of the way between the Yellow Sea, the Sea of Japan and South Korea. I wondered whether they ate dog in North Korea, perhaps that was all they ate. I wouldn't be squeamish about eating dog – I loathed dogs, having forever been put off by the breeds that stalked south London – however, I just knew dog would taste revolting. If that were all there was to eat in North Korea, with rice on the side, I would have a serious problem. I wasn't very keen on rice. Though possibly if food was so scarce in North Korea they would have eaten all the dogs years ago. Perhaps it'd be blissfully dog-free.

Plus there was Kim Jong-il. Or was there? Who knew whether he was alive or dead. Or if he was alive in what sort of state of health. Had he been rendered useless by a stroke, as recent reports had suggested? A pale shadow of his former, extraordinary self, lying semi-comatose, surrounded by weeping flunkies, in some outlandish palatial mansion. What a pity. I'd liked his style. His jumpsuits and bouffant hairdo – would he still have someone to attend to his toilet? How I'd liked his reputation as being something of a ladies' man – the fact he'd fathered numerous children and was now living, or maybe not, with a former movie star. I'd liked his power and the fact he'd so troubled both the US and China. And how if he went anywhere, which not surprisingly was not often, at least not far – who would have him? – he went by a lengthy, bombproof train. It wasn't that he'd been concerned about his carbon footprint – though given his nuclear ambitions, one could argue he'd been trying to do his bit to cut carbon emissions – he was scared shitless.

I too had a problem with flying – not so much with the fear of crashing, or the emissions, as with the horror of being cooped up with so much humanity in such a confined space. Alas, for years work pressures meant not going somewhere was not an option for me. However, respect due, Kim Jong-il had clearly made the most of his problem, which seemed to be the story of his life. Take his faltering eyesight. Now there was, or had been, a man of the moment, as Bobbie might have said, with those outsized frames and tinted lenses. It wasn't the geeky nerdy look, more the demented dictator. It increasingly seemed to me that demented dictators and untrustworthy tyrants provided not just inspiration but perfect safe havens, for a certain sort of immigrant.

As usual I'd woken up listening to Evan Davis, with thoughts of escaping. But having lost the instructions, I feared what might happen if I unplugged my radio alarm. It was tuned to some atomic bleep, emanating from Germany, and was accurate to three tenths of a second within a million years, or something. Except originally locating this signal had been far from simple. I needed a clock to tell the exact time, not just because I believed in punctuality, but also to set my watches by. Like clocks, I hated watches to tell the incorrect time, even by a few seconds, and I would alter my various timepieces three or four times a day. They were all wildly inaccurate, especially the most expensive, vintage ones, though that was the price you paid for rarity, I guessed. Beautiful hand-assembled mechanics, and exquisite aesthetics, but crap functionality – a bit like Bobbie.

How I'd loved, especially, my slim, gold 1952 Jaeger-LeCoultre, even if it did lose almost one second an hour. Bobbie might have said chunky divers' watches were in right now and I might have indulged that notion with a couple of rash purchases – an Omega Seamaster and a Tag Heuer Aquaracer, of all run-of-the-mill things, plus, I was deeply ashamed to admit, a fake Rolex Submariner – but the Jaeger was my all-time favourite. The real crocodile strap alone cost £200, or would have had I not convinced an antique watch repairer that he had scratched the underneath of the case when it went in for a service, and that the least he could do, by way of compensation, seeing as he was such a respected horologist, was chuck in a new, fully branded Jaeger-LeCoultre strap.

Jaeger were the only watch manufacturers who set their lugs 17 mm apart, which meant that if you wanted a strap to fit perfectly you had to have one of theirs. It was admirable, canny business practice. Of course a 16 or even 18 mm generic strap would have fitted fine – indeed when I got the watch it came with an 18 mm fake crocodile strap and nothing appeared wrong – except I knew it wasn't the real thing and this ate away at me for a number of months until I worked out a way of rectifying the situation. If I was going to own something, let alone actually wear it, of course it had to be spot on. Perfection was always my goal.

It was 08:49:27, atomic time. I'd found my all but ruined glasses on top of the small chest of drawers that doubled as my bedside table. However, the Jaeger was not in sight. Usually at night I placed it carefully by the radio alarm, hoping that somehow it would latch onto the atomic pulse and start to learn to tell the time more accurately. Where the fuck was my most prized wristwatch? I had this sudden, sinking feeling that I knew exactly where it was.

The lug holes on the 18-carat gold case might have been uniquely set 17 mm apart but they were hopelessly worn, and the real crocodile strap was already badly cracked. It wouldn't have taken much for the strap to come loose. I tried to calm my breathing. I was sick of rare, posh watches. They were unreliable, flimsy, expensive. And not much of an investment, as I'd recently discovered – though what was nowadays? Maybe I'd switch my allegiances to tough, sexy Japanese models – wouldn't I be so lucky – with their ridiculously inexpensive, but totally accurate quartz movements. Seiko, Citizen, were there any other makes? And who sold them? Every high-street chain I supposed, and for very good reason. I'd have to venture out to Oxford Street, the cheap end. I'd have to make my first ever visit to H. Samuel.

At least it wasn't raining. For once golden sunlight was flooding the room. There was a great rectangular patch shining on the bare white wall. Really, my blinds. I'd been meaning to change them for ages. Not only were they not blackout blinds, but they barely fitted the windows. Well, that's not quite true. They fitted the windows exactly, if you looked at them square on. However, they hung miles away from the windows themselves, due to a bizarre top window opening mechanism, which jutted out. Light flooded around the edges, especially when the sun was low in the sky. Obviously it wasn't a problem I encountered every day, even very often, though that didn't mean it wasn't annoying. Plus, I couldn't imagine the incompetence of the person responsible – of someone putting aesthetics ahead of practicalities. That someone actually did such a thing. Obviously you wanted something to look good, but it had to work properly as well.

My head was killing me and the unusual brightness was certainly not helping, nor the radio. I pulled the duvet over my face, shading the light and muffling the sound, but my exposed feet soon felt chilly. Plus it smelt under the duvet. At last I threw off the covering and climbed out of bed. I really did have a very bad headache, then I remembered the cheap Australian Chardonnay, on top of God knows what else, and tried knowingly to smile to myself. Though all I could manage was a grimace as other memories came flooding back.

Walking through to the kitchen I was shocked to see the Agent Provocateur shoebox on the sitting-room floor. I couldn't believe I'd carefully brought that back, yet had managed to lose my watch. Something was very wrong with me.

I knew I'd have to get rid of the box, fast too, but as it was here I didn't see the point in not re-examining the contents. Besides, I wasn't doing much else that morning. However, filling the kettle I still worried a little about how long I really had. Time was a constant concern for me and I wasn't accustomed to rushing in the mornings. It always took me an age to clean my teeth, floss, shave, shower and dress. Often I'd spend hours in my pyjamas, putting off the moment when I'd finally have to make a decision about what to wear, unless I had an urgent appointment with the horologist, or optician, or Waitrose. Or, thinking about it, Church's. I had a pair of fine English shoes I'd been meaning to take back for ages.

Moving into the sitting room I put my coffee on the desk and reached for my mobile. I texted Bobbie – *Frantic. In meetings all day. I'll call u later. Mx.* I picked up Bobbie's box and emptied it on the sofa, as there was no space on my desk. Not because it was messy, it was never messy, but because of all the work I'd been doing recently it was laden with neat piles of papers and folders, plus I was trying, and failing, to hook up to a new broadband provider and there were endless leaflets and printouts and superfluous wires and discs and filters and auxiliary modems to do with that.

Before I began sifting through the contents of the box – though pushed for time I was savouring the moment – I went back into the kitchen, got a cloth, returned to the sitting room and started wiping the wall above and just to the left of the sofa. It was suddenly getting to me. I had made little effort to remove the stains yesterday though I was beginning to realise that I'd probably left it too late. I don't know what I'd been thinking. The once immaculate white wall was speckled with spots of crimson. There were some splashes on the ceiling. Fortunately the sofa was dark brown leather, a Robin Day, from Habitat, and had been easy to clean. I had managed to wipe that, probably more out of necessity than some urge to clean up – the sofa being where I liked to have an afternoon doze. And being naturally fastidious about my clothes I obviously didn't want them to pick up any unnecessary stains. As it was that whole, dreadful incident had already caused me to dispense with a pair of tan cords and a rust brown, V-neck Smedley. Both items I'd deemed to be beyond cleaning.

Standing back, I wondered whether I could hide the stains with a painting. It would have to be large and cover also a fair proportion of the ceiling. A bespoke mural might have done it, but I wasn't sure whether I'd ever seen a mural that didn't appear atrociously amateur. Indeed, there was very little contemporary art of any form that I could tolerate – because it was either too obvious, or trying too hard to be obscure. The search for meaning seemed so arbitrary, and was usually engaged in by those least equipped to do so – today's artists, I'd always believed, had problems both analysing information, and articulating their response. It came down to communication – you never really knew what the hell they were really trying to say. If I had to have a painting I supposed I would pick some token of abstract expressionism, to complement the mid-century modern architecture of my pad. An Yves Klein would have done quite nicely, or a Pollock, or a late Rothko. Actually a late Rothko would have been my top choice, except the one or two I had in mind, when he eventually discovered lighter and brighter colours – probably because he could feel the end was in sight – weren't so very large and obviously didn't stretch round corners and across ceilings.

But given the state of my finances, and the current fickleness of the art market, I knew I'd be better off finding a B&Q and repainting the damn room myself. The flat hadn't been painted since I'd moved in and a bit of refreshing wouldn't have gone amiss anyway. Plus it wouldn't take forever either. Bobbie's flat might have been contained but mine wasn't exactly enormous. The bedroom and sitting-room were effectively one space, partitioned off by a sliding door. However it was an original sliding door, complete with glass panels at the top. Indeed everything about my flat was original, which was one of the reasons I'd found it so appealing.

There was a small galley kitchen, a narrow bathroom, a compact hallway and a balcony, with just about room for two chairs. The balcony led off the sitting-room section of the main room and occupied a space directly outside the kitchen and bathroom windows. With my flat being on the tenth floor, the views of the City and towards the high, leafy ground of Hampstead and Highgate were stunning – so everybody thought. I failed to see the grandeur, the expanse, the romance. There was a smudge of green, some way off, but few glittering towers of note. London wasn't New York.

At night there was more to observe, especially nearby. It was hard not to peer into other homes on the estate, across the concourse, and invariably see things of an intimate nature.

I had to turn my back to the sun pouring through the window, while leafing through Bobbie's secrets. Obviously the size of the windows and the light they generated in the flat were one of the most impressive aspects of the place and a trademark of the estate's architects, Chamberlin, Powell and Bon. These were the same people who later designed the Barbican proper, which was next door. But in many ways my estate was a purer form of British modernist architecture. At least that was what I was always telling people.

'Why pay Barbican prices,' I'd say, 'when you can have so much better for so much less?' I wasn't sure I entirely believed that. Anyway when it was sunny, as I was discovering, Chamberlin, Powell and Bon had in fact also created something of a design problem. I suddenly craved the greyness, the drizzle, the usual London fare. At least the flat was warm considering I didn't have the heating on. I'd been meaning to get a plumber round to fix the boiler for ages, but I hated plumbers and maybe, if this weather kept up, I wouldn't have to bother. I was becoming used to cold showers – not a bad thing, I supposed, if I were headed for North Korea. I couldn't imagine the domestic plumbing was up to much, though the North Koreans had, of course, managed to generate some kind of nuclear fusion.

Bobbie's stuff wasn't revealing anything of interest. Most of the letters appeared to be from her younger sister, who was dead, so I didn't see why she had been so protective of them. If that were all there was she should have just said so. Think of the trouble it would have saved. There had to be something else.

I came to another thick envelope of photos, but these too were all of Bobbie with her sister, or just her sister, who if anything had been even sexier than Bobbie. She had a fuller figure and a less austere haircut, though I had to keep reminding myself she was dead, long dead, tragically having fallen from a hotel balcony in Spain. There were yet more letters, cards, notes, photos. For a minute I wondered whether something fishy had been going on between them.

But Bobbie's sister's messages were not of a sexual nature. The collection was more like a shrine. I couldn't get over how stupid Bobbie had been about me discovering this stash. I went through all the stuff again to be certain then hurriedly rang her mobile. The answerphone eventually kicked in.

'Bobbie, it's Matt. I've got a couple of seconds. Look, I'm very sorry about last night. I don't know quite what happened. Hope you are all right. Can we meet? Give me a ring, leave a message, send a text, please. Love you.'

What was the point in denying we'd had an argument? In that flat of hers, with those shoddy walls, the whole street would have heard.

I kicked the Agent Provocateur box under the sofa as a temporary measure — that lush pink, that rich brown, the seductiveness of those colours was offending me — and went into the kitchen to get more coffee. I had yet to find a cafetière that was either the right size or sturdy enough. I had broken innumerable inserts and was never able to find replacements that fitted so had to buy whole new cafetières. The weird thing was that when you went into Habitat, or Bodum, say, on some other mission there were always piles of the appropriate inserts. I wished I wasn't so coffee-dependent, though too much could make me feel faint. I was feeling slightly light-headed this morning as it was but I helped myself to another full cup anyway. It was barely warm.

Returning to the sitting room, and my desk, I wondered what it would be like to have one of those massive, purpose-built cappuccino machines, with frothers and steamers and an endless array of flashing lights and gauges. Though I didn't feel I had anything to prove by purchasing such gleaming kitchen machinery, even if it was well made. Nevertheless, I would have had a quick look on the net if my broadband hadn't been down. There was no harm in arming myself with the knowledge of the best machine on the market. I was already certain it would be a Gaggia. It wouldn't take that long to find the right model. I never saw the point in trying to save money by buying either a cheaper model or a cheaper brand altogether. To me economy meant buying the best and watching it last. Of course that didn't always happen. Less and less in fact. What a shoddy world. Looking up from my desk and out of the window, at the strikingly low London skyline, being suppressed further by a seemingly mocking sun – this city was not designed or equipped for such strong, cheery light – I thought I'd abandon the idea of a Gaggia for the moment. The reality was bound to be a disappointment, plus I had work to do.

'How's Bobbie?'

'She's fine. Or was the last time I saw her.' I wasn't sure why I added that. Maybe I'd have to watch what I said more carefully.

'Are you not still seeing her?'

'Yes, I am, but there are a few problems. She's pretty young and I don't know, it's just one of those things. Maybe she's not right.' I took a sip of my wine. It was white, because Roger wanted white. He was on a diet, yet again, and thought white wine was less fattening than red wine. I'd said utter rubbish but seeing as he was paying, I'd let him choose.

'When are you ever sure, Matt? This has been going on for years.'

'I haven't been going out with Bobbie for years. It's been barely ten months. What do you mean?'

'Well, you're never sure, are you? Or haven't been since Francesca. And you weren't exactly sure of her, of all people. They are always too young, or old, or fat. They've never been too thin, I'll give you that.'

'Thanks.' I took another sip of wine. It was a South African Chenin Blanc, 2004. It was utterly boring but drinkable – I was amazed a restaurant of the calibre of St John stocked such crap and then charged such a price.

South African wines were never much of a bargain, from whatever establishment – the cheaper bottles often being quite foul. As far as I was concerned Chilean wine, white and red, more than had the edge on South African and for that matter Australian wine, though frankly if I ran a restaurant I wouldn't stock anything from the New World. There was never enough subtlety, finesse, or heritage. But I couldn't help admiring those Maipo Valley winemakers. They really churned the stuff out – millions and millions of bottles a year. What was the secret behind their reliability and productivity? The soil, or was it a state of mind? Maybe it was a hangover from the Pinochet days – a commitment to duty, and regimental subservience. Or perhaps it was simply a desire to catch up for lost time, because I didn't think a culture, a nation with a long tradition of a truly free market ever produced such results. Pity the North Koreans didn't make wine. They'd have swamped the world.

'Great plonk, isn't it?'

'Fine.' What could I say? Plonk was exactly the right word.

'Is the sex still good?'

I smiled, coyly. 'With Bobbie?' I was watching our waitress walk to the serving counter. She was wearing tight black trousers, and a white blouse. She had long dark hair, which came to more than halfway down her back. She reminded me of someone.

'Is there anyone else I should know about?'

That was it, the sales assistant from David Clulow. There was something unattainable about both of them. A frosty, superior, yet also oddly demure air. I liked a challenge. 'No, who do you think I am?'

'I think I know you well enough. You've always got your eye on someone.'

'Don't be ridiculous.' I couldn't stop smiling again. 'How's Emily?' Emily was Roger's wife. She was also always on a diet, not that sadly it ever did her much good. She worked part time for UNICEF, and she and Roger had two hideous, red-haired children. One, in theory, was my godson. I still hadn't got his christening present engraved. In fact I couldn't remember where I'd put it, or what it was. He was possibly six or seven. I had no idea when his birthday was.

'She's fine. A bit stressed, as ever. She's got a big trip coming up. She's off to Burkina Faso.'

'Yeah?'

'West Africa.'

'I know where it is. Rather her than me.'

'They run an amazing programme out there.'

'How long will she be gone for?'

'Two and a half weeks.'

'Shit, so you've got the kids on your own for that long?'

'Well they are at school and nursery, and Emily's mum's coming for a bit and we do have an au pair. It'll be fine. I've done it before.'

'Perhaps we can go out one evening then, have some fun.'

'Yeah, maybe. Where do you go nowadays?'

'Oh, I don't know, there are various bars around here in Clerkenwell, some in Shoreditch, the usual Hoxton suspects. But we could always start off at the Giraffe.' I smiled yet again. This bonhomie felt so false. Plus I wasn't good in male company. It brought the worst out in me.

'You don't still go there?'

'Only with you.'

He laughed this time and turned slightly redder than he was already. Sweat was beginning to glisten on his chubby cheeks. The Giraffe was a strip pub, with lap dancing in a side room. It was open all day and most of the night. Roger loved it and he loved taking me, because he made out he was too shy and embarrassed to go on his own, though he probably did anyway. It wasn't far from his office.

'Back to Bobbie,' he said, leering. 'Tell me, does she have a Brazilian? Or a Hollywood?'

How many times had he already asked me this? But having mentioned the Giraffe I'd obviously set him off on his favourite topic – female pubic hair, or rather the absence of pubic hair on grown women today. I supposed I'd done it on purpose. 'Yeah, of course. She is only twenty-four. Every woman under the age of thirty, probably forty nowadays, has a shaved muff.' Roger looked ready to burst. He was so easy to tease. 'Doesn't Emily?' Of course I knew the answer.

'What do you think?'

Emily didn't like me. I wasn't entirely sure she liked Roger much. 'Things are still all right in the bedroom department, though, aren't they?'

'Were they ever?'

I was so bored of Roger complaining about his non-existent sex life, but could never stop myself from goading him. 'She's sexy, in a wholesome sort of way. Come on, Roger, she's got nice tits.' They weren't very nice. They practically came down to her waist. They were a long-standing source of amusement among Roger's male friends. We wondered just what she did for UNICEF.

'Can't say I've been near them for a while.'

'How's that possible, living in the same house?'

'She's always too busy, or tired.'

'You should spice things up. You know, sex toys, bondage, a bit of S&M. Get her reinvigorated. You've been married for a while. No wonder it's gone a bit flat.'

'OK, I want the truth, have you had anal sex with her?'

'With who? Bobbie?'

'Who do you think?'

'Yes. Obviously. It was no big deal. It's become like normal sex for the under thirties. They expect it.' I hadn't had anal sex with Bobbie and I wouldn't be having anal sex with Bobbie. But Roger liked to live his sex life vicariously through me and I saw no reason to short-change him, especially right now.

'Does she come, when you're doing it? Do they come?'

'Women? They enjoy it more than you could imagine.'

'Emily thinks that men who want to have anal sex all have small penises.'

'Roger, are you trying to tell me something?' The frosty waitress appeared with our main courses.

'Thanks,' Roger said, as she put his plate in front of him.

She was younger than I'd first thought. We were having main courses because aside from being on a diet Roger supposedly was in a rush. He'd only agreed to have lunch with me because he hadn't heard from me for ages and happened to have a window. He actually used that word. I not only needed to get out, but I needed someone to buy me a decent meal. My week was getting worse by the minute. Roger said St John, which suited me fine, being just around the corner from my apartment. Plus I hadn't been to St John for ages. I was amazed to find the place still so packed.

'I know it's not the most original eatery, but it's consistent,' he'd actually said on the phone, and as if he would know about consistency. 'I'm sure we can get a table. I'll get Lily to book.' Lily was his PA. He always got Lily to book. It was both a power thing, because it wasn't as if he didn't have the time himself – by all accounts he did virtually nothing at work – and also a way of pointing out to me how important he was because he had a fucking PA. He was such an arsehole. Who would use a word like eatery too? Window, plonk, eatery – he lived by a different dictionary. He used to be tolerable, but success, if you could call it that, had made him not just fat but increasingly unpleasant, and insecure. Same with most people. Fortunately it wasn't a charge that could be levelled at me.

My eyes followed the waitress' behind, snug in those tight black slacks, until she disappeared amid a clutch of seemingly equally aloof staff. Turning to my pigeon I was immediately disappointed. It was tiny, and I'd thought St John specialised in serving gutsy, no-nonsense dishes. Times certainly were hard. How I wished I'd had the lamb. Someone was having lamb on a nearby table. What a portion, cut into thick, pink, juicy slices. And it came with a mountain of anchovy and caper sauce, and a few green leaves. Watercress?

Invariably I made the wrong choice in restaurants. Half the time I picked something already knowing I'd rather have something else. I think I did it out of a perverse wish to ruin a perfectly decent meal. When had I ever had a large, truly satisfying pigeon? Pigeons were never that large. If I ran a restaurant I'd only ever put pigeon on the menu as a starter. St John should have known better. At least I wasn't having the grilled plaice – too watery. But Roger didn't seem to mind. He had no palate, despite his fondness for smart restaurants. Though that was all show of course, proving to everyone, and himself, that he had arrived. But where? Advertising. Roger worked in advertising, as an account director, for a massive media group, teetering on the edge of extinction. Poor chap was only a bit-part player. At least I ran my own business. I could barely watch him tuck into his plaice.

'Great food, isn't it?' He probably knew more about wine.

'Want to try some pigeon?'

'No thanks, pigeon's not really my thing.'

Perhaps that was why I picked the pigeon, knowing Roger would never have ordered anything as gamey as pigeon. Plain food for a plain man. You were lucky if you got shepherd's pie at his house. Every meal was designed for kids. At least he and Emily ate meat, occasionally. However, I can't say that I was happy about going all the way to Crouch End to sample it. I'd been to their house twice. Both times it was a complete nightmare, just getting there. My first attempt was by public transport. From memory it took two Tube changes, a bus and finally a minicab – an hour and a half in total from central London. Though it might have helped had they told me that they lived in Muswell Hill and not Crouch End. No one in London actually lived where they said they lived. The second time I drove and got so lost at one point I found myself in Queen's Park. I don't know why I was always ending up in Queen's Park, when I would have rather been absolutely anywhere else.

The waitress appeared and asked if everything was all right.

'No,' I said.

'I'm sorry, what's the problem?'

'It's perfectly cooked, just the right side of pink, but there's not enough of it.' She waltzed off, smiling. She thought I'd made a compliment, so had Roger the dodger with the tiny todger, but I hadn't. I was being completely serious. I'd have to persuade Roger to let me have pudding. Cheese at the very least. Fuck his window. 'Did I tell you about North Korea?'

'No.' He wiped his mouth and proceeded to dab his forehead, with the same bit of napkin. He really was gross.

'You know I've been talking to a new VC outfit – maybe the last in the City with any cash – well it turns out they have ties in Pyongyang. Don't ask me how, perhaps that's why they're still liquid, but they do, and it seems they have an interest in the sort of exposure I'd be able to give them. It's possible that my business, and our particular expertise, might be able to dovetail with their aims, and if it comes off, we're talking about some serious money. Long term. Ultimately, of course, I'd be helping the North Koreans to export their ideas to the West. I like that, especially now. At the very least I should get a fascinating trip out of it.'

'You're going to North Korea? When?'

It continued to amaze me how Roger managed to hold down a job at all, even in advertising – though who knew for how much longer. I was the one who could have sold him anything. 'Should be very soon. They want to move on this as quickly as possible.'

'Can you just go, like that? Don't you need a special visa? Emily's lot have major problems.'

'I'm sure, but this is business. Money always talks. Plus I'm not going simply to snoop around. I'm hardly a journalist, or a human-rights activist. Or a bloody aid worker. They've already indicated that my getting a visa will be no problem. Essentially, at least if this comes off, I will be working for the North Koreans. It's in their interest.'

'How long will you be there?'

'I don't know, a couple of weeks, maybe more. So if you don't hear from me, don't worry. I'll be enjoying spit-roast dog, courtesy of Kim Jong-il. Pudding?'

Roger wasn't going to refuse pudding. The obese never did. He had the rich chocolate soufflé, I had a lemon curd tart. His looked considerably better than mine – still steaming, gooey, very rich, though he wouldn't let me try any and actually slapped away my probing spoon. When Roger's had more than a glass and a half of Chenin Blanc, or whatever it is that he regards as wine, he becomes absurdly childish and mean with his things. He'd obviously been overindulged as a child, and underindulged as an adult.

'For next time,' I said to the waitress as she collected Roger's gold, business account Mastercard – he wouldn't have bought me lunch out of his own pocket – 'could you please advise the kitchen to source some plumper pigeons. I like to get stuck into a good bird. Do you work the evening shift as well?'

'Sometimes.' She looked particularly shy, wary.

However, I had an inkling that she wouldn't be quite as shy in the sack. A welcome surprise or not, I suddenly had a terrible urge to find out. 'Tonight?'

I caught Roger's disapproving expression. How predictable he was. How easy to shock.

'Yes, I'm working tonight.'

'That's a shame. I was going to ask you out for dinner – to a place that knows how to feed their customers properly. What time do you finish?'

'That depends.'

'Matt, I've got to get going.' Roger looked at the waitress, clearly imploring her to hurry up with the chip and PIN machine, for her sake as well as his.

'Would you like to add a tip?'

'Don't, whatever you do, meet up with this man. He's dangerous.' Roger took the machine, laughing. He was bound to add a decent sum. He always did, being terrified of not making an impression. I wondered whether generosity born out of insecurity really amounted to much.

The waitress looked at me. She was clearly uncomfortable though she tried to smile. I smiled back. For once Roger had said exactly the right thing. She was interested all right. Perhaps I would call by later.

'You can't stop yourself, can you?' Roger said, as we were exiting the building.

The sun had been replaced by dense cloud. What a surprise. It would soon be dark. Rain seemed likely. The traffic on St John Street appeared already to have slowed in preparation for the downpour. 'What?'

'Picking up women.'

'Why should I?'

'Bobbie, for one.'

'The thing about Bobbie, Roger, is that she's never around when you want her to be.' I was always at my most randy after a couple of drinks at lunchtime.

'Good to see you,' he said, successfully hailing a cab.

Where had that come from, at this hour and in this weather? But I supposed Roger was one of those people who never had to struggle to get by. He was lucky. Things went his way. He'd always had it easy, except perhaps in bed, with Emily. But maybe that was all his fault. Maybe he'd become too expectant and lazy and fat. After all he wasn't even going to walk the few hundred yards to his office. Fat people never walked anywhere.

'I suppose you're not heading my way?'

'No. Back to the grind. Thanks for lunch. Send my love to Emily and the kids.' I was pretty certain Roger wouldn't be mentioning who he'd had lunch with today. 'When she's away, if you fancy a serious night out give me a ring.'

He eased his great bulk inside the taxi, huffing and puffing. 'If you're not in North Korea.'

'Yeah, that's right, I almost forgot. If I'm not eating dog.'

'Or fucking one. See ya.' He waved.

I was glad to leave him stuck in traffic, knowing he'd be anxiously watching the meter – in private I was certain he counted the pennies – and wondering whether he had enough time to pop into the Giraffe before he had to be back in the office. I couldn't believe he was once my best man, designate. But that was in another life. I looked at my watch, except my watch wasn't there – this was going to take some getting used to. I had to retrieve my phone from my coat pocket for the time. It was nearly three and I still had no messages or texts. The Giraffe would be emptying out nicely. Maybe I'd be able to surprise Roger, by securing a lap dance with the stripper of my choice before he made his entrance. With any luck he'd be so embarrassed to be spotted stepping into such an establishment, he'd buy me another. Hush money. It had happened before. But I wasn't going to start moralising, even if the hypocrisy of some people's lives never failed to amaze me.

My heart missed a beat as I neared the place where I'd lost Bobbie's fancy shoebox. I'd carefully deposited it, before lunch, on a street on the far side of the restaurant to my flat, deliberately going almost a mile out of my way. Plus I'd squashed it as far into the litter bin as I could without getting my hands too dirty. However, a couple of Community Support Officers seemed to be paying particular attention to the very receptacle, where it presumably still lay, crumpled and covered in crap. This had to be a coincidence – London was all about coincidences, wasn't it? Perhaps they were looking for a bomb. I hurried on nevertheless.

THREE

Toxic Debt

I left another voice message for Bobbie. 'Give me a ring, sweetheart, please. I'm getting worried.' Act and think normally, that was what I was telling myself, and everything would be all right. I still hadn't rung her work number. I was leaving that for another rainy day.

My estate was aglow with artificial light. Across the slick concourse I liked to think I was observing an ocean liner at dock, or an upmarket resort close up. It was seemingly so neat and friendly it had to be a place of fun and relaxation; one of those new city mega-spas, perhaps, and not a tired, ex-council concern, where mortal danger lurked around dark corners. With so many passageways, walkways and exterior stairwells it was a mugger's paradise – where wasn't nowadays? But I was trying to look at things on the bright side. Despite all that had happened I was making an effort to be positive.

There were two flats in particular that I could never help observing. One I could see clearly from my bedroom, or rather sleeping area, and the other from the balcony. Tonight I appeared to be in luck with both. I shifted between vantage points, not bothered about leaving the balcony door open and letting in the cold, damp night air. My heating was still not working, indeed I couldn't begin to imagine when it ever would. Fortunately it wasn't quite as cold as it should have been for the time of year.

In the flat I could see best from my balcony, which was almost directly across the central concourse, she was reclining on the sofa in just her dressing gown, a towel wound on top of her head. I knew that that was all she was wearing. From where I was I could see straight into her flat, if she kept her blinds open. She would regularly walk between her bathroom and her bedroom naked, as she had tonight, before pulling on her dressing gown. She must have fixed her head towel while in the bathroom. I couldn't have seen her do that, but I imagined her standing naked and wet while wrapping the thing around and around.

She had shoulder-length blonde hair and a good body. At least she looked pretty attractive from a distance, but when I'd seen her close up, on a passageway or the concourse, she wasn't quite so attractive, appearing older, greyer, shorter and stockier. However, in a way, that fuelled my fantasies about her. Because she lived on her own, and was of a certain age, I had this idea that she was lonely and rather desperate. She must have known she was visible for almost miles around. Total privacy was not much of an option here.

I was willing her dressing gown to fall open and for her to start playing with herself. My filthy mind. Not that it had ever quite happened like that, but as I knew better than most there was a first time for everything. She reminded me of Jeanette – in all the wrong, or was it the right ways. I wondered what would happen if I were to knock on her door and say, 'Hello, I'm from across the way. I couldn't help noticing you' – I'd give her a knowing look at this point – 'and thought perhaps I might come in.'

I'd once read, years and years ago, when I was barely a teenager, a story in a copy of *Forum*, which I'd found in my mum's bedroom, about a couple of neighbours. When their husbands were out at work one would visit the other and the first thing they would do, right on the doorstep, would be to reach for each other's genitals to see how excited they were. They were always only wearing dressing gowns, or coats with nothing on underneath and yes, they were always dripping and virtually on the point of orgasm already. I wondered how wet my Jeanette lookalike would be when I paid her a visit.

Shifting back inside to my other vantage point, I was pleased to see Mia was still doing yoga, or maybe it was Pilates, whatever. It was her attire that had first hooked my attention all those months ago – tight black cycling shorts and a white vest top, with definitely no bra underneath, and I presumed, because obviously that was how my mind was working, that she was wearing no knickers as well. Though I couldn't see that clearly. I had tried the zoom on my camera, but it was an old model and the lens not much use. I'd been meaning to buy some binoculars for ages. Leica made a neat pair, for birdwatching, which came with an equally smart black leather case. There was a Leica shop in Holborn I'd stopped at a couple of times or so. I had been thinking that I'd upgrade my camera at the same time, because Leica had also just brought out a new digital device, shaped a little like their classic rangefinders, but with ten megapixels and all sorts of manual override options. I hated the idea of having a point and shoot camera. I wanted a camera that could compete with the best professional models. It wasn't just for pleasure of course, I needed it for work too, and I wasn't going to be caught abroad, and God knows where that could mean, without a decent, reliable piece of equipment.

I hadn't got around to buying either yet because the last

few times I'd been into the shop the man behind the counter annoyed me intensely. Aside from his bulk I didn't have every confidence that he knew exactly what he was talking about. He had clearly been there for years, certainly for as long as I had been going in, but I had the suspicion that he was confused by digital technology. And, more importantly, he didn't take me as seriously as he should. He didn't seem to understand why I'd need such a sophisticated model. Actually, in the end he was rude. I wondered whether they'd still had the stuff on hold for me.

Mia was decidedly more discreet than Jeanette and usually kept her bedroom blinds closed and also the door at the top of her stairs – all the maisonettes across the way and on that particular level were of the same internal configuration. However, that shyness, that modesty only made me want her more – me and reserved women. Me and wanting something I couldn't have. Plus she was better-looking than Jeanette, not just at a distance but also close up, being dark-haired and slight and possibly Japanese.

She probably wasn't called Mia, but she reminded me of Mia, the Mia who used to cut my hair, when I had hair, at a place called 5th Floor. I knew that it might not go down quite so well if I happened to knock on her door, out of the blue. It would require much more groundwork – days, possibly weeks, if I had the time, because, sadly, she lived with her partner. He was a large, flabby white man, with a shaved head, a goatee and big, thick-framed glasses – of which Bobbie no doubt would have approved. He had erratic working habits and was often to be seen sitting at the desk in the lounge diner. This was the room directly below where Mia was currently standing on her head, lowering her legs to the floor backwards, and revealing the full, perfect curve of her bottom, so taut and stretched, I could imagine, but couldn't quite see, the slight swelling of her upside-down vulva pressing against the fabric. What a position. What architects. Chamberlin, Powell and Bon, born voyeurs, surely. But then wasn't that the case with all mid-century modern architects and their obsession with glass and open-plan living, with unobscured views, and with leaving everyone wonderfully on show, if not exposed and so frighteningly vulnerable?

Her bloke, this overgrown kid, could have been an architect, though most likely he was a web designer, as so many of the younger residents on the estate seemed to be. Birkenstocks, baggy jeans, big glasses, shaved heads, goatees, with petite girlfriends as complacent accessories. They were like a tribe. Give me a hoodie anytime.

At least Mia went for bald men with glasses. I didn't think she would have the slightest problem with me being tall and trim, alongside the fact that I obviously had a well-travelled sophistication, a certain intelligence, because frankly I couldn't believe any woman would prefer someone who was flabby, and pretentious. An adult still wanting to be a youth – I didn't get it.

It also didn't make sense that I was watching Mia, but still thinking about Jeanette, not the Jeanette lookalike across the way but the real Jeanette, from ages ago, and getting something of an erection. The power of certain memories, of old fantasies, never ceased to amaze me. I shot through the flat and out onto the balcony where I could see that my Jeanette lookalike hadn't moved from her sofa. A faint, flickering blue filling the edges of the spotlit room told me that she was watching the television. *I'm A Celebrity . . . Get Me Out Of Here!*? It was about that time.

Maybe it was the way she wound her towel on her head, and walked from room to room, or simply the way she seemed so blasé about being naked, that reminded me of the real package, because the lookalike wasn't quite in the same league. The real Jeanette was more petite, more refined, helped no doubt by the fact that she was loaded and had clearly always spent a lot of money on herself. Most markedly, perhaps, she had had much smaller breasts. In fact Jeanette had tiny breasts, though very prominent nipples, and she would absolutely never wear a bra and often, if I were sitting in the front of her car and she happened to lean forward to change gear, she'd slip a nip. Catching sight of them then was a real turn-on – coupled with the way she always wore short white dresses.

I found myself securing vantage points for when she climbed in and out of her car – she had a sporty little two-door, BMW 3 series – or when she was sitting casually on a sofa, so as to be best placed to grab an upskirt. Her knickers were usually white also, and oddly rather plain, and big. However, once, when she was crouching down to tell Stephen and me something – we were in the pool – I had an unforgettable, close-up view straight between her legs. She was wearing a pair of red knickers, which were made from a sort of crocheted material and were almost completely see-through, so I caught this mass of pubic hair, much of which was spilling out of the loosely elasticated sides. When she'd gone I had to climb out of the pool and rush to the toilet, where I ejaculated before I'd managed to get my trunks off. What a mess.

Jeanette knew what she was doing, of course. Like the time they took me on holiday to Spain, to a villa just outside Marbella – they had great taste – where every morning I'd see her drying her hair in the hall, just outside her bedroom. She would be naked and obviously knew where Stephen's and my room was and how, because Stephen was such a baby despite being thirteen or whatever it was, he had to have the door left open at night. I could see her from my bed, in the early morning Mediterranean sun, blow-drying her hair, curling bits and straightening other bits, all in the nude, with her large, dark nipples and smooth white bottom, all the whiter because of her bikini marks, and her forest of pubic hair, which was so much darker and wilder than the hair she was tending to with the humming dryer and an assortment of chrome hairdressing tools. It would take her ages, but it never took me long, despite being a little older and more experienced by then – and very anxious not to be noticed.

Even when Stephen finally realised how much I fancied his mum and remorselessly mocked me, I couldn't stop looking at her and hoping to catch sight of intimate bits of her, or longing for her to finally make a proper move towards me, which she would I was ever positive. I dreamed of her finding me alone in their pool changing room, or, when Stephen was busy doing something else, asking me to help her move some furniture in her bedroom, and once inside she would shut the door and slip out of one of her simple white sleeveless dresses, letting it fall to the floor, and there she would be, with those extraordinary erect nipples and in those red crocheted knickers, spilling pubic hair – petite and very foxy – and she'd be smiling, a come-on smile, and it was obvious what was going to happen next. The natural progression, I'd since learned, of desire over rationality.

The buzzer went, but I had reached the point of no return and shot into the toilet – at least I'd made it that far this time – and pumped the rest out as best I could and rapidly pulled up my boxers and trousers and flushed the toilet, and it was not until I was approaching my front door, ready to peer through the spyhole, that my heart started seriously thumping again, for the second time that day. I couldn't work out who the hell would be ringing my buzzer at this hour, not just the main buzzer linked to the intercom by the entrance to the building ten floors below, but the buzzer just on the other side of my front door. And I couldn't get the idea of Jeanette out of my mind, and how even expensively maintained bodies aged.

The shock, the violence of dashed hopes and expectations. I should have learned something by now. Obviously if I wanted to climb out of the loop – dreams denied and all that – drastic action was called for. Again. Besides I didn't want my true feelings and predilections, my real desires, revealed to the wider world. I was a very private person. Passionate, sure, committed too, but private. Though, I had a dreadful inkling that however hard you tried to cover your tracks, the story would not end there.

It wasn't possible they had come about Jeanette, was it? Too much time must have passed. Why was I even thinking this? I was losing touch with reality. Imagining the worst. Recent events had badly unhinged me. 'Yes?' I said. I could see two men, white, early thirties, bad haircuts, thick jaws, roughly shaved, not in uniform as such but both in taste-less, dark blue anoraks, pronouncing that they were low-paid officials of some sort. 'Yes?' I said again, louder, more assertively.

'Mr Freeman?'

'Who is this?'

'Are you Mr Freeman?'

'Why?'

'Could you open the door please?'

'No. Not until you tell me who you are.' The man not doing the speaking was looking around the corridor – working out whether I had another way of escape? I did, as it happened, an old fire-escape hatch leading to the exterior stairwell – those architects thought of everything. But to get to it would take some time. I'd have to shift aside my wardrobe, which was effectively built in and stuffed, albeit very neatly, with every item of clothing that I possessed, except of course what

I was wearing. It would have taken too long, aside from the fact that I was not prepared to throw my clothes onto the floor. I hadn't washed the floor in weeks. Something else, I realised, I should have done, as well as repaint the walls. My laziness, my incompetence, my stupidity was going to finish me.

'We're from TV Licensing. You do not appear to have a licence.'

Were they making this up? Was this some underhand way of gaining entry without a warrant? Were they plain clothes dressed, even more badly, as TV Licensing people? I wasn't that stupid.

'How do I know who you are?'

'Here's my identification.'

The man doing the talking unzipped his anorak to reveal a photo ID laminate hanging by a thin cord from his neck. He held it up to the spyhole. It could have been fake of course but I decided to open the door as far as the intruder chain would allow. I didn't want to arouse suspicion unnecessarily. Act normally and everything would be all right. 'Yeah?'

'According to our records you do not have a television licence.' While not stepping any closer he was craning his neck, attempting to see further into my flat.

'I don't have a television.'

'We have to warn you that if you operate a television without a licence you will be liable to prosecution. The fine is a thousand pounds. Our records show that there is no licence for this property.'

'That's because I don't have a television.' I knew he couldn't see my TV. It was in the far corner of the main room, well out of his view. 'Why would I want to watch the crap that they churn out? And I'm not even thinking about the shopping channels, I'm talking about BBC and ITV and Channel bloody Four.'

'I'd like to warn you again, that if you have a television, you will be liable for prosecution.' He was still craning away, his cohort puffing out his chest behind him. But they couldn't see anything incriminating, I was sure of that.

'Come on, mate,' I often found that when talking to a certain sort of jumped-up official I couldn't help but slip into their vernacular – mate was not a word I used regularly – 'why would I want one? To watch *I'm A Celebrity . . . Get Me Out Of Here!*, or *Celebrity MasterChef*, or *Strictly Come Dancing*, or *Soccer Aid*?'

I looked them up and down, these so-called TV licence people in their cheap anoraks and ill-fitting polyester trousers and dirty white shirts and scuffed, soft shoes, and with bad haircuts and breath and tiny spectacles that were simply years out of date. How they needed a makeover. How they needed Lisa Butcher and Mica Paris. Even Nicky Hambleton-Jones could have done some good.

'Or Gordon Ramsay's *The F Word*?' I continued. 'If I have to listen to another thing that man says. Or *Britain's Got Talent*. No it hasn't. Not from what I've seen. Or *The X Factor*.' How could I have forgotten that show with its millions of viewers? 'Oh fucking hell, not *The X Factor*. What a disgrace. And what a poor reflection on today's youth. Why does everyone want to be a fucking star? I don't. I just want to live in peace and quiet, a million miles from all that rubbish. I want to be left alone, to mind my own business. Understand?'

'Sounds like you've been watching quite a lot of telly,' the other man said, in a dull, retarded-sounding East End accent.

'Why do you think I've just dumped my girlfriend?' I was livid. 'When I went round to her place that was all that she was ever doing. Passively rotting what was left of her brain. Finally I had enough. And you're asking me whether I have a fucking television? I'm telling you this is a television-free zone.' I glanced over my shoulder as if to emphasise I meant my property, my patch, my territory. 'But if you want something to think about, if you want serious culture, at least an intelligent chat,' I could tell I was beginning to freak them out, 'well you've come to the right place, boys. And what's more I'm free. Not cheap, I wouldn't say that, but free, in the best liberal tradition. What do they charge for these licences anyway?'

'One hundred and forty-two pounds fifty,' the first man said.

'That's far too little, to take over lives. They should charge thousands. Tens of thousands. It should be a proper tax, for the damage television does. Forget offsetting carbon emissions, and protecting the environment, we need to find ways of counterbalancing all the bullshit on the telly. It's really not the planet that people should worry about but their own minds, and the minds of others. As ever the real problems are so much closer to home. And it's people like me, the ones who stand back and don't reach for the remote, who have to deal with the fallout. I haven't just lost my girlfriend, I've lost a city, a nation, a whole world nearly.' I was beginning to enjoy myself.

'Do you have any idea of the significance of this collapse? Why do you think there are so many hoodies stalking the streets of London? Why's everyone so frightened? Why's everyone so dissatisfied?' These two looked so pitiful out in the corridor, trying to be officious, trying to enforce what little power they had. What a couple of losers. 'I expect you'll be popping up on *The X Factor* next series, singing some cheesy duet. What would it be now, let me think. "Something Stupid"?' Actually I liked the song, even the Nicole Kidman and Robbie Williams version.

'Hey, Nietzsche,' the slow, retarded-sounding man said, 'bottle it.'

'We can get a warrant, you know,' the other man said. 'We have detector vans, hand-held devices, and huge databases at our disposal. We'll be watching you.' They turned as one and walked back down the corridor towards the lift.

Detector vans. What a joke they'd been. I shut the door and walked through to the TV and switched it on, but it was still Ant and Dec, watching the hunk Bobbie fancied wrestling with a snake. I paused, hoping he'd be constricted to death, before I killed the set, kicked the sofa to let off some steam and shifted across to the window at the back of the flat. Mia had disappeared so I walked through and out onto the balcony. Sure enough Jeanette, or rather my Jeanette lookalike, was still glued to the box. Just how engaged was this woman? And at her age. She should have known better. I should have known better.

Mia, my Mia lookalike, the very idea of striking up a mean-ingful or at the very least physical relationship with her, suddenly seemed more fresh and exciting, now she had slipped from view. To do what exactly? Take a shower, or was she in bed already, getting frisky with her fat geek? Why would I want to go for some nerdy geeky look? Bobbie had so much to answer for. And that woman at David Clulow — she wasn't going to get away with anything either. I'd be paying her another visit, sooner rather than later. I took off my glasses and tried to ascertain, for about the fiftieth time that day, exactly how damaged they were. It was obvious that one arm had been bent way out of shape and hurriedly bent back. I would like to have snapped the damn thing off completely, but my stock of spectacles, with my current prescription, were running dangerously low. What wasn't?

At least Mia, my gorgeous Mia lookalike, probably even better than the original thing, wasn't watching telly. Maybe she had something resembling a brain, which hadn't yet been completely destroyed. I'd have to keep a closer eye on her, because Mia was beginning to feel like the future, if not an accident waiting to happen. I chuckled to myself, suddenly wondering whether I had started talking aloud too. Surely Jeanette, like Bobbie, was the past. But I'd always had a problem with escaping the past — that loop. The comfort.

I wondered whether I should trek all the way over to Battersea Rise. Maybe it would be wise to be seen there, to be seen trying to do something. Would Gabriella be back? Invariably I was a man of action, not inaction. That's how I got where I was. I couldn't stand people who let life drift by them without getting involved. Besides I needed some air. Night air, even in the centre of this polluted city, had a certain tinge to it — a distinct, incomparably exciting edge. I suddenly wanted to gulp it down.

Pulling on my coat, my best Crombie from Crombie, which of course was the only outfitters who produced the original article, my mobile went. *Withheld number calling*, it said. It was 22:46 according to the bottom of the tiny screen — an infinitely more reliable source of time, I was coming to realise, than my old Jaeger-LeCoultre. I quickly slipped my phone back into my pocket, leaving it to ring out there. Shortly I heard it beep. Whoever it was had left a message.

Was I going to Clapham? Or St John? Now there was a thought. I could only guess at what time she would be getting off, that dishy waitress, with the teasingly frosty demeanour and fantastic figure — the second such female that had captured my fancy in as many days. Soon surely. Pigeon past ten o'clock at night didn't seem very palatable. But perhaps I had muddled them up in my mind, those two — Asian? — babes. Overwhelmed by the sudden surplus of fanciable waiting staff and sales assistants. Even so, I'd be pushing my luck. I'd had enough scrapes. Enough rejection.

There was no trace of the TV licence boys on the way out of my building or as I was exiting the estate. Yet gathering pace, I could feel my heart beginning to pump again and beads of sweat prickle my brow. Was I their only port of call? Who were they really? I didn't press the answerphone button on my mobile until I'd almost reached the entrance to Barbican Tube and was safely standing on the deserted corner of Aldersgate and Long Lane — those walkways, that concourse, the dangerous truth of my estate. I could still go either way.

'Leave her alone,' said a man's voice. Some joke. Though just the direction I needed.

A faint light was on upstairs. The landing. It was late, nearly midnight, and surprisingly cold. I didn't know what had happened to the weather recently. First it was warm and sunny, then, after a torrential downpour, distinctly chilly. I was missing the usual lame mugginess. I was missing the drizzle. I didn't like change and I knew I couldn't keep standing out on the street for much longer. I had generated some heat walking from the Tube — and what a novel experience the Tube at such a time had proved to be. I'd thought that drinking had been banned. But those who weren't comatose or engaged in heavy petting seemed to be swigging alcopops. What a sobering lesson on a stinking, crowded, late-night Underground train. I couldn't wait to disembark, but there were signalling problems at Willesden Junction and I was stuck between stations for almost an eternity. Was the Bakerloo Line actually worse than the Northern Line? Now finally free, and absolutely freezing, I was desperate for a drink, and for something considerably stronger than Smirnoff Ice. Funny how such horror was so easily dismissed.

What I couldn't ignore, however, was the inadequacy of my Crombie. The coat might have looked fantastic and fitted beautifully, but it was showing signs of weakness. It simply didn't work. Where was the warmth? If Crombie couldn't

make a decent Crombie anymore, who the hell could? H&M?
I blew into my hands and watched the escaping air rise into
the night.

There was nothing unusual about the house from the
outside tonight, as if there should have been. I really didn't
know what I was expecting. Signs of forced entry? Police
tape? A cop on guard? My mind was running away with me,
taking me on yet another hideous, stalling detour. I needed
to get back to the present, the icy here and now.

I'd forgotten, as I always did, how quiet this part of London
could be after *Newsnight*. How tree-lined the streets were
and how big and well preserved the houses, though mostly
terraced, appeared. This was where strung-out, over-lever-
aged people bred, in comfort, without having to lose all their
social credibility. Or so they thought – the fools. This was
where I could have ended up, in a different life, with a
neurotic, nagging, deceitful wife and who knew how many
children. Children I'd have to lug to Queen's Park every
weekend, when we weren't in the country, so they could
jump around on a hideous plastic play area with thousands
of other screeching, spoilt kids. There I'd be, left on the
sideline with their scooters and squashy tricycles, discussing
the latest disastrous derivative trades, while leering at tasty
young Slovakian au pairs' arses, with other stressed dads
doing their smug but ultimately thankless bit. When all we'd
want would be to slink off to the Salisbury. I'd had a lucky
escape. I'd bailed out at the Notting Hill stage. Bayswater
anyway.

Not so Joe. Joe ruthless Ryan. He'd picked up where I'd
left off. Before I'd left off in fact. Had he kept the light on,
expecting, even daring me to show? Was he drawing me in,
hoping I'd get caught this time? I wasn't a complete sucker.
He didn't scare me. Nor did his threats of exclusion orders
and restraining orders, whatever they really meant. He would

never be able to tarnish my reputation, my standing in the business world, as he'd proposed, even if he were a lawyer. And so what if he believed he knew what I'd done, once, twice, a few times before – the pathetic accusations. How the guilty liked to apportion blame. But he wouldn't catch me, nobody would. I laughed.

She must have been in there too, of course, snug and secure, snoring away – ha, I laughed again because she did snore – and their children, finally conked after hours of tea and tantrums. How many did they have already, two, three? If Joe insisted on threatening me I knew how to make things very nasty indeed. He had no idea who he was dealing with.

I started to shiver, while observing all this that could so easily have been mine – the immaculate, early Edwardian property, complete with original stained-glass front door, that had been elaborately fortified. The downstairs windows, again probably fastened by stops and screws and bruise plates, were well curtained against any draught and prying eyes. But what were they really protecting? Not a privileged life of happiness, fulfilment and security, but a terrible fucking lie. Had Fran told Joe about her bulimia, her dyslexia, her lack of ambition and thirst for attention, her obsession with hair removal, dieting, tooth whitening and *What Not To Wear*? Her addiction to shopping, alcohol and adultery? Though he must have already known about the latter affliction. And to think how generous and understanding I'd been, to think of the long hours I'd spent listening to and comforting a supposedly distressed, deeply troubled young, or youngish woman, when really she'd just been betraying me.

And for Joe to keep denying that simple truth, even that he'd slept with her that time they'd gone to a conference in Birmingham, or on that occasion Fran had said she was staying at her brother's when I discovered her brother was abroad. For Fran and Joe then to turn round and report me for harassment, for actual bodily harm and criminal damage no less – it was so cruel and unnecessary, especially considering how much Fran had meant to me and what I would have done for her. She should have been my wife for God's sake. I'd have loved and cherished her, as I was all set to promise to do in a fancy little west London church of her choosing. She was the world to me. How dare she and Joe abuse those feelings, that trust. How dare they mock me. No more.

An alarm was blinking halfway up their wall. An aged Vanguard box, too inadequate for words, but it was a signal, another signal pointing the way. For a couple so cultivated, with such trappings, they were remarkably slack when it came to protecting their assets properly. Maybe that was always the way with the monied – on paper anyway. Easy come easy go. There were chinks everywhere. Queen's Park was a total sham.

The road was impossibly still, the air framing my every breath. Now was the time, a voice was telling me. Move. Quick. Little bird.

FOUR

Frozen Liquidity

Eternity was something the North Koreans certainly took seriously. No matter that the president Kim Il-sung had died in 1994, he was still president, assigned the role for, extraordinarily, eternity. He had long been titled the Great Leader while his son, who might also have died, Kim Jong-il, was the Dear Leader, forever too. Who was next, Kim Jong-nam, I supposed – Kim Jong-il's Mickey Mouse-loving eldest son. What was he going to be, the Disney Leader? Maybe the whole place was an American invention, propaganda to make the dream still endlessly attractive, if not attainable. With China now sold out, and Cuba all but a busted flush, North Korea was the last bogeyman of communism.

North Korea seemed almost too bad, or good, depending on your perspective, to be true. There were over forty-three million North Koreans, rigorously kept in check. No one ever defected, no one ever stepped out of line. No one ever said a word against the Great Leader or his Dear Son, or probably the Disney one, though Kim Jong-il had not been averse to a little unconventional fun himself. There were the wives, the mistresses, the luxury Western goods, the barrels of cognac, not to mention those Elvis spectacles and jump-suits, even if they were in a drab khaki. Obviously there was no point holding all that power if you couldn't enjoy your-self occasionally – or indeed if you couldn't abuse it. And Kim Jong-nam was clearly following in his father's foot-steps, with his love of all things Disney, and, allegedly, porn and James Bond movies. Though, maybe this was all part of the American invention. Was Pyongyang really party central for South East Asian drug traffickers, money launderers, counterfeiters, nuclear-arms dealers and terrorists – crim-inals and evildoers of every persuasion? I'd be in good company if it were. What a blast.

Unable to sleep, I'd been doing my homework. It had been slow going because my broadband connection was still not connecting and I had to resort to old-fashioned dial-up. The last time I'd rung the technical helpline I asked them how I was meant to run a business without broadband and they said I hadn't registered for business use. I was down as a leisure user, operating from a residential address.

'Just because I'm not down as a business user,' I'd said, 'doesn't mean I won't be using my broadband for business. Millions of people work from home nowadays, and you're telling me we all have to register separately as business users?' Apparently business users got preferential treat-ment when there was a fault and as I was a leisure user I couldn't expect any favours – despite the fact that my broad-band hadn't been working for two and a half months. I could barely hear what the man had been saying anyway, from some call centre in India.

I'd asked to speak to the supervisor and was put on hold and had to listen to Beyoncé singing the same dirge twice. The male supervisor who eventually came on had a Geordie accent, which was even more impenetrable than the person I'd been speaking to earlier. What's more he kept calling me 'mate' and even 'Matt'. Did I call him Gazza, or Wazza or Bazza?

He was no help whatsoever. He couldn't even tell me when it would be fixed. 'How long is a piece of string?' were his actual words. He then told me there was huge pressure on the exchange because I lived in a very congested area. As if I didn't know.

'I've wasted hours and hours on your bloody helplines, for what? Because I fancied a chat? Because I'm lonely?' I said at one point.

'You'd be surprised,' he said.

'Believe me, I have got better things to do.'

'I'm sure, Matt, but we're doing everything we can.'

I asked for compensation.

'Now you are being silly,' he said.

'No, far from it.'

'Matt,' he said, 'listen mate, contractually we've provided everything we set out to by way of equipment, and we've activated your ASDL line. It's an engineering problem, at the exchange, or somewhere on the line, and this is being looked into.'

'When?'

'All I can say is action is pending.'

'I can barely hear you. Fuck it. I want to cancel my subscription.'

'You can do that at any time. It's a free service.'

'And how long will that take?'

'You can cancel it now but we will have to notify the exchange. That'll take ten days.'

'So it's going to take me ten days to get out of this mess.' Where was Kim Jong-il when I needed him?

'That's the way it works, Matt. You'll find it's the same with every provider.'

'I didn't ask for your broadband. I was rung up. The woman

practically begged me to have it because I was such a loyal and valued customer. What a fucking joke. Do you think I treat my business partners so incompetently, so callously? No, of course I don't. I've had three months of constant aggravation from you. And it's been far from free, the money I've spent on helplines, the time I've wasted when I should have been working. What the hell do you suggest I do now?'

'It's entirely up to you.'

'It's entirely up to me? No it's not. Sadly it's up to you, you cunt.' I could see how people, how nations occasionally had to rely on force. Having a nuclear option suddenly seemed entirely reasonable to me.

It had been one of the most exhausting phone calls I'd ever had, and had got me absolutely nowhere. The whole issue was probably not helped by my dusty PowerBook, loaded with anachronistic software and on the verge of a seizure. Nothing was made to last for more than five minutes. I slammed shut the heavily scratched and worn lid. It was impossible to work. No wonder my business had been having a few problems over the last two or three months, not least regarding cash flow. I walked over to the window. The blinds in the sitting-room section of my flat were no better than the blinds by my bed. Daylight was now streaming round the edges, not quite sunlight this morning, but not the normal blank, endless grey either – how I was missing that, that muggy dreariness, that certainty. Wild, unpredictable weather better suited less crowded, remoter places. I tugged the cord and opened the blind fully. There was no sign of my special neighbours. No sign of anyone. It was still early. And chilly. This new weather was not letting me forget about my broken boiler today.

White goods were no better than brown. I hadn't had the boiler installed of course. It had been here when I'd arrived, but it didn't appear too old, not that I knew anything about such appliances. German badged, if not made, it shouldn't have broken already, and nor should the zip on my duck-down, Prada, sleeveless puffa, which I found myself having to wear indoors, day and night. I would have kept the Crombie on but by the time I eventually got home, no thanks to Transport for London, I was so disgusted with its lack of warmth, and its heaviness and stiffness, which seriously hindered my agility just when I really needed it – plus after discovering, in the brightly lit lift on the way up to my flat, that it had acquired a couple of grubby marks – that I bundled it up in a black bin liner and chucked it down the rubbish chute.

In their wisdom Chamberlin, Powell and Bon had designed rubbish chutes for every floor of my building. Open a metal hatch out in the emergency stairwell, stuff your rubbish into a compartment, shove the thing shut, and whoosh, there it went. You had to wait for a few seconds before you heard it clatter and clunk into a container at the bottom. Window blinds, and maybe the odd, dark passageway aside, I had yet to find a major fault with the architects, with their vision. This was what modern, communal, inner-city living should be all about – convenience, space, clean lines, light, warmth. Except, long gone were the original communal boilers that had provided round-the-clock heating and hot water. And long gone was any real sense of communal living. No one gave a shit about anyone else, let alone the shared infrastructure, those corridors and walkways, stairwells and concourses. But this was just a snippet of the wider picture, of what was happening across the capital. What was wrong with people? Why did everything have to change, for the worse? Prada, of all labels, couldn't even get it right with a simple zip.

OK, the puffa was from the cheaper, red label sportswear range but it shouldn't have broken. I would have taken it back of course, despite the fact that I'd bought it in a sale a couple of years ago. However, I'd recently vowed never to go into the flagship Bond Street store again. This was where I'd originally purchased the puffa and where in their latest sale I'd picked up a tweed jacket – not from the sportswear range but the main luxury line. It was made from a heavy, grey and white pure new wool cloth, woven apparently in the Outer Hebrides, and it had faux frayed elbow patches, two buttons, a half-lining and no shoulder padding. Though technically unstructured it had plenty of shape to it, screaming country casual for the urban sophisticate. At least it was as close to a traditional tweed jacket I was going to be seen in this or any other year. As much as I admired the quality and build of much country clothing I hated the country and I definitely didn't want to look as if I lived there, full-time.

The unpadded shoulders, nevertheless, were a problem. They were too big. In fact the jacket was a size too big, being a 40 and not a 38, but because it was Prada, I thought it would be OK. While the chest and arms were fine – and it was rare that jackets had the right-length arms for me – the shoulders most definitely weren't. Anyway, it was half price, some £480 had been knocked off, and I couldn't help myself, especially as they said they'd take in the shoulders for free.

A guy came up from the basement and the minute he started explaining how he'd actually do the alterations I knew it was going to be a disaster. He talked about tucking in the sleeves at the top but then lengthening them at the bottom. It seemed all the wrong way round to me and I immediately began to doubt his tailoring qualifications. Needless to say when I picked up the jacket a week or so later the shoulders were far too tight and the material appeared rucked and badly finished right around where the sleeve joined. I freaked. Especially as I'd already paid for the jacket.

Some other man to the one who'd sold me the jacket in the first place said, in what I was convinced was a fake Italian accent, 'I'm sorry, sir, but this alteration was exactly to your order. I've just checked with the tailor, and he said he followed your instructions, even how you told him to take in the shoulders.'

'What do I know about tailoring?' I'd said. 'He's meant to be the expert. Does this look like it fits? And what about the rucks here?'

'I've been informed that you were advised by more than one member of staff that the jacket fitted well originally and didn't need to be taken in. But you insisted on having it altered, which, because we value our customers, we agreed to do for free.'

'I'm a 38. This jacket is a 40. It was too big and now it's too small.' I didn't bother to tell him that the customer was always right, whatever.

'The tailor has informed me that it's not now possible to let out the shoulders, the material has been cut away, as you requested.'

People had started to look at me. With that particular boutique even then being hardly the busiest place on Bond Street, it was not possible to be discreet.

'There's nothing we can do, I'm sorry. It was a sale item and sale items are non-refundable.'

'So what am I meant to do? Live with it? I want my money back.'

'I'm afraid that's not possible. Not only is it a sale item, it has also been altered.'

I'd never hit a sales assistant before and I didn't hit this man very hard. It was more of a slap with the back of my hand, which I sort of disguised as part of my desperate struggle to tear off the ruined piece of clothing as quickly as possible. He was too shocked, I think, to realise quite what had happened. But I couldn't stand it when places such as Prada proved so unaccommodating. It was particularly shoddy behaviour, from an establishment that tried to project such a refined, stylish image.

'Keep it,' I shouted, letting the jacket fall to the floor. 'But don't expect to get my custom again.' I couldn't afford to waste £480, but I didn't see why a trickle of Prada customers shouldn't be made aware of how they treated their non-celebrity clients. What a two-faced world. Bond Street, surely, represented everything that was wrong with shopping and stardom, aspiration at least. Where was Kim Jong-il, or anyway Kim Jong-nam and a levelling dose of communism?

Was I jealous, because of my humble pedigree and dwindling bank balance? Not a bit. I simply believed in treating people with respect, though of course not respect in south-east London, knife-wielding gangsta terminology. Besides, I didn't like to be let down. Prada had been on my radar for so long. In fact, thinking about it, didn't Prada perennially do a line of militaryesque khaki-wear, with neat rows of buttons and completely superfluous epaulettes? Hadn't Prada invented the concept, in the fashion sense? Maybe they'd even supplied Kim Jong-il with his jumpsuits. It wouldn't have surprised me, given their ruthlessness and his showmanship. Then who was I to question the ethics of doing business with the North Koreans? Or of wearing fancy but barely functional gear?

Obviously there was no way I was taking the puffa back. I shouldn't have bought that either. I'd never much rated the sportswear range and I hated wearing any item of clothing that had the label on the outside. Look at me, I'm wearing Prada. How insecure would you have to be? But I didn't think Prada was quite as sad in that respect as, say, Burberry, even though I'd always fancied a proper Burberry trench coat. I ran my hands over the man-made shell of the puffa, encasing, supposedly, the duck down. Maybe I would take it back, but to the Prada concession in Selfridges. What would they know? Unless they had never stocked this particular item, which was possible. I didn't remember seeing it there and I was in Selfridges enough. Why Selfridges was still always so busy I had no idea, especially when it was only one obvious concession after another. It was as if the department store operated in a different universe, a universe inhabited by people who never worked but only shopped for luxury goods – except for the sales assistants, if that could be called work, rather than simply attitude.

I left my desk and walked towards the balcony door, rubbing my hands together. They were freezing – I had terrible circulation, for someone so young – and the skin was dry and chafed and badly scratched. I'd been washing them too much recently, in cold water as well, but on closer inspection, under natural daylight, not thoroughly enough. There were still some flecks of something dark under the nails.

For a brief moment I wondered whether I was seeing things, whether, indeed, like in some horror movie guilty bloodstains would keep appearing on me despite my best efforts to scrub myself clean. I could imagine fine splatters of blood breaking out on my face, trickles emerging on my arms, pools gathering by my feet. Walking back through to the bathroom I wiped my nose on my left hand and was relieved to see I'd left a fresh trail of blood. I must have had a minor nosebleed and because I was working so hard on the Korean project while endlessly having to wipe my nose on the backs of my hands because of the cold, not noticed that I wasn't dealing with just snot.

Whether I was growing more paranoid or not I knew I'd have to repaint much of the room, today. DIY was not my thing – was it really anybody's except perhaps Joe's, who must have been forever patching up his perfect home? But

I knew that this was one occasion when I couldn't call in the decorators, even if I'd had the funds. They would have asked too many impertinent questions, as they always did, even the Poles. I really didn't want to be quizzed by a bunch of odd-job men. I could just imagine how it would go, along with the accents they'd put on.

'Hello, hello, hello, what's been going on in here?' would say one of the decorators, the fatter one, trying to sound like a chummy 1950s detective. 'Someone slit their wrists in front of the telly? Wouldn't blame them. Or was it a domestic dispute? Think your girlfriend was running around behind your back? What'd you do, stab her in the neck?'

They wouldn't believe me if I'd told them I'd flung a glass of wine across the room because the wine was corked. How could they comprehend the annoyance I felt at finding my very last bottle of Château Perron 2003 tasting sharp and vinegary? It wasn't the most expensive bottle of wine I'd ever bought by any measure, but the previous bottle of Château Perron I'd opened was beautifully balanced between old vines and new methods, it was ripe, with impeccable oak, fruit and sophisticated tannins. There was serious depth and a very long, complex finish. It was everything and more I wanted from a reasonably priced claret. Except on opening my second bottle that evening my high expectations had been dashed in an instant. It was almost too much to bear and worse than not having drunk any wine that evening at all. And not, I was sure, a story many builders or decorators, Polish or otherwise, would empathise with.

Indeed all the builders I'd ever had the misfortune of coming into contact with, especially those who weren't Polish, were lazy, unreliable, bullying and expensive, not to mention completely dishonest. Why we had come to rely on them to quite such an extent I had no idea. Building and decorating were not complicated jobs, not the small stuff. Anyone could do it, if they were malicious enough. Builders, sales assistants, technical support supervisors, they were all as bad as each other. I really had to learn to forget about empathy, about understanding, about simply being reasonable. As usual my expectations were far too high. What was wrong with this place? What was wrong with humanity?

When my mobile went and said *Withheld number calling*, yet again, I was instantly reluctant to pick it up, of course. Who could be calling me at this hour? In fact what hour was it? In the panic I couldn't see the time on the screen. Though it had to be pretty early in the morning and there was usually only one person who rang me at that sort of time. Thinking about it, he was just the person I needed to speak to.

'Hiya,' Sean said. Like Roger he failed to sound and act his age. What was it with my friends and family?

'Hello Sean. You sound odd. What's wrong with the line?'

'I'm ringing via my computer, on a Skype connection, it's never as good as a normal line, but it's virtually free, even calling abroad. Don't you have one, with all the foreign calls you must have to make? Don't you know anything?'

'It doesn't make that much difference to me. I can usefully write all that stuff off to tax. Besides I need a crystal-clear line, with the people I have to talk to.' Sean would sign up to anything if it were cheap enough.

'Why am I ringing your mobile anyway? I tried your landline. It was engaged. It's been engaged for hours. I thought maybe there was a fault.'

'I was on the Internet. Maybe I didn't shut it down correctly.'

'Yeah, but what's that got to do with it?'

'My broadband's playing up.'

'You mean you were on dial-up?' He laughed. 'For

someone who does what you do, I can't believe you're not more sussed.'

Sussed? What sort of a word was that? My brother, honestly, hard to think of him as a grown man. 'I cope fine. Anyway I don't see the point of endlessly having to change your software and reconfigure your computer and fork out for the latest technical who knows what. It's all bullshit, designed to make you feel inadequate. And it especially offends my rather acute sense of prudence. I manage to run my business just fine, on a tight budget.'

'Good. I'm very pleased for you, and me actually.'

Mostly I thought my brother and I were poles apart but very occasionally I thought we had something in common. He could be to the point, and amusing with it. 'What time is it there?' I said.

'I don't know, nine thirty. Have I called you too early?'

'No, I was awake, working.'

'It's Saturday. On what?'

'This and that.'

'Yeah?'

'If you must know, a North Korean thing's come up.'

'North Korea? Wow, that sounds interesting. How was Dubai by the way? I haven't spoken to you since you've been.'

'Dubai? That was ages ago. I can barely remember. It was fine, I think. Busy. Very swanky hotel, and hot of course, though not inside. Everywhere is chronically over air-conditioned, it's worse than New York. But you know what they're like, these trips — lots of people promising you things and the reality not being quite so good. I'm waiting for a couple of contracts to come through.' I don't know why he always managed to put me on the defensive, and make me feel so inadequate.

'So you don't regret trying to go it alone?'

'No, of course not. Why should I? I'm my own boss. It's

what I always wanted.' I especially hated to talk about business with my brother. What did he know, he was a fucking sculptor. Sure, he'd invested some money in my business, but he, indeed anyone would have been mad not to. He saw the obvious opportunities, plus he was loaded. Tight but loaded, which was probably why he was loaded. It was always the way. 'Kids all right?' He had three children, two girls and a boy. Or was it two boys and a girl? I could never remember how old they were, or in which order they came. I struggled with their names too.

'They're great. Johan's started at this football academy, he's got real promise, a right little Ole Gunnar Solskjaer in the making, perhaps he'll play for Rosenborg one day, or Man United, that would be something, wouldn't it, and Ellie's turning into quite a princess. She's so pretty and Christina's going through a very cute phase too, if a little temperamental. I think out of the three Christina's got the most artistic promise.'

'How old is she?'

'She's two and a half. But you should see her paintings, technically they're terrific. In fact you can. I've posted them on my blog. I've completely redone the site. It looks great and is getting so many hits already. I've changed the whole concept. It's no longer just about my work, but about my whole life, my interests and influences, my family and friends. It's what a lot of artists are doing in Norway right now. Already masses of people, even strangers, have contributed words and pictures. In a way it's like a scrap-book, very free-flowing and sketchy and constantly evolving. Organic is the obvious word to describe it, but I hate using that word. It's so overused. Let's just say it's both intimate and expansive.'

When my brother started talking about his fucking work, let alone his family, not that obviously he saw much of a distinction between the two, he never stopped. I held the phone away from my ear and yawned.

'The idea,' he continued, 'is that any potential customer knows exactly what they're investing in – me, effectively. As you know, my work is my life' – yes, I did know – 'it's all-encompassing. That's what I try to project on this new site anyway. You should check it out. Contribute something if you want.'

I couldn't think of anything worse. And I don't know why I'd also just thought my brother and I ever had anything in common, however remote or tiny. We didn't. If it weren't for his investment in my business, I'd never have picked up the phone. As it was I'd been thinking for some time about asking for a further injection of cash. Like everyone else I suddenly had a problem with liquidity. Plus he couldn't seriously have thought he would see a return for his initial measly sum quite so soon. I was operating a proper, grown-up business, reliant on transparent market forces, not an inane lifestyle project, which for some completely bizarre reason was proving to be so popular, in Norway. The Norwegians couldn't get enough of my brother and his sustainable wooden sculptures painted in nursery colours, more often than not, I suspected, actually by his offspring, and accompanied by home videos showing everybody having a fun-filled time dancing around them.

There was a whiff of fascism about it all – the forced, mass jollity, dictated by my crazed brother. He'd have given Kim Jong-il a run for his money. And what exactly did Sean's acceptance, his popularity, his authority in Norway say about that particularly strange little country? As far as I could tell it was an absurdly childish nation of non-dissenting Boy Scouts, and the odd, busty Girl Guide. No one, it seemed, had ever fully matured. Everyone, by and large, still ran around in shorts with penknives holstered to their belts, getting ready to bed down for the night in creaky wooden huts, painted an unpleasant, ubiquitous scarlet. Chamberlin, Powell and Bon would not have been impressed.

And why was everything so shockingly expensive in Norway, especially alcohol? Why was drinking so discouraged, when surely nothing could have been more necessary to liberate both minds and bodies? Adults, so I'd gathered, would actually sit around at night drinking coffee and eating cakes, leaving their children to run amok, at least once they'd played their part in whatever so-called artistic ritual they'd been assigned to. It was all the wrong way round. There was no proper conversation, no culture.

Plus given that the country was so rich, why was everything so demure? Why was everyone so poorly dressed? Were there any Norwegian fashion designers of note? None that I could name. And why, given all that cash, those vast oil and gas reserves, did they eat such unrefined food? Smoked lamb, dried reindeer, blubbery whale steaks – those were the delicacies. To think that North Korea had such a bad rap for being backward and isolationist, and incapable of properly feeding and clothing their people. At least the weather in the Korean peninsula had to be better. As much as I loved grey, drizzly days, blinding sleet and ice storms were not my thing.

My brother was welcome to Norway. Indeed, clearly he'd more than found his true home – with his plump, humourless Norwegian wife, who still wore dungarees and pigtails and was endlessly baking inedible rowanberry cake. Amazingly she was why he'd been attracted to the country in the first place. What was she called? Britta? Bridget? Brigitta? 'How's, how's your wife?'

'Anna's really well. In fact she's pregnant. That was one of the reasons I was calling.'

'That's great.' What else could I say? 'So you'll have how many? Four? Blimey, that'll be a handful.'

'Oh, we're really looking forward to it. We're absolutely thrilled. Anna and I both burst into tears when we found out, and then we took the kids to the hut for the night and fired up the wood burner and sat around hugging each other for hours, thinking of the future and our ever-growing family. It was very moving, very spiritual. You must come out, when the baby's born, if not before.'

'When's that?'

'Not until July. We'd hoped to give birth on 21 June, that's what we'd planned, but it looks like we missed it by a couple of weeks.'

I didn't know how much more of this I could take but seeing as he was on the phone and in such a good mood it occurred to me that now would be as good a moment as any. 'Sean, actually, I did want to talk to you about work some more. Did I tell you, I had to draw up another business plan the other week? The fucking bank was getting a bit huffy about its exposure – who isn't? – and while they could see the potential and know that I'm on the verge of securing a couple of major contracts, money is not coming in quite as expected and to cut a long story short they've given me to the end of the month before they pull the plug. To be honest, they've already frozen my account, which seems a little unfair, especially as I really need to get this North Korean proposal completed.'

'Shit.'

'I'm really sorry to have to bring this up and I know how helpful you've been already, but I don't want you to lose your stake anymore than I want this thing to collapse.'

'You want to borrow some more money, is that it?'

'Not borrow. I'm offering you a bigger slice for a further investment. I wasn't going to bother you with this. There are plenty of other people I can turn to, but seeing as you're on the phone, I thought I'd give you first choice.'

'Matt, before I think about this seriously, there is another reason why I rang. I've been talking to Fran. She's been calling me.'

'You're joking? What the fuck does she call you for?'

'She was worried about you. And herself, frankly.'

'I don't get it. We split up years ago. She's completely out of my life. I've almost forgotten about her. What's she doing ringing you up?'

'She says she's seen you in her street again, a number of times in fact. She thinks you're stalking her. Her word, not mine. And someone's been vandalising Joe's car. She doesn't want to go to the police, not after what happened the last time. She still cares about you.'

'No she doesn't. She never did. How could she have and behaved the way she did?'

'Let's not go into that. She wants you to leave her and Joe alone, Matt. They have got young children.'

'Haven't they just. But suspiciously not that young.'

'She thinks you need help, that you must be going through another bad patch.'

'This is ridiculous. And how insulting. Suddenly I'm the problem, am I?' I was probably shouting by now. It was an outrageous accusation.

'Matt, I'm only trying to help you.'

'I have not been stalking my ex-fiancée. I haven't been anywhere near fucking Queen's Park for years. I can't stand the place. It gives me the creeps. Believe me, she must have been seeing things, again. Maybe she likes the idea of me still being obsessed with her, because it fuels some narcissistic need. As you know she has a long history of neurosis, if not mental instability. Thought about that? But if it makes you feel better, I promise you, I don't wish to go anywhere near Queen's Park ever again. What more do I have to say? I'm not a stalker and never have been for that matter. It's not my style. The accusations she bandied about last time were bad enough. I can't believe she's actually been ringing you up. When exactly did you last hear from her?'

'It doesn't matter. The point is she obviously felt worried, and threatened.'

'Who doesn't, in this town? Look, I don't know what to say. It's like nobody ever believes me. Maybe things haven't been going all my way recently, but I don't need people to be talking about me behind my back. Especially not my brother and my devious ex-fiancée. You shouldn't be talking to her anyway. Where's the familial allegiance? The brotherly love? Whose fucking interests do you really have at heart?'

'Calm down, Matt. Sorry. I'm sorry. I didn't mean to upset you. How's Bobbie?'

'Bobbie? Why does everyone ask me about Bobbie all the time? I'm not seeing Bobbie anymore, OK?'

'I didn't know.'

'Well now you do.' I pressed the end call button. What was the point in continuing the conversation? When he rang back, as I knew he would, I switched off my mobile and flung it on the sofa. I'd have to keep the landline jammed on dial-up and find another investor, fast. Roger? He had declined originally, claiming, ridiculously, that it might lead to a conflict of interests. However, I was godfather to one of his atrocious children, and he had nearly been my best man. Did that still make him my best friend? I should have dropped a few hints over lunch yesterday. At least I'd bothered to get in touch with him. Maybe I'd have to send the kid a present, if I could remember his name. Shit, that meant I'd have to go to Toys R Us as well as B&Q today. Way off-piste for me.

There was no movement across the way. It was too early for Mia, and Jeanette, though being the much older of the

two, was usually up well before Mia, especially on the week-
ends. I thought of Bobbie's maisonette, how deathly quiet
it would be, whether Gabriella was back from the States or
not. Like Bobbie she never got up early unless she absolutely
had to. Even when I was a student I was an early riser,
cracking on with my reading, my essays, my dissertation. I
couldn't stand slothfulness, or the thought of the best years
of my life slipping by in a sleepy haze. I thought of Fran and
Joe's pitiful household, entrenched in the rapidly souring
pretension of Queen's Park, and I wondered just how quiet
that would be at this time. I laughed. Perhaps I'd found my
true purpose, peacemaker. Or concerned interventionist
anyway.

Maybe I would have to redraft not only my North Korean
proposal but my whole business plan, yet again. I knew I was
a stickler for detail, though I could see how this redrafting
game could quickly get out of hand. Yet I couldn't quite relin-
quish the idea that my business held the key, despite the
recent turbulence of my private life. My future, my well-
being and indeed the well-being of quite a few others, had
to be linked with whether it all finally worked, or not.
Growing up when and where I did, and living for so long in
central London — the city that had unquestionably led the
way, at least in the field of mugging the poor and stuffing
the rich — no wonder I had always been obsessed with
escaping the pitfalls, perfecting my ideas, and publicly
standing tall. However, I was finally running out of options.
The equilibrium I had most recently established and enjoyed
seemed to be in the process of being ferociously ripped from
me. Once more.

In many ways Bobbie was the least of it. She was always
going to be the least of it, being so dumb. Not as dumb maybe
as the TV licensing heavies, definitely not as dumb as them,
but dumb enough. In fact I was staggered she could have

been quite so devious and deceitful, which was why, of course, I'd had to end it so drastically. I wasn't going to be taken for another ride, particularly by someone like Bobbie. But that was all now behind me and I had to regard the encounter, the liaison, as of little consequence, if I was ever going to contemplate what was left for me, let alone move forward. Sorry Bobbie.

I began pacing my flat. Not like a caged lion exactly, more like a condemned prisoner. Was this how it felt? My pad was almost too minimal for its own good. Why couldn't I live in a plush house in north-west London, even if it was hocked to hell and had a smashed window or two? Why couldn't I have a wife and kids, a surprisingly fickle Jack Russell, a company BMW X5, one of the very latest off the production line, broken wing mirror or not? Would I care about the deep scratch running down the nearside? Or the flat tyre? Did we all have one now anyway?

Why couldn't I have a credit crunch-defying salary, with a host of share options, even if they were effectively worthless? Why couldn't I pop into Paul Smith, or Prada, or Burberry, or fucking Gieves & Hawkes for that matter, when it wasn't an end of season sale and purchase whatever I needed? In fact, not needed, but simply wanted. Why couldn't I have an industrial-size Gaggia for my immaculately fitted Linea kitchen and a seventeen-inch MacBook Pro with a 2.0 GHz Core Duo processor to sit sedately on my original leather and chrome Eames desk? I wasn't going to jump on the bandwagon and blame the recession.

I wanted to know why I couldn't go abroad, to places like Paris or Rome, or the fucking Seychelles and stay in five-star accommodation where my every whim was met with fawning servitude. I worked hard. I had always worked hard. Like a fucking dog. But it wasn't enough. It was never enough.

The Seychelles? I was looking across the acres of damp

concrete – it was still damp despite the upturn, or down-turn depending on one's preference, in the weather – to the banks of maisonettes that Chamberlin, Powell and Bon had so imaginatively and ingeniously designed, but there was still no sign of life in the two flats that had captured my imagination. I rushed from room to room, or in reality from one section of the room to another. What was I to do? I could sort out my clothes again. I was sure that there were a couple of things I no longer needed in my wardrobe. I hated giving space to anything that was past its best. Plus with more shelves and drawers freed up and with clothes that suddenly needed replacing I'd be fully justified in taking a trip west, and not just to Oxford Street, the cheap end. As if I was really going to search out a Toys R Us and a B&Q. Where were those places located, together? Deepest south-east London. I faintly recalled, though I had absolutely no idea why, that there used to be such a coupling on the Old Kent Road, just up from PC World and World of Beds. Near a World of Leather too. All these worlds I'd never entered. What was I missing? Slashed prices? Bargains galore?

I wasn't after bargains, I would always much rather buy something of real worth, something that oozed quality and craftsmanship and timeless style. Something that would last. As for the Seychelles – I didn't really care to stay in a fake rattan hut, on the doorstep of a tepid sea stretching benignly to the horizon. I would be bored rigid, and that would be before I'd even mingled with the other guests – from Eltham and Billericay no doubt. I could just imagine the place would be crawling with overpaid, overweight taxi drivers, who'd still be finding something to moan about – the king prawn curry, and the fact that they'd be missing the Arsenal replay with Luton. Frankly, I'd swap the Seychelles for somewhere like plain old Mallorca any day. I didn't see the point in trying to be adventurous, or especially glamorous when it came to leisure travel. Everywhere had been discovered, and invariably already trashed.

Mallorca. Suze. The two, sadly, now went together. But I couldn't believe I hadn't thought of Suze before. Yes I could – I never thought of Suze, unless I was really up against the wall. I did a little jump and heel click, what I thought of as my Fred Astaire move, though it might have been more in the vein of Billy Elliot.

All was not lost. I attempted a growl. And another. And clawed the air with my half-clenched fingers. Perhaps that was what tigers did, not lions. Animals weren't my thing. Neither was Suze, by a long shot; still I was going to break the silence, the impasse, for once, and give her a ring. Wasn't I the proactive peacemaker. Not finding my untrustworthy Jaeger on my wrist – would I ever get out of the habit? – I rushed through to my bedside table and checked my atomic-controlled radio alarm. It was 09:12:43. She would be up, and alone. She was always alone, waiting for someone to call, waiting for me to call. How she loved me, regardless.

FIVE

Moral Hazard

'What have you done to your face?'

'Let me sit down first.'

'Oh my God, Matt, you're still bleeding. You should go to hospital. See a doctor at least.'

'I'm all right. Really. I will be all right anyway. I just have to get my breath back.'

'What the hell happened?'

'I need a drink. Shit, I'm shaking.' I held out my hands as if to emphasise the point. They were shaking, though no more than normal.

'Of course. Of course. What do you want?'

Suze let go of my arm and reached for her bag – a scruffy, faux suede affair, probably from H&M. I doubted she ever shopped anywhere else. 'I don't know. A whisky. A large one, with a drop of water, no ice. A Laphroaig if they have it.' They wouldn't. It would be Bell's, if I was lucky.

She handed me a surprisingly clean, white cotton hand-kerchief before she stepped over to the bar. Trust Suze to have a hankie handy. I dabbed at my cheek and wiped my nose before checking the cloth. There was probably more snot than blood. But my cheek felt swollen and my nose was very sore and blocked. I had to breathe through my mouth. I must have sounded like a right jerk. Fortunately the Earl of Rochester was almost completely empty. Where was everyone? Shopping? Still living on credit? Slouching down Sloane Avenue? I felt a momentary pang of jealousy.

Suze handed me my drink, wrapping my hands around the chipped glass for me.

'Sip it slowly,' she said.

She sat down facing me, gently helping me lift the glass to my thick lips.

'Slowly.'

I wrenched the glass away from her and took a long glug. There was too much water and the whisky was Bell's all right and the glass, besides being chipped, was too small and warm, no doubt having just been pulled from the dishwasher. It was all wrong, but my fault, I supposed, for presuming I'd get a decent whisky in a proper glass with just the right amount of water. It was a horrible, poky pub I'd had the misfortune of visiting once before with Suze. She loved the place, the way it attracted proper locals, so she'd said, not that there were many about now, and the way it had never been trendied up, or gastro-fied, considering its location. As much as I loathed gastropubs, I didn't see the appeal of this place's 1970s-era sticky floral carpet and dim beige and maroon walls, complete with cheap prints of hunting scenes. Looking at the worn, empty bar stools and dark, stained tables, it didn't seem, for once, that I was in the minority. What was wrong with a bit of tasteful pretension, some recession-defying glitz? I had suggested we meet in the Blue Bar, at the Berkeley, but Suze said she wasn't budging from her beloved Pimlico, that Belgravia was for twats with still far too much money, and she wasn't even talking about the

Russians. If I wanted to see her I'd have to do the travelling.
I knew it would be a big mistake.

'So what happened?'

'What's the time?' It wasn't just my Jaeger that was
missing. When I went to my watch drawer earlier today my
collection seemed alarmingly to have dwindled. In fact there
wasn't one significant timepiece left – not the Omega or the
Tag, or even the chunky Glycine. I couldn't believe I'd sold
them all already, especially as I didn't now have my Jaeger.
But that was the problem with living so near to Clerkenwell
Road. There wasn't just one but two second-hand watch
stores. I knew the guys who ran both well, not that it ever
stopped them from charging me full whack and then
rescinding on their premium buy-back offers. They must
have made a packet out of me alone. And they weren't the
only concerns squeezing what they could out of me.

'Nearly seven,' Suze said.

'Sorry I was late. Not that I could have done anything about
it. Shit.'

'Matt, what happened?'

Suze was staring at me with her large brown eyes, putting
on her soppy, doleful look.

'They must have taken my watch as well.'

'You were mugged? Where?'

'After I got off the bus. I got off early – having spent an
age waiting for it in the first place – thinking I could take a
short cut, behind Buckingham Palace Road, by the coach
station.'

'You're joking? You were mugged? Round here? In
Pimlico?'

'Do I look as if I'm joking?'

'Sorry.'

'So did they beat you up, too? Oh Matt, how many of them
were there?'

'There were two, three big, stocky, white guys, speaking with thick, Eastern European accents. But I wasn't simply going to hand them my stuff.'

'You got in a fight? They hit you?'

'They pushed me to the ground and I suppose sort of shoved my face into a paving slab. I'm not sure they hit me exactly, but they kept me down while they went through my pockets.' It wasn't so far from the truth. I had ended up on the floor, after an altercation.

'They got everything?'

I stood up, wobbling, and frisked myself. I felt my phone in the outside pocket of my jacket, pulled it out, looked at it in what I thought was a bemused way and put it back. 'Yeah, except my phone. They were disturbed, thank God – it's a real wasteland out there isn't it? – and ran off. A car drove past, a shiny, dark four-by-four. It didn't actually stop of course. What if I'd been really injured? What if I was dying? But I suppose the people who drive those things gave up caring about the human race years ago.'

'Matt, I'm so sorry. You've called the police?'

Why were people always saying sorry to me? 'No, Suze, I came straight here. I didn't want to be even more late.'

'That's ridiculous. We need to call them.'

'There's no point. They'll probably be on a coach to Vilnius by now. Or Belgrade. They'll never be caught. When I've been mugged before no one was questioned, let alone prosecuted. The police barely bothered to show any interest – more put out that I'd reported such an everyday crime. Look, I'm a bloke. I haven't been raped, or anything like that. Think how many people are in my situation across London right now. Hundreds, possibly thousands. Are the police really going to do anything constructive? They're overwhelmed. Besides, those guys weren't even knife-wielding hoodies, and they only got my wallet. So I lost some cash, but I can cancel my credit cards.' As if I would have needed to do that.

'And your watch?'

'Oh yeah, well that's a shame. But what can you do? The sad thing is those bastards won't appreciate it. They'll probably chuck it, thinking it's some worthless piece of old junk.'

'That's sad. I'm sorry.'

'Don't be. It's life.' I finished the whisky. Suze hadn't touched her vodka and tonic. She normally drank gallons of the stuff.

'But you can't just sit there like that. You look terrible. Your face is a mess.'

'I'm fine. I feel much better already, honestly. Let me go to the toilet and have a wash, that's all.' I stood up again and made more of an effort not to wobble and walk straight and seem in control of my limbs and mind and no longer in shock. I didn't want Suze ringing the police behind my back. It was just the sort of thing she would do, thinking she was being helpful and that she only had my best interests at heart and knowing how I never liked to make a fuss about anything.

The toilet was cold and too bright and stank of piss and damp, but it was empty. There was no soap and the sink was filthy and the taps dripped. What a pub. I pissed in a dirty, stained urinal, and took a closer look at my face in the small, smeared and cracked mirror. My right cheek was grazed and my bottom lip swollen and I'd obviously had a bad nosebleed, though that was all. Nothing was broken. Remarkably, the lenses in my glasses weren't even scratched. They'd flown off and this time they'd landed on a neatly trimmed box bush.

The hot water was far too hot so I splashed cold water on my face. It stung, but probably only because it was so cold. It felt good and soon the water ran clear, though of course there was nowhere to dry my face. The paper-towel dispenser was empty and there was no World Corp hand dryer so I had to use the sleeves of my jacket, which reminded me that I was wearing my Belstaff. An item of clothing I'd yet to feel comfortable with. It was Bobbie who'd persuaded me to buy it, as part of her campaign to make me look younger, and trendier, and tougher. Also, she was a real sucker for advertising and revamped trad brands on the up and up. However, stiff, waxed cotton made a hopeless towel. The inside lining of the jacket was better, though it still smelt of the wax. I loathed the smell and the way that whenever I wore the Belstaff my hands became sticky and dirty-feeling. However, the material appeared to have stood up to my flooring. Perhaps it wasn't solely a fashion item. Maybe the advertisements weren't so off the mark. Maybe, given my current circumstances – my ever-growing need for protection – I'd have to wear it more often. Besides, without the Crombie, and with the Prada puffa all but useless, I didn't have many winter coats left. My wardrobe really was becoming a little bare.

'You look much better.' Suze had got me another shot of poorly blended Scotch. She was certainly thoughtful, too thoughtful most of the time. 'Almost handsome.' She laughed, her low, hooting rat-a-tat-tat. In fact it was more a nervous affliction than a laugh. It was a dreadful sound.

'It wasn't as bad as it looked. I told you I was all right.'

'That doesn't mean you shouldn't call the police. You've had your wallet stolen, and your watch. More importantly you've been attacked. You can't let people get away with it. And anyway, what if they attack someone else? Wouldn't you feel bad, even a little bit responsible?'

'How would I be responsible?'

'By not helping the police catch them in time, as – what do they call it? – a preventative measure.'

'Suze, they were Eastern European. I bet they were waiting to get on a coach home, saw me, thought he looks easy pickings, got what they wanted, something like that anyway, and bolted back to the station and onto some rank, clapped-out bus to Lithuania. The whole notion of preventative measures is absurd anyway. What do you do, lock everyone up, in case they might be compelled to commit a crime? Another crime?'

'I don't know how your mind works. What I said was completely logical. You always have to take everything too far.'

'Thanks a lot.' I touched my cheek for effect.

'Sorry, I'm just concerned about you – stupid me – and what these people did. I live in Pimlico. I don't like the idea of muggers prowling the streets. What if I'd been mugged? I could have been raped. I don't want them to get away with it, wherever they're from, or going back to. Zero tolerance, that's what I say.'

'Well, don't count on the police.'

'I thought Boris was adopting a stronger line. What's the point in having a Conservative mayor, if they're not tough on law and order?'

'Do you think you've missed your calling, Suze? Cheerleader for the Tory Party? You're certainly strict enough.'

'I'm being serious, Matt. You know I'm not a fucking Tory, but the streets need to be kept safe, people need to feel secure. Otherwise everything starts to collapse. End of story. What is Johnson doing?'

'Look at what he's got to work with. If you ask me it's not just about numbers, but brains. Perhaps they should up the qualifications.'

'We all know about your qualifications, mastermind.'

The pub was not as empty as it was when we'd first arrived, but it was still hardly heaving, which was just as well because the other drinkers seemed a particularly sad, decrepit lot, especially for this part of town. Pimlico was in a time warp – the low-rent boozers, the dilapidated town houses, the dark, deserted pavements. The vicious crime. Where was the gentrification? It might have suited Suze, but not me. I didn't want to be dragged back to a winter of discontent. Yet we were not a million miles from Sloane Square and the King's Road, once a favourite stomping ground of mine. How I'd loved the boutiques, the exuberance, the posh totty. There was nothing to remind me of that scene in the Earl of Rochester tonight. The locals were all either grossly overweight, or worryingly underweight. Most showed signs of some form of abuse. If Suze thought this was authentic, that we were among real people, in a proper pub, it was not an authenticity I was after. But of course she was something of an abused old lush herself.

'Suze, let's get out of here. This place is depressing me.'

'I like it.'

'I know, only too well, but maybe we can get something to eat.'

Once on the pavement Suze froze. 'You don't think they followed you here?'

'Who?'

'The people who mugged you.'

'No, don't be ridiculous. They ran off, in the opposite direction. There's no way.'

'Why didn't you drive over? You usually do.'

'Someone vandalised my car. Didn't I tell you on the phone? They slashed a tyre and ripped off a wing mirror and put a very nasty scratch all down one side. It's in the garage, being fixed. Sounds like it's going to be there for ages too. Car repairs are such a rip-off.'

'You're joking.'

'No.'

'You're not having a lot of luck at the moment, are you?'

'No.'

She put her arm through mine and snuggled close. This was not what I needed, though I didn't attempt to break free. I could smell the alcohol on her breath and wondered whether she'd been drinking before I'd met her. Probably.

'Are you sure you're feeling up to eating?'

'Yeah, I'm starving actually. Plus it might do me some good. Where do you reckon?' Suze was a tall woman, almost my height. She wasn't overweight especially but she was heavy-boned — at least that was how she described herself. It was a struggle to walk down the pavement with her attached to me so tightly.

'Pimlico Tandoori?'

'I'm not sure an Indian's quite what I want.' I really hadn't trekked right across London, on public transport, when it finally came, and nearly being killed in the process, just to have an Indian. 'How about that Italian place, Olivo is it? Or that French restaurant, La Cuisine?'

'We'll never get in, on a Saturday night, and anyway it's very expensive. Olivo isn't exactly cheap either.'

'I'd pay if I could. You know I would. I'm sorry I don't have my wallet on me. It wasn't as if I forgot it on purpose.'

'This time.'

'What was that, Suze?'

'It's all right. Don't worry. I'll pay.'

'We don't have to have three courses. Two would do.'

'You don't change, do you?' She laughed, startling a passer-by. 'You're never happy unless you're spending a fortune. Or someone else's. I seem to remember you still owe me some money from Mallorca, as it is. In the region of five hundred pounds I think.'

'Haven't I paid you that back? I always pay back my debts.'

'No.' She laughed again, the hooting, rat-a-tat-tat, but louder and finishing it off with a disgusted-sounding snort. She had a habit of doing that also.

'Oh?' £500? It was hardly a lot of money. I couldn't believe Suze had brought that up, tonight of all nights. I should have known otherwise. It was just the sort of thing she wouldn't let me forget, whatever might have happened – and I thought I'd thought of everything. 'I'm really sorry. That's awful of me. If I still had my wallet we could have gone to the cash-point right now. As it was I had a fair amount of cash on me anyway – a couple of hundred pounds at least. Sorry, Suze. It must have slipped my mind. I've been so busy recently with work – it's a tough environment out there all right. But that's no excuse. I feel terrible. I do, Suze. Sorry.' So it was infectious – I suddenly couldn't stop saying sorry myself. I leant over and kissed her on the cheek. That usually did the trick. Wow, I had a thick lip.

'Sadly, Matt, it's what I've come to expect from you.'

This wasn't like my Suze. 'Don't give me a hard time.' We had reached the junction of Holbein Place and Pimlico Road. We turned left and headed past the once-fancy antique shops, now looking tired and neglected, and headed in the direction of La Cuisine, which I knew was also on the way to Olivo – was it too late to persuade her of the merits of rustic Italian cuisine, even if it didn't come at rustic prices? We were also going deeper into rustic Pimlico, closer to Suze's grotty little flat. 'I'll pay you back, of course I will. I always have done before.'

'It's not just the money, Matt. You never ring me up. You're not interested in seeing me. Unless you want some-thing. Sex, usually. Then money.'

'That's not true.'

'How many times have I seen you since Mallorca? Once? Twice at the most. I don't want to be possessive, you know me, but the minute you find yourself a girlfriend you disappear off the radar. What's her name this time? Bobbie. That's it.'

I felt a sharp pain in my leg. Had I torn something in the

tussle? I slowed and Suze slowed too. She was still clamped to me like a limpet. 'I'm not seeing her anymore. It was only a very brief, silly thing anyway.'

'So why has it taken you so long to get in touch? Because you didn't want to pay me back the five hundred pounds you owe me?'

It was my phone. I could feel it buzzing in my pocket. What perfect timing. I pulled it out and released myself from Suze and stupidly pressed the green button without looking at who it was. But I was so relieved to find some space of my own on the damp pavement. The drizzle was back. 'Hello?'

'Next time you're dead.' It was a man's voice, again, though because of the traffic and Suze breathing down my neck, and a sudden inability to think clearly, it didn't register. I pressed the red end call button and immediately flicked to the incoming call list. It was a withheld number. I switched the phone off and stashed it deep within the Belstaff.

'Who was that?'

'Wrong number, I think.'

'What did they say?'

'Nothing. Nothing that I could understand anyway. They were foreign. Asian? Korean perhaps. Actually that's possible, I suppose. I might be doing some business in North Korea. Did I tell you? Maybe it was a contact, who must have thought I spoke the language.'

'Is something going on that I don't know about?' Suze had crossed her arms in front of her, obviously huffy, and was blocking the way forward. 'I know you have a problem facing up to things sometimes.'

For a moment I thought about turning and running for the safety of Sloane Square. 'No. What do you mean?'

'I don't know.' She was almost tearful. 'I don't hear from you for ages and when I do you turn up in this state and pretend you can't understand English when someone calls you. I heard what that person said.'

'What? What are you talking about? What who said? The North Korean? You tell me.'

'Something's not right, Matt. Why can't you tell me the truth?'

'Maybe I should just go home. Let's call it a night, Suze.' I stepped back, ready to walk away, but knew I wouldn't, knew I couldn't. Besides I had a clear idea what was coming next.

'No, Matt, don't. I'm sorry. It's just I haven't seen you for so long and you turn up like this, getting odd phone calls, and, I don't know. I'm so confused. Come on, I'll take you to La Cuisine, if we can get in.'

We were practically outside. Behind the windows, dripping with condensation, I could see flicking candlelight, people, fine French food. It was exactly the sort of place I needed to lose myself in for a while and enjoy at least a small semblance of extravagance. Everyone else seemed to be, despite all this talk of recession and belt-tightening. It wasn't real yet, not from what I'd observed in the boutiques and restaurants, the malls at Canary Wharf of course – not to mention Bond Street. People were still spending, lavishly. Except me. Why was I the only one being hit so hard? In the pocket and round the head.

I would go for something classic and filling like a chèvre and leek tart, followed by coq au vin. From memory they did it well at La Cuisine. I'd have frites as a side. Not quite the done thing I know, but I preferred frites to dauphinoise, especially with a dish such as coq au vin. They soaked up the sauce so well, presuming the sauce was worth soaking up and that they were still using a proper burgundy rather than some cheap table plonk. Besides I knew Suze loved frites, but would never order them, because of her weight – those very heavy bones — and seeing as there was no way I was going back to my pad tonight I knew I needed to charm her and pander to her peculiar fancies in every way I could.

'You're not just using me are you?' Suze was smiling.

'No. I adore you.' We were on her sofa. I was wedged into the corner. She was sprawled virtually on top of me. When she wasn't kissing and licking my good cheek I could smell alcohol and garlic and something much less pleasant on her breath. I was too full and frankly too drunk for this. But if I hadn't been drunk of course, there was no way I would have let it get this far. It was always the same with Suze. She pounced just when you let your guard slip.

'Really?'

'Yeah.' I kissed her back, on the lips. She had large, soft lips, and parted them immediately while pulling the back of my head forward so I was sort of clamped in position. How had she got her hand round there? I thought I'd blocked that manoeuvre, knowing what Suze could do with her arms, knowing how strong she was. And then I felt her tongue probing deep inside my mouth, finding the space my missing molar made, and at the same time she was sort of panting and her hair — she had long, ridiculously thick, dark brown hair, beginning to grey — which had come loose was all over my bruised and scratched face, and my thick lip, not to mention my nose started to hurt again with the pressure. God, it was awful, and reminded me of exactly what I didn't want to be reminded of. I attempted to break her off. Eventually she pulled back and smiled at me, a knowing smile that implied she was at last getting what she wanted. And that not only was I enjoying it more than I'd ever dare admit, she was only warming up. Obviously this wasn't the first time I'd been in such a situation, but it was still very scary.

The thing about Suze was that while on the one hand she could come across as vulnerable and hopeless, indeed almost pitiful in her desperation to please – the sort of person you could instantly feel sorry for – on the other hand she was pretty manipulative. One of the reasons why we'd been friends for so long was because we both understood each other and how we could use that to our own advantage. It was a two-way street, except I always forgot quite how powerfully she could come on, and in retrospect, I supposed, Mallorca had, if anything, made it abundantly clear that the relationship wasn't entirely equal. No wonder I hadn't been keen to hook up with her since. Money was the least of it, as it always was with me.

Over dinner Suze had managed to somehow keep steering the conversation away from the direction in which I needed it to go – as well as managing to eat most of my frites. This was a shame because my coq was rather disappointing. What meat there was was dry and the sauce oddly bitter. Maybe they had used poor-quality wine, or probably wine that was corked. Unfortunately there were other problems too. La Cuisine might have looked intimate and romantic, but as far as I was concerned it had turned into a camp pastiche of a cosy French restaurant – the waiters performing as if they were extras in *La Cage aux Folles*. Was it possible to get good, properly authentic French food anywhere anymore? I wondered whether it was still possible to be served by people without attitude.

'Shall we go to bed?' Suze's big doleful brown eyes were tinged with excitement.

I waited for that laugh and snort. But there was no going back. I'd have to see it through, despite my mind suddenly refusing to leave the horror of Mallorca behind. That trip might have been my idea, not that Suze needed much persuading, so perhaps I'd asked for it. But the humiliation.

On the first evening, on the terrace, overlooking Deià, a glass of cava each, she'd said, 'I think I must really like pain. I like it when you hurt me, when you're rough with me, when you can't control yourself, Matt.' And I'd thought I'd been gentle with her up until then. More fool me. However, for a brief moment on that terrace I'd thought that inflicting pain on someone, in such beautiful and luxurious surroundings, would be especially thrilling, which conceivably was why I'd orchestrated the whole thing. But it wasn't and the more Suze seemed to enjoy it the less I did. I couldn't believe how enthusiastic that woman could be in such increasingly extreme circumstances. I couldn't believe how much pain she could endure. It was a terrible turn-off and made me long for Fran even more. Fran who'd barely lift a finger in bed, at least when she'd been with me. My lovely, sweet Fran who'd lie stiff as a board until I'd come.

Besides, I'd felt that I'd finally let Suze in on a secret. She knew something about me that really no one else did. At the very least she had encouraged me to reveal a chink, a weakness so I could be played with and abused, in the most disgusting ways.

In our gently air-conditioned room, stuffed with basic Mallorcan furniture, giant plasma screens and crisp white linens, with a view down an incongruously green valley to the ever-sparkling Mediterranean, she had teased and taunted me. In earshot of other guests. In this particularly exclusive and refined environment. 'Do it then,' she'd cried. 'Fuck me up the arse. I know that's what you want. Every man does.' She'd been squeezing my balls, digging her nails into my scrotum, while shoving a finger from her other hand actually inside my own anus, without having thought to spit on it first. What agony. 'Come on, Matt, make me scream.' And she expected me to pay my full share of the holiday? I could have killed her. I should have killed her then and there.

'Suze, when are you going to get rid of those cats?' Her two cats were on her bed, the foot of the bed maybe, but still the bed. They were huge and stank. One was a dusty grey, the other black with white paws. One was called Starsky, the other Hutch, which proved not only how ancient they were, but how ancient Suze was as well. They hated me as much as I hated them. In fact I was scared stiff of them. 'Suze, get them off the bed, please.' I was happy to remove the dolls and cuddly toys but I wasn't going near those cats. My head suddenly began to pound. Not just from the alcohol. It had been a very long day.

'Matt, they're only cats.'

'I don't care.'

'You're not really scared of them, are you?' She was bending suggestively over the grey one, stroking the back of its neck. Purring. 'Come on, baby, off the bed, Matty doesn't like you. And you too, Hutch.' She turned to me, smiling. 'We have to make room for Matty. He's a very big boy, with very wicked ways. We don't want to make him too angry, do we?'

Suze was drunk. She was quite possibly drunker than I was. Maybe once in bed she'd simply fall asleep. No. That was too much to ask for. She wouldn't fall asleep. Who knew when she last had anyone in bed with her? I really wasn't feeling my usual self. Hadn't for days.

'Tell me about Bobbie,' Suze said, undressing.

Her jeans were too tight for her and as usual she wasn't wearing any knickers. I used to find this exciting but now I found it gross. She wore fancy bras, I'd give her that, but once free her breasts were almost unwieldy. Naked she dived under the covers. For someone with such a violent sexual appetite she could be surprisingly shy about her body. 'Hurry up, Matt, it's freezing.'

I took off my zip-up, dark brown Paul Smith jumper, or

technically was it a cardigan? There appeared to be a rather nasty rip on one cuff — how had I not noticed that before? I removed my Smedley Oxford, folding and laying the items on a chair, before I unbuttoned and stepped out of my Margaret Howell jeans. Apparently they were pure, ring-spun Japanese denim. Certainly they had cost a fortune, though they were wearing in well and seemed to have escaped damage from the altercation. I folded them too, carefully hanging them on the back of the chair, before joining Suze under the covers. I didn't remove my vest or my boxers.

'I always forget how long it takes you to get into bed.' She put her arm around me and wriggled close and swiftly her leg was over my right leg and she was pressing herself into me. 'Is Bobbie gorgeous?'

'Why do you want to know?'

'I'm always curious about your women. How did she like it? Was she easy to please? Or did she have any special requirements?' She laughed, that hooting rat-a-tat-tat, and planted her soft wet mouth on mine before she had time to snort.

Completely swamped, I resigned myself to the fact that I'd have to air my own special requirement in the morning. I wasn't going to get anything meaningful out of her tonight, if ever. She might have been able to provide me with a temporary safe haven, though I supposed it was always doubtful as to whether she'd be able to lend me any cash. Apart from the fact I already owed her £500, she clearly had no spare money. She wasn't tight, not tight like Sean, she was just perpetually skint.

Suze didn't quite work for a charity, she worked for the Arts Council, in the drama bit, in some ludicrous administrative role, which involved doling out money to aspiring dramatists and actors — most of whom, as far as I could tell from what she'd told me, were completely talentless — and painfully ill-conceived theatre groups. The majority seemed more concerned with self-help than putting on perform- ances. If only she could have doled out a bit more money for herself – she was some actor all right.

Her flat was a nightmare of impoverishment, not helped by the fact that it was in an ex-council block – certainly not designed by a trio of inspired, modernist architects – in a sprawling estate the wrong side of Ebury Bridge Road, not that I was entirely sure there was a right side. This was a chunk of Westminster barely touched since the days of Orwell. It made Bobbie's flimsy abode look like a designer penthouse. Just being at Suze's made me feel down and out.

'Bobbie had this thing about asphyxiation,' I said, strug- gling vainly for more space.

'Now I'm getting excited.' Suze swung her leg right across me and sat up, pushing the duvet back and leaning forward and pinning my arms by my sides. 'We've never done that, have we.'

Fully straddling me she began rubbing her groin on mine. It wasn't an entirely unpleasant experience, except for her heavy breathing – she had mild asthma, which would invari- ably flare up when she became excited – and her hair that was all over my face. Why she couldn't cut and dye it, perhaps in some sharp, funky irregular style, I had no idea.

'Did you fuck her at the same time? Is that what happens?'

'Is what, what happens?' What mild arousal I felt was tempered by the discomfort – Suze was just so heavy and hairy and unwieldy – and my distress at falling for such an easy option, again. Plus my wounds were making themselves felt. I was in terrible pain. Besides I was finding it hard to follow her train of thought, or my own for that matter, except I suddenly knew I needed to get out of this fast. 'Suze, my face hurts. You're hurting me.'

'I thought that was the point. Maybe you fuck her up the arse at the same time. Is that how she likes it? Is it?'

'Is what?'

'You know, when you do this thing?'

'Do what? What thing?'

'Strangle her.'

'Oh for fuck's sake.'

'Or does she strangle you?'

'You're hurting me, Suze, get off.'

'Like this.'

'No.' I could barely speak. Suze had leant forward, put her knees on my arms and her hands around my neck. She was tightening her grip and letting her hair smother my face and pressing her crotch harder against mine. For some extraordinary reason I felt I was getting an erection, but my penis was trapped inside my boxers, under the full weight of Suze and I was very short of air and feeling all the whisky and wine from earlier, plus my bruises and scratches and thick lip and crocked nose, and yet I wanted to beat her at her own game. I wanted to fuck her and strangle her back, if that's what she really wanted. No wonder she never had long-term relationships. She was far too demanding, and complicated.

She eased her grip slightly. 'Tell me the truth. You weren't mugged tonight, were you? I bet you got into an argument with someone and they thumped you. And you never had your wallet stolen, you just didn't bring it because you didn't want to pay me back that five hundred pounds. Or couldn't. And you wanted a free meal on top of everything else. I know you pretty well, Matt. Well, you're going to have to pay me back in kind, aren't you now?'

She licked my sore cheek and then forced her tongue into my mouth and as deep as she could get it, way past my missing molar, and I felt the heaviness of her breasts rolling on my chest, and pressure on my neck again, except she had one arm across my throat and with her other hand she was fumbling to free my penis from my boxers. It needed to be freed. And with almost the next move I found I had entered her and my erection felt so full and bursting and I really couldn't breathe, except I could hear her saying, 'fuck me, Matt, fuck me,' and I could feel her rocking backwards and forwards on my cock, and she had both hands round my neck once more, and that was when I stopped struggling and started to blank out, and it felt like I was swimming, though it was so warm and peaceful and effortless and suddenly next to me in the water was Bobbie, beautiful, stylish, young, thin, trim Bobbie, with her pale, almost luminous skin and dark brown hair cut in that pin-sharp lopsided bob, and she looked just so desirable, and perfect and, as ever, unattainable, I knew I was going to come. I couldn't possibly help myself. And immediately the pressure eased and I sunk a little further into the rank mattress.

'Fuck, Matt. Have you come already?' Suze stopped.

'I don't know,' I spluttered. I was flushed and my face wet.

She climbed off me and shoved her hand between her legs. 'You have, you idiot. And you weren't wearing a condom. Shit.' But her voice changed and she began to smile. 'I didn't know you felt quite like that about me.'

'Like what?' I still hadn't completely caught my breath and couldn't understand why I appeared to have been crying.

'That you wanted to impregnate me. That you want to have a baby with me. That you love me that much.' She laughed, rat-a-tat-tat. 'Look at you, all overcome with emotion. Matt, it's not like you. How sweet.' She leant forward and kissed me on the forehead, with those big, wet, soft lips, as if I were a child. 'Haven't you changed your tune. A baby, Matt. Our little child.'

I grabbed her by the upper arms and pulled myself up

and kicked the duvet out of the way and swung her over so I was on top of her.

'Steady on, big boy.'

I pinned her arms by her sides with my knees, exactly the way she had done to me. She wasn't resisting exactly, but wriggling and flaying around like mad. It was hard to keep my balance. 'You want me to hurt you?'

'If you've still got it in you.' That laugh again, but softer, weaker thankfully.

Her hair was everywhere and it was hard to get a good grip of her neck and keep her arms pinned to her sides by my legs and to keep her from throwing me off. I don't know why she started to resist more strongly. I'd thought that this was what she wanted. 'Am I hurting you yet?'

'Yes,' she whispered.

I could feel her try to nod her head too, to nod an affirmative, but I had a pretty firm hold of her now.

She was going red in the face and flushed and sweaty from before, and with her tits blancmanging on her chest. To think she thought that I loved her, that I wanted to have a child with her – was she being remotely serious? To think she could possibly have been some replacement for Bobbie, for beautiful, chic, neat, well-trimmed Bobbie. To think she actually thought that I'd finally made up my mind to settle down with her, in her shabby, damp council flat, infested with cats and stuffed with cuddly toys. To think I was meant to be her saviour, her knight in shining armour, to rescue her from her sad, lonely, impoverished, single life, me of all people. What a spectacular joke.

And what was worse, what was so much worse was the fact that I had another erection already. It was poking up between her breasts. I looked down at it with such embarrassment, with such shame, and scorn. My stupid cock. Suze's heavy, obliging body, even if it was in a firm grip and short of oxygen. Was this really turning me on, again? This pseudo control, this fake violence? The fact that Suze was such a willing participant? No. I hated fakes. I hated actors and acting – the fucking Arts Council for aiding it all. Everything had to be real with me.

Maybe I needed to try a little harder. We'd done all the spanking and whipping and tying up before, much to my utter humiliation and her amusement, and probably lots of other people's amusement too. Those walls in Mallorca were paper thin. It was all so very public. Though this asphyxiation stuff was new. At least it was new in this context, in this absurd relationship. Of course I needed to try harder at it and knew I could – I'd learned, the hard way, to be ever resourceful. Up until now I'd barely been bothering. But it was not the same knowing she was enjoying it. I released the pressure slightly and she coughed and gagged and tried to say something.

'Careful, Matt. Be careful.' Was that it? Was that what she was saying?

Though I wasn't sure what she could have been referring to because, while maintaining her arms by her sides, while maintaining control, I had managed to get her legs either side of me, and had them shoved wide open revealing every last bit of her – and I slammed into her before quickly tightening again my grip around her throat. I was going to make her pay for this, this time all right. Oh, the terrible embarrassment and teasing, the tragic assumption of hers that I was somehow into it, this role playing, this pain, and into her, forever. Love? A child? Our child? What a monstrous thought. I could never let that happen. Never, never, never. I huffed and I puffed – now who was the child? – and I pumped and I squeezed with all my might until I heard something snap. But could I come again? No. Could I fuck.

SIX

Emergency Bailout

Chelsea Bridge at dawn was not providing the uplifting, picturesque cityscape I'd hoped for. Looking east, the low, leaden river seemed to merge with a fat, grey smudge of sky, dominated by the scruffy shell of Battersea power station, and those vast, redundant chimney stacks. Why hadn't they bulldozed that hollow edifice long ago? Did we really need to be reminded of London's chronic dependency on fossil fuels, of the old source of pea-soupers and acid rain? What was it with posterity and hankering after yesteryear, especially when, by all accounts, it was even worse than what eventually followed? And what was it with the redevelopment, the multibillion-, probably now multitrillion-pound plans for fancy homes and retail space, for theme parks and pleasure domes, topped off by a giant glass funnel set to shatter that supposedly beloved skyline? Still sunk in bureaucracy and stalled funding? Nothing was going to be moving forward in this slump, even if, as I vaguely remembered reading in a freesheet, the Americans were aiming to build a bunker for their diplomats on the edge of the plot, having cashed in their super-prime located Grosvenor

Square fortress to a property developer with the wholly appropriate name of Candy. Weren't they behind the times. As ever.

Where was the rising sun? It certainly didn't look as if it was going to break through soon. I had long learned not to care about the weather, even if I was occasionally surprised by some strange flux – a sunny spell perhaps, or a truly frosty winter chill. Though there was something about dawn that always snagged. It had to mean something, the beginning of a brand-new day. I wanted it to fill me with optimism, to make me feel truly alive, and not simply even closer to death.

Would the world of amateur dramatics be at a loss without Suze? What a thought. Though for that matter, would the fashion industry mourn the demise of Bobbie? The list could go on, and on. Stephen, would Stephen ever stop missing his precious mother? One step at a time, I thought, keeping Battersea Park to my right. Large trees were becoming more discernible, their bare branches silhouetted against the gathering grey. The odd bird was tweeting, an attack dog barked, thankfully far in the distance. Empty buses rumbled past, a clapped-out Mercedes saloon with Lithuanian plates was sitting at the Esso garage, not by a pump but on the front of the forecourt, facing the road and blocking the pay window. Ready for a quick getaway? No one seemed to be about.

Quickening my pace I soon came to the Queen's Circus roundabout. There was no choice to be made, no quandary at all. Gathering conviction, feeling stronger, I continued along Queenstown Road, pulling my Belstaff tighter around me. Not because I was cold especially, but because of some absurd need still to be comforted. What was happening to me? Under the railway bridge I could see a tramp, lying motionless in a huddle of damp cardboard, a Sainsbury's shopping trolley nearby. I shivered. I actually shivered, thinking for a moment that our predicaments weren't so far removed. If I didn't watch it I'd be out on my ear, living rough – and that was if I were lucky.

'Get a grip of yourself,' I said, maybe aloud, though no echo returned from the stale gloom. Act normally and everything will be all right. I trudged on and up the gentle incline as Queenstown Road approached Lavender Hill. The traffic was increasing, though I imagined there would have to be more going on at such an hour in downtown Pyongyang. With everyone being in forced labour, weekend or not – the commitment to a tightly controlled economy – hurrying to or from work, except perhaps Kim Jong-il, who'd be still up partying with his cronies. Or would he be comatose, the life, what a life, draining away?

Why I now found myself almost hurrying I wasn't sure. There was no one following, on foot or in a vehicle, I was certain. There was no sign of the Mercedes – was it a coincidence, the Lithuanian plates? Or was the threat from wayward Eastern Europeans even more pernicious than I'd previously considered? No one had me in the sights of a high-powered, telescopic lens, surely. Except, I couldn't stop looking behind me, or scanning the road ahead. Or casting my eyes over the terraces and semi-industrial buildings to my left and right.

After a short row of scruffy shops I came to the Queenstown, a gastropub Bobbie and I had frequented a number of times, and I cut my pace. The place was obviously shut at this time, and if it were up to me it would remain shut. The food was atrocious, as was the ambience. The so-called dining space was too hot and cramped and loud. They actually thumped out music. Needless to say Bobbie loved it. She thought it was cool, the food yummy, and she particularly liked how it was always heaving – with people her own age. Plus she more than approved of the lurid, contemporary decor, which effectively obliterated the fact that it must once have been a rather grand Victorian pub. But what did she know about fine food? Or interior design? What did she know about life? What did she know about me?

Suddenly there was no traffic and certainly no pedestrians anywhere near, so grasping the opportunity, which had to be something of a speciality of mine, I slipped down the narrow side alley between the gastropub and the row of shops. There was a wooden gate at the end, piled high with barbed wire, and a fat, aluminium kitchen chimney sticking out of the wall about a third of the way along. Even the exterior shell was covered with thick, yellowy black grease. The alley stank of piss already.

Because I was looking at the gate and the barbed wire and wondering what it would be like to be incarcerated for twenty-four hours a day, seven days a week, fifty-two weeks a year, for who knew how many years, it took me ages to notice a hair was stuck to the end of my penis, right across the opening of my urethra, and that I wasn't exactly aiming straight, with two jets coming out at odd angles – one landing on the gate, thankfully, but the other on the right leg of my Margaret Howell jeans. Pulling the hair off midstream made even more of a mess of the ring-spun Japanese denim and I got urine all over my hands too. Buttoning up, I realised I should have washed myself more thoroughly before leaving Suze's. I had to wipe my hands on the lining of the Belstaff – what a tough, multipurpose jacket it was proving to be – before I hurried out of the alley, keeping my head down, and pulling the Belstaff tightly around me once more and trying to stretch the impossibly stiff outer waxed cotton lower, because it must have looked like I'd pissed myself, rather than had an accident with a stray pubic hair, of considerable strength and thickness. I immediately turned left in the sudden brightness, before shortly feeling a weight, a hand on my shoulder pulling me back.

'Hey, just a minute.' It was a male voice, youngish. Aggressive.

South London, at some absurdly early hour in the morning, was I going to be mugged? Again. Crime in the capital was totally out of control. You couldn't even go for an early morning stroll without being attacked. And to think of all the tax, all the council tax I paid to protect myself and others from these random acts of robbery and violence. What a city. What a country. What a sham. At least it was a local accent, nothing Eastern European about it. Though maybe local was worse, round here. I tensed, turned on the spot, while ducking to try to shake this hand, this grip off my shoulder. It didn't work, in so far as the pressure remained pretty much the same. In fact it probably stopped me from tripping.

Oh. The hand, the voice belonged to a policeman. In shirt-sleeves – at this time of the year? – with one of those chunky, stab-proof body armour vests on, he looked even younger than his voice had sounded. But he was taller than me and broader, and had a full head of sandy-coloured hair – not to mention the fact that he was well protected. He also had a colleague, older perhaps, old enough to drive anyway, who was sitting in a patrol car, which must have pulled up in front of the alley while I was having a piss. Typical. Cops were never around when you needed them, and somehow always about when you didn't. Like taxis.

'What were you doing down that alley, mate?' The boy nodded over his shoulder.

'Relieving myself.' I tried to sound as calm as possible, but I didn't like policemen much more than I liked muggers, be they south London gangstas or Eastern European hoodlums.

'It's against the law to urinate in a non-designated public place.'

'I wasn't aware that that alleyway was a public place, designated or not. It looks pretty private to me.'

'Does that building belong to you?'

What an absurd question, I wasn't going to bother to answer. I shrugged. Really, did I look like it belonged to me? And if it did what would I be doing pissing on my own doorstep, so to speak? What was I meant to say, I was inspecting my property, officer, and was suddenly caught short? 'You see, I have a prostate problem,' I actually said, 'and when I need to go I really need to go. Sorry. And, no the building doesn't belong to me.' I could have added, that if it had belonged to me I'd have hired a proper chef, lowered the volume, decorated the place with a little more style and sympathy, and racked the prices up, even today, in a bid to discourage hordes of inebriated young professionals, who couldn't tell the difference between a bottle of Chianti and a bottle of Rioja. Or for that matter a business consultant and a serial killer. The lack of discernment was truly shocking. And to think that someone still employed them. Now.

'Where have you just come from?'

'A friend's.'

'And where was that, exactly?'

'Pimlico.' I was liking his tone less and less.

'And where are you going?'

'Another friend's.'

'At this time, on a Sunday morning?'

I looked at my watch, or where my watch should have been. 'What time is it?'

'Seven-o-two.'

'I'm going to be in so much trouble.'

'Where does this friend live, precisely?'

'Which one?'

'Where you're headed?'

'Clapham. Or I suppose it's Battersea Rise, if you want me to be precise.'

He took his hand off my shoulder, at last. 'Let me get this straight. You've been visiting a friend in Pimlico, where precisely?'

I couldn't believe he wouldn't stop saying precisely. His colleague in the patrol car was on the radio, but I couldn't hear what he was saying. 'Just off the Ebury Bridge Road.' In situations like this I'd always found it best to stick to the truth, or as close to the truth as possible. That way you didn't tie yourself in knots, and you could answer any awkward questions with so much more conviction. I wasn't a very good liar.

'And you're off to where?'

'Precisely? A friend's in Battersea Rise.'

'At seven o'clock on a Sunday morning?'

'Yes, at seven-o-two, or is it seven-o-four by now?'

'And you thought you'd stop to urinate in an undesignated public place on the way?'

'I have a prostate problem, as I said. It's rather enlarged. I'm sorry. But it's not as if there are many actual, properly designated public toilets around here. Or anywhere else in London. Where was I meant to go?'

'I'd watch what you say. I could easily arrest you. You have committed an offence, and you are acting suspiciously. Who are these so-called friends, then?'

Did he think I didn't have any friends? Did he think I lived on the street? 'It's complicated. To be honest I've been a little bit of a naughty boy.' I coughed. 'Playing away from home, if you know what I mean.'

'Yeah?' He looked at his colleague in the car, who was still on the radio.

'I hooked up with an old girlfriend last night and one thing

117

led to another, and now I'm on my way to my current girl-friend's to try to smooth things over.'

'What happened to your face? Which one of them hit you?'

'You won't believe this, but I was running for the bus, this was last night, on my way to this old girlfriend of mine, the one who lives in Pimlico, and I ran into a lamp post. I nearly knocked myself out. At least it won me some sympathy. Too much I suppose.'

'What about your hands? Why are they all scratched up?'

'That's a separate incident.' I sighed. Exactly what else did he want to know? 'The old girlfriend's got a couple of cats who are very territorial. They don't like me at all.'

'Have you got any ID on you?'

'What do you want?'

'Driving licence?'

I had to undo my jacket to reach the hidden, zipped pocket at the back. I'd put my wallet in there to keep it well out of Suze's way. This jacket had everything – I still couldn't get over the fact that it had been hanging in my wardrobe pretty much unworn since the day Bobbie had persuaded me to buy it, months ago. And now Bobbie was no longer around not only had I rediscovered it but my appreciation of it was growing by the hour. I could just imagine how suitable it would be for travelling in hostile environments. Though I wasn't sure whether I'd be able to regard North Korea as hostile. Not, I laughed to myself, if it was to be my new home, away from home. I'd have to embrace the place with warmth and optimism, much as Suze had first embraced me last night. Deep down I was sure the jacket would eventually reveal a major fault. What didn't?

Opening my wallet – a once smart, particularly soft lamb-skin affair from Paul Smith – I discovered that I did indeed have my driving licence. How much would that be worth on the black market? 'Here.' I handed it to the boy.

'Is this your current address?'

'Let me have a look.' He held it for me so I could read the address. Not only was the address from about three flats ago I didn't think the picture looked anything like me. I had hair. And so many less wrinkles. 'No, I've just moved and haven't had time to get the address changed. I do a lot of travelling and constantly need my driving licence. I will inform DVLA as soon as possible.'

'It's against the law to not keep your driving licence up to date.'

'Yes, but as I just said I've very recently moved, actually I've moved a lot recently. It's not the easiest thing to do, to keep sending your licence away, with the post being what it is and also with DVLA not being the most efficient organisation in the country.' I was beginning to get extremely annoyed. I was being held up. There were things I needed to do. Fast. Plus, didn't these two idiots have anything better to investigate? Surely there were numerous serious crimes that they could be attending to, instead of hassling me for having a pee in a rank alleyway.

He handed my driving licence to his colleague who was still in the patrol car, but no longer talking on the radio. 'We're going to run a check on this, if you don't mind moving over to the wall.'

'What?'

'Over there, please, and can you turn round, so you face the wall, and place your hands apart and on the wall at head height?'

He was going to frisk me. I couldn't fucking believe it. I looked in both directions, wondering how far I'd get if I legged it, and indeed whether I'd manage to evade them for a sufficient period of time, for at least long enough for what I urgently needed to do. That was the thing with me, when I got it into my head that I had to do something, I became completely focused. But it didn't seem likely I'd get far. While at school I was regarded as something of a sprinter, I was way past my peak of physical fitness, plus Suze had seriously worn me out. And aside from youth these plods did have the added advantage of wheels. So I did as he asked and let him rummage around in my pockets. I had nothing to hide.

Having looked over my mobile, wallet and keys and as he appeared to be counting my change, the radio crackled into life.

'It's a code three,' the guy in the car said.

The policeman who had been manhandling me shoved my things into my hands and rushed round to the driver's door. I couldn't work out why he'd been the one to get out and accost me anyway. Maybe he'd stopped because he wanted to have a piss himself and much to his shame and annoyance I'd been in his way. Even police must get caught short.

As the roof lights began to flash but before the car pulled away his colleague stuck his thick, young neck out of the window, tossing me my driving licence. 'You won't be so lucky next time,' he said.

Really?

LONDON SHARES CRASH AGAIN said an old *Evening Standard* hoarding fluttering in the gentle breeze outside an already open newsagent's. But still, I couldn't help thinking, life went on. Or didn't. Same as ever. How many times had I read such headlines? Yet, I wasn't in the mood to be reminded of any insecurity, any further calamity. My world, my business survived on confidence. What didn't? Would my latest project now be in jeopardy when I was banking on it to pan out? Exactly how susceptible were the North Koreans to the vagaries of global money markets? Presumably they'd be in a better position than most. Surely that was the point of maintaining one of the very last, effectively closed economies. Obviously competition, not to mention slack regulation, hadn't provided all the answers. Kim Jong-il had been no fool. Would he, or his successor, continue to withstand the pressure, from China, from South Korea, from Vietnam, from the US, to open up and shift towards a market economy? Would the Dear Leader, or his successor, not now have ample evidence to prove that in fact they were right and the rest of the world was wrong? The regime would only have to point to the *Evening Standard*, the fine print.

Why, I wondered and not for the first time, did everybody hate North Korea, or at least its ruling elite, so much? What had they done to us? I wasn't aware of ever being threatened by North Korea, not in a remotely meaningful, concrete way. They hadn't even restarted the Yongbyon nuclear reactor. Besides, all the officials I could be certain to meet, would, I imagined, only ever be wholly courteous and pleasant, and quite likely very self-effacing, in that South East Asian way. Bad breath would probably be the biggest problem I'd have to contend with. Though that had to be entirely excusable of course, given the diet, plus possibly, poor dental care. For some reason I couldn't imagine the North Koreans flossing their teeth with any regularity or passion. I'd have to re-educate them – which, after all, wasn't far off what I was planning to do. Together we'd make some force, and then we'd be able to stand our ground.

Inside the newsagent's, stacked on the racks, I couldn't see anything strikingly new on the credit crisis from the headlines in the Sunday papers. Would it all blow over again, with the pundits, not to mention the public fast becoming attuned to the ever more frightening tales of financial destruction? Where was the reality? People hadn't yet been hit hard enough, if at all. Bond Street, for so long my Mecca, my mania anyway, still seemed to thrive. As did the malls at

Canary Wharf. I hadn't yet been to Westfield and maybe I'd never make it to White City, but I was aware of the sheer scale of it, the crowds and mayhem. Everywhere shoppers continued to taunt me with their purchasing power, their endless credit, their bucking of the trend. Nevertheless, I was annoyed with the newsagent for having left that sign out on the street, adding to the drama – the melodrama – and my own fears. Had he done it on purpose, knowing that someone just like me, suddenly with everything at stake, would wander past? What was the big story this morning? Who'd been voted off *I'm A Celebrity*. It was Bobbie's heart-throb. I had to laugh, briefly.

The newsagent's smelt of spice and sweat. The man standing behind the counter was fat, white and bald. He was unshaved and radiated bad health and ill intent. Where were the police when you wanted them? Where were the Pakistanis? Was this man an interloper, or simply a throw-back to a bygone age? Boom to bust etcetera, we were going full circle. He looked on edge, as if he wasn't fully at ease or familiar with his surroundings. A dusty Alsatian lurked next to him. Had he not been so big and armed with such a fero-cious canine I might have had a sharp word with him about that incendiary hoarding. As it was I opened the fridge and extracted a bottle of Lucozade. I hated Lucozade, marginally less than I hated Red Bull, but was suddenly feeling rather light-headed and in urgent need of aspartame. The neon drink was in one of those plastic bottles made to look like glass – I couldn't believe what they faked nowadays. The thug demanded £1.35, and it wasn't even cold. The fridge was not the only thing in the shop that was not functioning properly.

Stepping back out onto the street I kicked over the hoarding and set off fast towards Battersea Rise, glugging the Lucozade as I went.

*   *   *

Bobbie's road was as dismal as ever, those poky terraces, the dead air of thwarted ambition, but I felt renewed, reinvigorated, up for anything. It wasn't just second wind, it was almost like I was a new me. What was in that bottle? There was no traffic, no pedestrians, though a few curtains and blinds had been drawn open and I saw lights and movement in living rooms and kitchens, the odd child watching telly, and a woman, my age perhaps, or probably younger – who wasn't nowadays? – with brown, shoulder-length bed hair. She was wearing a dressing gown and I couldn't tell what she was wearing underneath, if anything. I hoped it might swing open and reveal all as she turned or stooped. But when she saw me staring at her she rushed out of the room and I continued to Bobbie's building.

There were no lights on, in either her flat or the flat below and every curtain and blind was pulled. I so wanted to see Bobbie, to make amends, to beg forgiveness, for not having trusted her, for being such a fool, that I was prepared to forget completely about the time, and the place, and march straight up to the front door and stick my finger on the buzzer. It took me a few moments to realise and then remember that the buzzer was not working so I began knocking. And kept knocking. Nothing.

Retrieving my mobile from a well-secured side pocket of the Belstaff, I switched it on, for, I realised, the first time since yesterday evening, waited for the signal, and rang Bobbie's mobile. It went straight to answerphone. 'Bobbie, hi darling, look, you know how sorry I am about what happened, but I'm downstairs, on the street. Let me in please and I'll explain everything.'

What was the point? So I rang the landline. I thought I could hear the phone ringing in the flat. With my mobile still pressed to my ear and pacing the very short path from the pavement to the front door, I slowly became aware that

I was being observed, by the old woman in the upstairs flat in the house immediately to the right of Bobbie's. I waved. She didn't wave back, nor did she stop looking at me. I'd seen her peering out of there before. Didn't she have anything better to do? But I didn't mind her attention. In fact I'd sort of hoped she'd be on hand to witness my presence, my return. As I turned my back on her Bobbie and Gabriella's answerphone kicked in. I ended the call and stood staring at my phone, like an idiot. While I'd been making the call, it appeared I'd received a message, or a number of messages. They could wait. I rang Bobbie's landline again. On the fourth or so ring it was picked up, which was not quite what I was expecting.

'Hello?'

'Hi,' I said, brightly.

'Who's that?'

'Matt. It's me, Matt.'

'Matt? What's the time? What are you doing calling?' Clearly I'd woken her, from a very deep sleep. A drug-induced sleep most likely; she was forever popping temazepam, or some clone, which she'd mostly acquired illegally. No doctor would prescribe the amount she got through. She could barely speak.

'I'm looking for Bobbie, Gabriella. Is she there?'

'I don't know. No, I don't think so. I thought she was with you. I just got back from the States, late last night. God, I'm completely whacked.' She yawned, loudly.

'I'm outside.'

'What?'

'Downstairs, outside. I've come to see her.'

'What's the time again?'

'I don't know. It's quite early. I've been trying to reach her for days. I'm not sure how to put this – we had an argument, not a major one, but you know what she's like.'

'Maybe she is here. I feel so groggy, God. Let me take a look.'

There was a clunk, as if Gabriella had placed the handset on a hard surface. The old woman next door was still staring at me, so I waved once more, and this time she disappeared behind the curtains – net it looked like, but in this part of town? – though, I was sure she was still watching. She must have been a sitting tenant, council, or I supposed housing association, from the pre-gentrification days. She'd be moved into a care home eventually and the flat would be sold to a couple of young professionals desperate to claw their way onto the property ladder in a cosy part of town. Or it would have been just a few months ago. Who knew what was going to happen now. The parameters were shifting, or so the *Standard* kept saying. As much as I didn't like the idea of a couple of smug, young corporate lawyers nesting in Battersea Rise, I wasn't particularly fussed about the plight of a nosy old bag. Maybe it wasn't too late. Maybe I could hurry the process along. I doubted that she would be missed.

I heard footsteps, movement, Gabriella picking up the phone. 'No, she's not here.' She yawned again. 'I didn't think so. I haven't seen her since I've been back.'

'There's no sign of her?'

'She's not here. Sorry.'

'Right.'

'Sorry, Matt. God, do you want to come up, as you are here already?'

Gabriella had never liked me. She obviously didn't want me in the flat. But I wasn't going to turn down the opportunity. 'Would you mind? This is really embarrassing, but I need to use the toilet also. Sorry. I won't hang around for long. You just go back to bed.'

'OK. I suppose it's all right. I'll chuck down the keys.'

After much longer than I thought would be necessary the

blind was pulled up and there was Gabriella, what a mess, in that huge white T-shirt she always wore in bed. Bobbie and I had speculated that it must have belonged to an old boyfriend, but who knew what had happened to him. She hadn't shown much interest in men since I'd been with Bobbie. The window was slowly opened and she leaned out and dropped the keys, right into my hands, which was something Bobbie had never managed to do.

I let myself in and was immediately hit by the smell of the communal hallway. It was a mix of stale food and air freshener, plus something fetid. Among the letters kicked to one side were a couple for Bobbie, a bill and a hand-written envelope. I quickly retrieved them and unzipping and popping my jacket stuffed them in an inside pocket. There were numerous letters for Gabriella also. Clearly she hadn't bothered to pick up her mail when she'd arrived back last night, so she wouldn't have noticed that there was anything for Bobbie. This was good. This was working out better than planned. I didn't bother to pick up Gabriella's post for her either, though I was pleasantly surprised to find she had left the door to the flat ajar for me. Another thing Bobbie invariably never managed to do.

Of the two flatmates I was suddenly thinking that I'd probably chosen the wrong one. Gabriella was so much more considerate and co-ordinated, and trusting, and eager to please too no doubt. But she was not my type. She was too unrefined, too unpolished. Her frizzy hair was badly cut and highlighted. Her face was awash with freckles. She was short, verging on the dumpy, and she had – I could never fail to notice thanks to the fact that she never wore a bra under that old T-shirt – these oddly wide-spaced tits, which appeared to point away from each other. I wondered whether she was not wearing any knickers also, under that balloon of stretched and tatty cotton, and what sort of wild and frizzy growth I could expect to find between her legs. Should I have been so inclined to find out.

'Thanks, Gabriella. Go back to bed. Please. I'm really sorry about this, but to be honest I've been a bit worried about Bobbie and sort of found myself walking over here, before I knew what I was doing. I didn't intend to get here quite so early. It's not as far on foot as I'd thought. I should stop being so rude about south London being the back of beyond.' The fetid smell was considerably worse inside the flat. I couldn't believe Gabriella hadn't aired the place since her return. What a slob.

'What happened to your face? And your hands? What's happened to you, Matt? Have you been in a fight? You look a mess.'

This was rich, coming from her. 'You won't believe this, but I was running for a bus yesterday and I ran into a lamp post. Nearly knocked myself out. Oh, and I've acquired a cat. It scratches like hell.'

'I thought you hated animals.'

'I do. Particularly this cat. When I say acquired, that's not quite what I mean. I'm looking after it for a neighbour. This old lady, she suddenly had to go into hospital, for an operation. She was desperate and I didn't really see how I could refuse. I'm sort of hoping the thing will fall off the balcony.' I laughed.

'Do you want a drink? A coffee?' She was leaning against the wall by the foot of the stairs, scratching the back of her head. Her eyes were barely open.

'Honestly, Gabriella, go back to bed. I'm just going to go to the bathroom and do my business and leave Bobbie a note – maybe she's gone to visit her mum – and then I'll be out of here.'

'Can't you get her on her cell?'

'I think she keeps switching it to answerphone when she sees it's me phoning. Or it's off.'

'Matt, maybe she's avoiding you. Perhaps you should just leave now. I probably shouldn't have let you in. If she doesn't want to see you, she doesn't want to see you, no? You really should leave her alone. Respect her wishes.'

I stumbled over to the sofa and sat down heavily and put my elbows on my knees and my head in my hands and sucked in a long breath of the stale, fetid air and tried my hardest to produce some tears and make sobbing sounds. 'I love her. This is making me so unhappy I can't stand it. I want everything to be all right between us. To be how it was. You knew how we were together. We made a good couple. We were serious about each other. I was beginning to think that this was it, you know, marriage, kids. A life.' I had to get into Bobbie's bedroom. I would have said or done anything.

'I'm sure everything will be fine.' Gabriella moved slightly towards me, but she didn't get too close, and certainly didn't put her arm around me, or touch me, or anything physically comforting like that. Was my story, my tears not good enough?

She was wearing knickers, I was suddenly sure because of the way the T-shirt clung to her arse. I could see the edging. How disappointing. How typical, of someone who seemingly paid so little attention to their erotic allure. But that didn't mean they couldn't be removed, in an instant. So what if I could still smell Suze on my fingers. I was suddenly feeling very carnal. What more was there to feeling truly alive than sex? 'Do you think she's been seeing someone else?' I croaked. 'Is that where she is now? Has she said anything to you, Gabriella? What do you know? You must tell me. Please.'

'Matt, I've been away. I haven't spoken to her in weeks.

I'm too tired for this. I shouldn't have let you in. It was a mistake. You've got to go. Now.'

'I'm sorry.' I stood and started for the stairs, the top floor of the maisonette. 'I won't be a moment, I promise.' I sniffed, loudly.

'Matt, hurry up, please. Please be quick. You shouldn't be here. Bobbie wouldn't like it. You're making me nervous. I'll wait down here.'

How exactly I was making her nervous I didn't know, though I was more than happy with her opting to wait downstairs. Removing my glasses as I went, I wiped my eyes on my sleeve. Oiled cotton was clearly not the most effective or pleasant fabric for wiping away tears, so it was fortunate that there weren't any.

Maybe I was imagining it but the fetid, decayed smell seemed markedly to get worse as I climbed the stairs and hit the landing. Was it possible Gabriella hadn't noticed the smell? In her doped state. The bathroom was my first port of call. Christ, I needed another piss already. What was wrong with me? Just how quickly did cystitis develop?

There was a definite burning sensation as I peed, but not much urine came out. After shaking myself and buttoning up I smelt my fingers. Yuck. Maybe I'd caught something from Suze. I thought about washing my penis then and there in the sink – it wasn't as if I hadn't done precisely that before, as I'd always been particular about my personal hygiene – though I made do with just washing my hands. Time was obviously short. Walking to Bobbie's room I couldn't help scanning the landing ceiling, noticing that the hatch into the loft appeared to be a bit grubby around the edges, though in reality the whole landing was grubby. Trust a couple of girls to live in such squalor. Though that made me feel better about things. I was pleased it was all so foul, and particularly pleased that Gabriella was zonked. But zonked enough?

Maybe she'd have to drop a few more tabs this morning.

Bobbie's room smelt of Bobbie. Of how she'd smelt the last time I saw her anyway. Mum deodorant, VO5 shampoo, Clinique rehydrating face cream, Chanel No. 7, a hint of sweat. A trace of fear? I laughed. Why had I suddenly developed such an infuriating croak and cackle? Had I caught that off Suze too? Maybe fear did have a smell, all of its own.

Everything appeared to be in place. Or at least there was nothing obviously out of place. It was a mess, but only in the way Bobbie's room was always in a mess. The bin was still overflowing and the top of her chest of drawers was cluttered with make-up and hairdressing implements, and cheap jewellery and balled tights and a small, dusty mirror in a chrome frame, and endless scrunched receipts and old tickets and small bits of paper. And there, I was sure, was a corner of a Durex packet. It can't have been. I would have definitely noticed that before.

However, picking it up, and examining it closely, there was an uncanny likeness. Durex Elite purple had to be virtually unique. Plus there was some white lettering in what I was certain was the Durex font. Bobbie and I didn't use Durex. We used Mates, if at all. What the fuck had been going on? Too distressed to contemplate exactly what it might mean, I hastily dropped the incriminating evidence onto the floor. I should never have doubted my convictions. Nothing ever escaped me. Of course she'd been having an affair, all the while misleading me and lying to me – indeed betraying me in the most callous and hurtful way possible.

The door to her wardrobe was slightly ajar. I opened it expecting I wasn't quite sure what and found most of her clothes not on the racks but in a heap at the bottom. Naturally this wasn't a complete surprise, not least because of her extraordinarily sloppy attitude towards looking after her clothes – and those people who loved her. Mixed in were empty hangers and numerous, odd shoes. What chaos. Quickly with my right foot I shoved the stuff further back and closed the wardrobe door properly and then didn't move an inch.

Where was Gabriella? I could hear myself breathing. What with the shock of finding the used Durex packet on top of everything else, I was struggling for breath, and my heart was thumping like mad. As silently as possible I stepped over to the open doorway – why had I left the door to Bobbie's room open? – and held my right ear to the landing void, but all I could still hear was my own breathing and banging heart and a voice in my head saying, 'You won't be so lucky next time.' No?

On my knees I peered under the bed. There were dust-balls, more scraps of paper, a long, slim, battered box – what the hell had been in there? – an odd sock, a pair of tights, a CD or DVD minus its case and in the far corner my useless Jaeger. There it was. I had to practically crawl right under the bed to reach it. Bobbie must have kicked it that far, maybe thinking, in the heat of the moment, that I wouldn't notice and that she'd at least be exacting some sort of revenge, if not providing proof that could be used against me later. Proof of what? That I'd been in her room? That we'd had a fight? How sly and calculating and, yes, actually malicious was that? All character traits that I should have picked up on far sooner.

Bringing my old watch into the light I could see that the long piece of strap had come away from the lugs. The spring bar was still intact, though it appeared that the case itself, or precisely the edges of an 18-carat gold lug hole, had given way. Gold was too soft a metal for a watch case, particularly antique gold. What a failure. What a disappointment. Especially as I had always thought that things used to be so much better made. Watches, clothes, spectacles, you name it. Maybe I'd deluded myself. Everything was as shoddy then as it was now, more so probably – without modern engineering and manufacturing processes, and space-age materials. I wanted to kick the Jaeger back under the bed and forget about it, though I knew that that wouldn't be a great idea given the circumstances, so I stuffed it in my jeans pocket. A Seiko was looking more and more necessary. And I wasn't thinking of a stainless-steel case, but titanium.

'Matt, how are you getting on?'

Gabriella was still downstairs, and it didn't sound like she was about to come up. Shame actually, I could have done with an outlet for my anger. I was ready to explode.

'I'm nearly finished,' I shouted back. 'I'm just writing a note. I couldn't find a pen.' There was a pen, an old red Bic biro among the rubbish on the top of her chest of drawers. It took some scrawling on the back of a torn envelope to get the ink running smoothly and for me to clear my head and calm myself enough to put pen to paper in a coherent, lucid and thoughtful fashion. If I was going to write a note of course it had to be properly considered. Not that Bobbie would ever be able to appreciate any such thing.

Dear Bobbie, I wrote in the red ink, which was a bit gaudy I knew, *where are you? I couldn't stand it any longer and came round on the off-chance. Very sad not to see you here. I'm sorry if I've upset you or angered you in any lasting way. I'm so sorry we had that fight. Please forgive me, though I'm not quite sure what I've done wrong. Can we talk at least? I feel I'm owed some sort of explanation. I miss you more than you could imagine. I want us to be together, forever. I love you. Matt.*

What a load of cobblers. How over the top. How unlike me. I left the note on her bed, had another quick glance around the room, turned out the light and stepped straight into Gabriella, the sneaky dope. Look what I was being presented with, when I was all fired up.

SEVEN

Chaotic Unwinding

It was not dark though not exactly light either. That perpetual twilight had returned and the temperature had risen a touch, as had the humidity. The cloud cover appeared permanent. Though I thought I didn't like change, I wasn't so happy with this overwhelmingly dim dampness. Out on the balcony, scanning the wet, grey concourse, I felt I was back on too familiar territory. I suddenly didn't want to be stuck in an unheated flat, on my own, on an autumnal Sunday afternoon.

Company was what I craved, yet I had this terrible sinking feeling that I was fast destroying the few crucial relationships I had left, that I was increasingly alone and disconnected in this city. At that very moment I wanted to be in a country cottage, by a roaring fire, the Sunday papers to hand, or at least the TV remote, having just strolled back from a quaint sixteenth-century inn, called probably the King's Head. This would have to be in the Cotswolds – I'd been to Stow-on-the-Wold with Fran all right, I'd checked out the heritage, those endless drystone walls, the real ale. My pregnant wife – a softening of the haunches and a swelling of the breasts well advanced – though not necessarily Fran, would be in the kitchen, her back turned, making gravy on the Aga. A forerib of beef would be resting on the slate counter – because although this would be a trad cottage, it would have been tastefully modernised. The two children we already had would be amusing themselves quietly in their bedrooms. The exhausted dog – let me see, a cheeky Jack Russell, called Brand – would be at my feet. My fat, authentically mud-splattered BMW X5 would be out in the drive, ready to ferry us back, at the end of the weekend, to our immaculate, north-west London house, where the underfloor heating would be timed to kick in well before our arrival. Was this how it had been for Fran and Joe? Before the scratches started to appear. Before the windows began to shatter and bricks amass in plush downstairs rooms. Who actually lived with all that comfort and security? That familial perfection? The insult to people like me. No wonder I had to take action.

But I had now moved on from all that. Hadn't I learned a few lessons, at least quelled my anger? I could have punched myself. This wasn't the moment to become reflective, even remorseful, let alone to fantasise about how things might have been. No time for weakness. I had to pull myself together and soldier on. Top of my agenda was to finish that damn business plan, attract proper funding, even if I didn't manage to nail a sizeable contract, and get the hell out of here. While I still had the chance.

Waiting for my PowerBook to fire up I wandered back onto the balcony. I thought things hadn't looked quite right earlier, even through the gloom – no wonder I'd wished to be miles elsewhere. Jeanette's blinds had been up as usual but there had been no sign of life in the main room or any other rooms for that matter. Indeed no lights had been on the whole time I'd been observing, yet the TV had been playing away in the semi-darkness — a blue-tinged flickering was clearly discernible, and the only movement. What had she been doing?

However, in the last few minutes the room was filled with light and people and despite the distance it was obvious something bad had happened. Something very bad. A few people were in uniforms, others, probably higher ranking detectives, were in drab suits and casuals. This was a Sunday afternoon. But where were the forensics in those white overalls, with masks covering their mouths, latex gloves on their hands and plastic bags over their feet? Either they hadn't been summoned yet or were on their way, with the police currently on the spot only just discovering the full extent of the gory details, and deciding what would be needed to conduct a careful and thorough gathering of evidence. Certainly, I was surprised by how many police seemed to be there already, and how exactly they had hit upon the scene. Had someone tipped them off? I didn't know what I'd been doing.

Very exciting, and terrifying. And just what I needed to liven up a dank, solitary, alcohol-free Sunday evening. I had been on the verge of hunting around the flat for loose change to see whether I had enough money to buy a half decent bottle of wine, which would have meant something Chilean, or more specifically an oak-aged Cabernet Sauvignon from the Colchagua Valley — a Threshers staple. I might have been a little short of cash and on the point of having to make a few sacrifices but that didn't mean I would be left knocking back sweet sherry, yet. Even in my straitened circumstances I had certain standards to maintain.

However, what was going on across the concourse had distracted me from my craving for the grape — as I was looking, riveted, the blinds were rapidly lowered, almost simultaneously throughout the maisonette. Fuck it. I scanned other properties and balconies on the estate to see whether anyone else had witnessed the ongoing drama. It didn't appear so and with the interior of Jeanette's maisonette suddenly firmly closed from view I wondered if it were possible that the whole episode would go unnoticed and be hushed up. Surely not. It wouldn't be long before word got out – after all, it was the sort of estate that letting agents described as friendly.

Police would start door-to-door investigations – who had seen or heard what – because I doubted it was going to be an immediately solvable incident. Jeanette lived alone. She had no obvious boyfriend or boyfriends, friends or enemies. Few people ever visited her. She barely went out. Yet there she was – I could see it all so clearly in my mind – lying naked on the floor beside her bed, in that space between the built-in cupboard and the cheap divan from Dreamland, with her legs and arms splayed awkwardly and a pair of black lacy knickers shoved halfway down her throat. So it couldn't be suicide or accidental death, I could just imagine the coppers crammed into the room slowly deducing. Or natural causes.

'It's murder, mate,' one of them, a lad in his late twenties with closely cropped hair and a cheap, ill-fitting suit, would say. 'First degree.'

'No chance it was sex games gone wrong?' another, the one female detective present, would offer. She would fancy herself as something of a sex-crimes expert, forever alluding to the possibility of a carnal motive.

'This wasn't about oxygen deprivation, for kicks,' a third, the oldest and most senior detective on the scene, would add. He would have known all about the tremendous sexual highs, and lows, that could be gained from blocking the windpipe when you're on the verge of orgasm – being an ardent practitioner in his spare time. And, more than likely, seeing as he was an experienced and canny professional also, rather than just a pervert, he would have a very clear idea about the appeal, to a certain sort of individual, of pushing the boundary further and further until the point of no return. It was a fine line.

'Definitely not,' the old DCI would continue, shifting his considerable weight from one leg to another, 'this was a callous, brutally violent act of sexually motivated murder. It looks like she's been gagged and raped, vaginally and anally. Can you see the tear marks on her perineum? The dried blood?' He would have stooped closer. 'Though it's not clear whether this was before or after death, or both. We're dealing with a highly dangerous psychopath. It won't have been the first time he's struck and if we don't get our arses into gear, guys – OK? – it won't be the last. We're fighting time.'

'Any indication of whether he knew the victim?' the lad, probably, would add.

'What do you reckon? There were no obvious signs of forced entry,' the self-proclaimed sex-crimes expert would acknowledge. 'Except the front door was left open. At least that's what the neighbour who called the police said. She says she found the door open, went in and discovered the body. She's pretty shocked. A couple of WPCs are with her now.'

How could anyone be so stupid as to leave the front door open? From my understanding of crimes and crime scenes, the longer they went undetected the less chance there was of collecting valuable evidence. DNA, from hair, flakes of skin, saliva, blood, semen, not to mention threads of fabric, fingerprints, shoe imprints, specks of dirt, these things quickly became contaminated, if not disintegrated beyond use, despite what the experts would have us believe. And who wasn't to say I hadn't had recent contact with Jeanette anyway? Maybe, still feeling fired up, I had popped round there to surprise her.

Maybe, when she had opened the door in that ridiculously loose and revealing dressing gown – what a tease – I had uttered the words, 'Hi, I'm from across the way. I couldn't help noticing you and what you were doing on that sofa,' and given her a knowing look, before adding, 'and wondered whether I might come in.'

She'd take my hand and place it inside her dressing gown, straight between her legs. She would be suitably wet. Then she'd lead me through to the main room and upstairs and bang into her bedroom where she would throw off the dressing gown and pull me onto the bouncy divan. The reality, however, was always going to be a crushing let-down. That was life.

I walked back inside, closing the balcony door. There was no lock on this door. There was no point. Nobody could break in here, unless they abseiled down from the roof, six more storeys above, or were aided with a massive, telescopic ladder. Did they even make ladders that large? If anyone was going to break in it would have to be via the front door, or the small fire exit that led out into the emergency stair-well. Or, I supposed, by knocking a hole through the bathroom wall of the adjoining apartment, if they were absolutely desperate to gain entry. And for what? I had virtually nothing left. I'd flogged most of my valuables and binned most of my clothes. Though there was me, of course. They could always be coming for me.

At least when company did arrive the place was looking surprisingly shipshape, thanks in no small part to Moran's on Old Street. I'd thought that B&Qs were everywhere, like Sainsbury's, or Tesco, or Toys R Us, but could I find one yesterday morning? No. Typical, wasn't it, that when you actually needed a B&Q there simply wasn't one. It was like taxis, of course, and buses and Tubes and trains, and girl-friends and wives and children and feisty little dogs and fat four-by-fours and elegant town houses and cottages in the country, not to mention a lucrative contract alongside a healthy bank balance – a burgeoning, if you like, trend-bucking business. There was just so much you always needed and never remotely got close to attaining, however hard you tried. And I was trying. Not vainly, because results were beginning to appear. Things were changing, forever, though not necessarily for the better.

Amazingly I'd quite enjoyed applying a tub of white emul-sion to the sitting-room walls and ceiling. There was some-thing very satisfying about painting over past mistakes and blemishes, covering up accidents and the reminders of unfortunate incidents, while also of course paying respect to Chamberlin, Powell and Bon. Seeing as they had gone to so much time and trouble to create the perfect urban living environment, an inner-city idyll, the least I could do was look after it and behave in a suitably restrained and minimal way. Though before I was completely carried away with good-will and executing good works, I got arm ache. This led me to formulating a particularly wicked though far more exciting idea, so I hurriedly finished up and dumped all the dirty gear, including what was left of the Dulux Brilliant White, down the rubbish chute, inadvertently managing to splatter much of the corridor. No one, I could be certain, would make a fuss.

My PowerBook had gone to sleep already. I hadn't even typed in my password. I wasn't going to work on any busi-ness plan or proposal now. I couldn't concentrate. North Korea would have to wait. I walked over to the main window, but leaving the balcony door closed this time. Even from here I could see that Jeanette's blinds remained firmly down, though behind light was clearly being pumped out. Had they rigged up some floods? Had the forensics arrived? And if so what were they really going to find? I needed a drink, and not just a bottle or two of Montes Limited Selection Cabernet Sauvignon 2007. I needed a Martini to kick off the evening, an extra dry Martini consisting of perfectly chilled Tanqueray, just the tiniest hint of vermouth and a twist of lemon – I wasn't into olives, olives were for girls and James Bond – and preferably from somewhere like the Blue Bar at the Berkeley, or Claridge's Bar. I'd long believed that the only place to get a proper cocktail was a hotel bar and the better the hotel the better the bar and therefore the better the cocktail, as long as the hotel wasn't the Dorchester. I didn't like the Dorchester – too many celebrities and too much swank. That was where the Joes of this world drank – or did when their expense accounts had allowed them such licence – thinking they were somewhere special, somewhere exclusive.

Exclusivity and expenses, I'd seen where it was heading. I wasn't foolish enough to have been caught in the tide and swept along. And maybe I'd been deluding myself about places like the Berkeley or Claridge's too, especially after I'd sunk a couple of stiff ones. I could see how they weren't exactly for me either – too much faultless service – and that I'd be far better off sticking closer to home. It paid to be parochial in London, to keep your ambitions within sight, your pecker up. I wondered what time St John closed tonight, because although I wasn't particularly hungry I wasn't in the mood for drinking alone. Once someone had lodged herself in my mind I found that she was there, teasing and plaguing away, until I'd put the issue to rest, so to speak. It was much the same with things, with fancy clothes and luxury goods, even bog standard consumer durables. We all still needed things.

A couple of years ago, maybe it was more like four years

ago, because it was around the time Mother died, I remember becoming quite fixated about bags. For some reason I seemed suddenly to need both a briefcase-type bag, at least a bag I could carry my work papers and pens and books and laptop and associated paraphernalia in, and also a bag I could use for a short business trip, or anyway for a few days away. This would have to be small enough for hand luggage but also large enough for essential clothes and toiletries, including a spare pair of shoes – I always travelled with at least two pairs of shoes. Also I didn't want to look like your average executive pulling a Samsonite, like an unwilling pet. I wanted my hand-luggage bag to be both stylish and practical and, yes, I supposed then exclusive too. Actually the same went for both bags, the larger and the smaller, because at the time I could see that I was going to be lugging them all over the world, in both benign and hostile environments.

To begin with I looked for compatible if not exactly matching bags – indeed probably not matching because that would have been rather too contrived, and quite possibly a little naff. No different really to logo flashing. Plus, it was important that if I was travelling first or business class they'd wave me on with both no problem. And if I wasn't travelling up front I still wanted to be able to keep both as hand luggage, which meant the bag for my work stuff had to be pretty discreet, though obviously still robust, and of course stylish. In many ways, I felt it was even more important to make an effort to look good when travelling, than when simply staying at home. Favours were more forthcoming. You got further.

I had had no idea of the problems I'd encounter acquiring these very necessary accessories. It was hard enough finding one remotely suitable bag, let alone two. Strangely the world of luggage was new to me. Until then I'd got by with I'm not quite sure what. Perhaps I wasn't travelling so much so I hadn't noticed that I was lacking essential equipment. Or, I seemed to remember, I'd had an old leather holdall – by, actually, Ralph Lauren – that had finally fallen to pieces, at least it did after I'd got very cross with it when I was coming back from somewhere and had noticed that one of the straps was loose – the stitching had come undone – and a corner of the bottom panel had nearly worn through. I could have lost everything.

John Lewis was a disaster. Someone, in fact it might have been Sean, had suggested that John Lewis, the Oxford Street branch, had a great luggage selection, and was relatively cheap. Of course I should have known better, and it wasn't even as if I was economising then. Work was good, I was still shimmying up the greasy pole, being offered ever more innovative incentives and bonuses and pension plans – that corporation. And Mother had recently died leaving me a packet, or so I'd presumed, and naturally I wanted the best. Samsonite, Angler, Travelpro, Atlantic, Swiss Army, Delsey. There were endless everyday brands I obviously wasn't interested in, so I said to the assistant, 'Is this all you have?'

'Was there something particular you were looking for?' she said. She was a large, busty, middle-aged black woman, with shiny ginger highlights in her hair and lots of almost matching chunky gold jewellery.

'Yes. Very.' But I knew there'd be no point in trying to explain exactly what.

'Do you want a suitcase, or hand luggage, or a briefer? Samsonite is very good. Or there's Delsey. Delsey's popular. And the John Lewis brand comes with a five-year guarantee.'

'It's OK, thanks. I'm just looking.' I was hurrying towards the exit, but she was on my tail.

'Angler's very affordable and a lot of men are going for the Swiss Army bags at the moment. Is it for you?'

'Yes, no,' I said, running into the computer section. Swiss

Army? The idea of me rushing off to a meeting in Milan, say, with a Swiss Army branded piece of luggage, probably in camouflage, because that was what seemed to be all the rage, was almost laughable, if it wasn't so tragic.

For days I toured London looking for luggage shops, but was continually surprised by the lack of interesting brands, the garish patterns, loud logos and frankly the shoddy quality. Everything appeared to have been mass-produced in China with second-rate, man-made fibre. The few leather items that I did come across were either far too heavy and the wrong shape, or too stiff, or simply a foul colour. Where was this stuff treated? The Tanning Shop? However, the more I pursued the matter the more obsessed I became. The perfect bags had to be out there somewhere; there was always an answer, or so I thought. I even contemplated having them handmade specially, except the only outfit that seemed remotely keen and capable was based in Neal's Yard, and there was no way I was going to walk around with a couple of bags made by Birkenstock-wearing hippies, even if they'd followed my instructions to a T, which they wouldn't have, because hippies never listened and always thought they knew best – same as artists, and advertising executives, and corporate lawyers, and bankers and politicians and Dear Leaders, you name them. Why couldn't I find a company that made traditional-with-a-modern-twist handmade luggage? I couldn't even find an old-fashioned saddlery.

Had Internet shopping been more advanced then I would have trawled the net, presuming I had the right software. As it was I finally returned to Selfridges where I was talked into buying a Tumi laptop bag in a sort of sci-fi grey with red edging and a matching, overly padded hand-luggage bag, with wheels and a telescopic handle. And I had expressly not wanted matching luggage. I wasn't keen on wheels either, or all the padding. What was wrong with carrying your own stuff? Yet the sales assistant – a slight young man with heavily gelled fair hair – said this Tumi luggage was almost indestructible, being made from a ballistic nylon that they used in bulletproof vests. However, when I got it all home, I must have still been living in Bayswater then, just a short stroll from the Heathrow Express at Paddington, I realised I hated it. I liked the idea of it being indestructible and also the fact that it had cost a fortune – so it had to be in a whole different league to those brands at John Lewis – but it looked ridiculous. I didn't know what I'd been thinking. And I'd so been looking forward to not having to worry about not having any suitable luggage. The grey was too light and the red edging too extreme and the ballistic nylon felt, well nylony. That style of bag might have appealed to a spoilt Japanese teenager, but it didn't appeal to me whatsoever.

The problem was I'd used the bigger bag to take the smaller bag home, testing the wheels and the handle along the way. And frankly the handle didn't seem all that solid and the wheels wobbled alarmingly and I could just tell that the light grey nylon was going to get filthy. I didn't mind a material looking worn if it wore well, like properly treated and tanned leather, say, or traditional canvas, or waxed cotton, but nylon, even or rather especially ballistic nylon? Forget it.

So I thought I'd put the bag through its paces and test the strength of the handle and the play on the wheels and what would happen to the grey if it were subjected to a bit of tossing around in the yard. After all, this was probably mild compared to what the baggage handlers at Heathrow, or Pyongyang International for that matter, would subject the thing to – except they wouldn't, of course, be getting their hands on it, as it was only ever meant to be hand luggage. However, the hopelessly young sales assistant in Selfridges' luggage department – what was his ambition in life? To front a boy band? – didn't necessarily know that. If I'd had a gun

I'd have shot the damn thing to see what it was really made of.

To be fair the handle and the wheels held firm, though the supposedly indestructible ballistic nylon didn't stand up quite so well. It marked atrociously. But I didn't even wait until the next day before returning to Selfridges. I knew I couldn't possibly have spent a comfortable night still in possession of those bags. I needed an immediate refund or at the very least to exchange the items, though I had no idea what for. More Tumi? But a different line? I remembered feeling sick as I hurried back to Oxford Street, that ludicrous grey, with flashes of red trailing behind.

'I'm sorry,' I said to the man, the boy — even then everyone was younger than me — 'the bags are not right. My fiancée hates them.' This of course was long after I'd kicked Fran out. 'They are all wrong.'

'Do you have your receipt?'

'Yes.' I handed him the pristine receipt and lifted the bags, the one inside the other, onto the sleek black counter.

He looked at the receipt and said, 'You bought them today?'

'Yes, from you.' I couldn't believe he'd forgotten me, or the particular purchase.

'Why does this one look so used?'

'You persuaded me to buy them. And you said if there were any problems I could have a full refund.'

'But they have been used.'

'Hardly. I only bought them today, obviously.' The conversation went on in this vein for a considerable while. Finally I said, 'You told me they were indestructible. Bulletproof, is what you said. How, if that's the case, is it possible that in the matter of only an hour or two they look like this, if they are really as tough and practical as you made out? What's the point in having such smart and expensive luggage if it looks

145

like this after its first outing? What would it look like if I took it on a trip to Iraq, or Afghanistan, or the Democratic Republic of the Congo? And that's beside the fact that my fiancée hates the colour. She's right. For once. What a ridiculous fucking colour for a bag. It's only ever going to show up dirt, like shit on a toilet bowl.'

'You don't need to swear.'

This was a grown man I was talking to, or should have been. Not a child. He was employed by Selfridges, or a concession anyway. 'Yes I do,' I said. How I hated it when people, when sales assistants of all people, told me not to swear. There was every need in the world to swear. Never was an expletive or two more appropriate. 'Get me the fucking manager.'

Eventually the manager arrived – a short, meek-looking man, closer to my age. Where did they get them from? 'Yes?' he said. 'What can I do?'

Believe it or not, I had to go through the whole saga again, about how his colleague had forced these products on me, telling me how tough they were and how clearly they weren't, anyone could see that now, and how disappointed my fiancée and I were, how it was going to ruin the anniversary of our meeting, which was already in the balance anyway because my mother had recently died, and I just couldn't take any more stress. I might have choked back a sob or two.

He gave me a full refund, as I'd only had them for a couple of hours, saying, he agreed, they weren't a great advertisement for Tumi and that he'd take up the matter with the manufacturer. 'Maybe there's a problem with this particular line,' he actually said. 'We haven't stocked it for long.' He might have been short and meek, with a slight stammer, but I could perhaps see why he'd risen to the rank of manager. He was brilliant at his job, a credit to his profession. I walked out of Selfridges with my faith in that department store fully restored and feeling in a surprisingly good mood.

But it didn't last for long. Not even as far as Bond Street, because there was still this dilemma about my luggage, or rather lack of it. Rarely had I ever bought something and been completely satisfied. Usually I went back for a refund or to exchange the item, which was invariably when the swearing started. All this could have been avoided of course if manufacturers made things properly and shops were better stocked and they employed more knowledgeable staff. However, I was still without some proper luggage and knew I wouldn't be able to relax until I'd found exactly what I'd been looking for originally, not that I knew what that was anymore. How I wished my work, my hectic international travelling hadn't made all this so necessary. If only I'd had a job and a lifestyle that didn't involve so much go-getting.

Yet many more days later and I found myself in the Tumi shop on Piccadilly, and obviously not for the first time. The thing was, I still liked the idea of Tumi, certainly the concept of this supposedly indestructible, bulletproof material, even if the colours and finishing touches weren't always to my taste. Needless to say I bought another hand-luggage bag, with wheels, and another laptop bag-come-briefcase. Except these ones were in a straight black ballistic nylon and had no fancy edging or thrills. They were no-nonsense. But my euphoria at this purchase hadn't lasted forever, because I could never help feeling that the black was too black, and that ultimately Tumi was too executive a brand for me. I hadn't wanted to look like everyone else when I jetted around the globe.

Walking over to my wardrobe, I reached up and pulled down the hand-luggage bag from the top. It weighed a ton – certainly far too much for a handy carry-on. There was a puff of dust and I was slightly surprised to find it still there in one piece. Having brushed it clean with my hand I put it on the bed and unzipped the main compartment. I always felt it wasn't as roomy as it could have been too. However, considering how much my wardrobe had shrunk recently, I'd probably be able to pack most things, especially if I used the laptop bag as well. Then I'd really look the part, wouldn't I, though clearly not a part that came naturally to me.

I wondered how popular Tumi was with travellers to and within North Korea. I somehow doubted I'd see too many Tumi bags on the streets of Pyongyang. What would I see? I had this sinking feeling that much of the place would be shuttered and deserted, grey everywhere, like the grey on my first Tumis, except without the fun of the red trim. Was I making a mistake? Perhaps I was just hungry. Was St John open on a Sunday night? I doubted it, which meant I'd have to leave that particular South East Asian diversion for another day. Considering I didn't have any money, or certainly not the sort of money to do any serious entertaining with, probably it wasn't such a bad thing. Obviously I wanted to make the right impression. There was no way I wanted to appear cheap. I was not my brother.

Threshers and a single bottle of Montes Reserva would have to suffice after all. Still, had I had a little more cash something sparkling might have been more appropriate. A celebration of sorts was in order. Though I wasn't going down the cava or prosecco route, even if they had any on offer, which they usually had. I loved champagne, but I was very particular about which label and vintage. Non-vintage, I was happy to stick with Moët & Chandon. My favourite vintage champagnes were Bollinger and Dom Pérignon, but if pushed I'd sink a vintage Lanson or Mumm. Cristal, of course, was obviously not for me. Too crass.

Halfway across the concourse I suddenly changed direction by 180 degrees and instead of heading for the small row of shops on Goswell Road I walked towards the Golden Lane exit. This route wouldn't just take me past the front of Jeanette's apartment, even though she was on the first and second floors, it would also give me a clear view of the back of her block and the access points to her landing and door. There were no police on view from the concourse and Jeanette's blinds remained closed though I could see outlines of people behind, in bright light, and stepping out of the estate there were a number of police vehicles parked up on Golden Lane, including one of those white forensics vans, not that it was exactly marked as such.

Some reflex made me pat the pockets of my Belstaff and jeans, and I wished I'd taken the trouble to have yet another shower, but one cold shower a day was more than enough for anyone. Of more immediate concern was the discovery that I still had Bobbie's mail stuffed in the large inside pocket – was this what was termed a map pocket? How could I have forgotten about the mail? I was such an idiot. And I'd so wanted some time to go through it carefully. OK, from memory there were what looked like a couple of bills, but there were also a couple of letters, one with a typed name and address and one handwritten, which could have been interesting. However, I didn't want to be caught with them on me, red-handed so to speak, though nor did I want to be caught dumping them in a bin. I hurried past the vehicles and just before I turned into Baltic Street I looked left, through a gap in the perimeter wall where once there had been a metal gate, and caught sight of the exterior first-floor corridor, which led directly to the back of Jeanette's. Sure enough I could see a couple of men in uniform, and some blue and white police tape, tape of some sort anyway, and also a number of neighbours further down the corridor who were jostling for position, frantically rubbernecking. Honestly, my neighbours.

I wondered how far the police had progressed with their investigations. Whether they'd discovered any hard evidence. The female detective would have bagged and sealed the sheets, looking for further signs of sexual deviation, while the old DCI would secretly be delighted that at last he had a serious crime to solve, and fast. He'd show them what he was really made of and would already be in the process of pulling out all the stops – summoning more manpower and detailing various personnel to explore numerous databases. Heaps of information would have to be sifted and analysed and as a priority any locals with histories of seriously abusive and psychopathic behaviour, along with all known sex offenders, would have to be tracked down and interviewed. Plus, though not quite so urgently, anyone with a criminal record for harassment or stalking or even burglary should also, he'd detail, be quizzed.

The victim's background would need to be trawled over with a fine toothcomb. Every member of her family, all her friends and acquaintances, work colleagues and contacts should be scrutinised. What chat rooms and websites she regularly visited if any, he'd stress, could provide clues, and of course all email and phone records, because he already had a very strong feeling that the victim knew her attacker. Or at least her attacker knew her. And then of course the net would have to widen and the media be informed and manipulated. They'd employ shock tactics, they needed some tabloid hysteria. He would probably be looking forward to his starring role, though wishing he'd dyed his hair more recently. There was far too much grey in what hair he had left, but he found that he had to be careful how dark he dyed his hair because his eyebrows and beard were flecked with grey as well and he'd already been caught out, more than once. Those parties he went to.

If I'd been in charge the last thing I'd be doing would be worrying about my appearance. I'd be exploring all possible escape routes more thoroughly, believing that that might provide a vital clue, and calling up what CCTV was available. Though I'd have quickly discovered that the back corridor and the way down onto the concourse were not covered by any camera, and neither was the entrance to my block. That particular camera had been vandalised months ago and not fixed despite persistent complaints about the lack of security on the estate and how with so many covered walkways and dark corners it was a mugger's paradise. Many residents wanted the place pulled down and replaced with something more people friendly, more modern – what a joke. However, not everyone was too bothered and I certainly didn't see how Chamberlin, Powell and Bon were to blame. It wasn't their fault society had degenerated in the way it had since the days when purity of vision, social cohesion and optimism went hand in hand.

Only the main surrounding roads, Golden Lane, Old Street, Goswell Road and Beech Street were covered, and I suspected intermittently at that. Not every CCTV camera in the City could be recording all the time, surely. Especially not on a Sunday. While the Corporation of London was not exactly the poorest borough around, I'd always felt residents were of less concern than either the people who commuted in and worked there, or the tourists. As I'd found to my cost it was much easier to get a business parking permit than a residential one.

Aside from the £670-a-year charge I had to produce endless documents proving I was a bona fide resident. Obviously that wasn't as straightforward as it could have been with the sort of tenancy agreement I had, so I'd had to go to WH Smith, the big one by Holborn Circus, and buy my own and forge a signature or two, which made me realise just how easy it would be to create a new identity for yourself. Utility bills were a breeze, with so many companies falling over themselves for your business. However, as I'd since discovered, opening a bank account with a false name wasn't as easy as acquiring a resident's parking permit. I had yet to secure a false passport.

My car was parked on Great Sutton Street, or was the last time I looked, which was on that fateful evening I terminated my relationship with Bobbie, and it did occur to me that perhaps I should walk over now and check when the permit was going to run out, and the tax disc, as I had a feeling both were nearing the end of their validity and I didn't want to attract any unnecessary attention. Though surely the Corporation of London would inform me as to when I had to renew the parking permit, even if it was a temporary one, and DVLA about the vehicle tax. Not that DVLA knew where I currently lived of course. All these forms and taxes, permits and licences, all this bureaucracy – why did everyone have to know so much about you? It was impossible to remain off the radar, so to speak, unless you'd been working at it for years. And then there was always someone, somewhere keeping an eye on you.

By the junction of Baltic Street and Goswell Road, leaving any sense of a heavy police presence and a rapidly unfolding tragedy behind, it also occurred to me that I should at least check to see whether my car had been vandalised again. Though what was the point? I didn't give a stuff about the car, it had already been ruined – and more than likely by someone who did know where I lived. Not all vandalism was random. Giving up any idea of trotting off to Great Sutton Street and just as I was turning left into Goswell Road, sparse traffic adding to the sense of Sunday evening gloom, my phone rang making me jump almost out of my skin.

With Bobbie's letters still burning against my chest, I

quickly pulled out my mobile. *Withheld*, it said – not surprisingly. I looked up and down Goswell Road and Aldersgate. The few people about didn't appear to be taking any notice of me. There were no suspicious-looking cars or vans idling on double yellows. Yet I was convinced I was being watched. And probably not by someone in an official capacity.

'Yes?' I said.

'Mr Freeman?'

'Who is this?'

'Is that Matt Freeman?'

It was a man's voice. Possibly the person from last night, though he seemed to be less threatening. But I was breathing so hard I couldn't hear properly, plus there was a sudden splurge of noisy traffic. Where had that come from? I supposed it could have been anybody on the other end. 'Yes?'

'Is your address 132 William the Great House, Golden Lane Estate?'

'Why? Why do you want to know?'

'You are Matt Freeman?'

'Yes, I've already told you that. Sorry, I'm on the street, I can't hear you very well.' I always tried to be as polite as possible. Manners got you everywhere, or used to.

'When will you be at home?' Was his tone becoming more threatening?

'Why? Why do you want to know that?'

'When will you be at home?'

'I've just said, what's it to you?' The traffic had died again.

'You have ignored all our previous communications.'

'I don't know who you are.' This was getting absurd.

'We need to pay you a visit.'

'What?'

'You are in possession of certain items that aren't yours.'

All I could think about was Bobbie's box, and of course I no longer had that. Were they after her letters? The ones I had in my pocket? 'I'm going away, on business. I'll be away for weeks.'

'Where are you now?'

'On a street, as I said. Look, who exactly am I talking to?'

'We're in the area, we can meet you.'

'No,' I said instinctively. Of course I said no. 'I'm not in the area, nowhere near. I'm on my way to the airport. I have a plane to catch. I'm in a massive hurry.'

'Which airport?'

'Which airport? Jesus, Luton. Luton Airport.' Of course I'd never flown from Luton Airport. I wasn't sure it still existed.

'You can't avoid us forever, Matt. Lies aren't going to get you anywhere. We'll find you. We'll always be able to find you.'

I was passing Costcutter and just a few steps from Threshers. They weren't in the area. That was the lie. If they were I'd have been lynched by now. These people, honestly.

'Matt, we can make your life extremely uncomfortable. You can't escape forever.'

'Yes I can, arsehole.' So incensed, I wasn't sure what I was saying. 'You'll never find me. I'm far too clever for you.' Why I'd bothered to be polite to this man in the first place I had no idea. As ever it had got me nowhere. I knew times had moved on, that I was dealing with scum. 'Fuck off and leave me alone.'

'You're running out of luck, Matt. We're on your case, you worthless piece of shit.' He laughed, and I was sure I heard someone else laughing in the background. A female?

I pressed the red end call button, which is something I should have done straight away, and watched the screen to make sure I'd properly disconnected, which was when I noticed I had at least one answerphone message and remembered I hadn't listened to my messages from earlier.

Normally I'd always listen to an answerphone message as soon as I knew I had one, knowing it could be an important business call, and how time was money, in my line of work, and that I could be missing out on a one-off. If I was trying to contact someone to offer them work and they failed to get back almost immediately I'd go elsewhere. Having left this message, or messages untended, indeed having forgotten entirely about them, was indicative of just how much my mind was focusing on other things. What a day. What a past few days. I slipped my mobile back into my pocket – business would have to wait. There were still many more pressing things to do.

As if by magic there on the pavement was a bin, a bin encased in a mini concrete shelter, and though it was pretty full I still managed to stuff in Bobbie's unopened letters and cover them up with other people's crap until there was no sign of them. Pulling my hand out I sniffed my fingers. They smelt of fag ash and rotten fish, and I really didn't want to think about what I was suddenly reminded of. Oh, I should have known so much better.

I was still reeling and disorientated from the phone call. How dare someone ruin my quiet Sunday evening. Did I feel really threatened? No. I wasn't scared. I wasn't scared of anybody, because only I knew what I was capable of and what I was culpable for – I didn't possess anything that wasn't mine. I was extraordinarily thirsty. One bottle of Montes Reserva Cabernet Sauvignon 2007 was not going to be anything like enough. It never was, which was why, when the dope behind the till was too busy picking the dirt from under his nails, while being blasted by Beyoncé from the shop's Bose speakers – and I thought Threshers was on the rack – I managed to lift a bottle of wine, the very first I got my fingers on, from the bargain basket by the front of the shop, and tuck it into the map pocket of my Belstaff. How this jacket continued to amaze me and what full use I was making of it. Though it would let me down one day, I could be certain of that. Nothing was that good. Nothing was perfect.

Only when I had selected my bottle of Montes and glanced back at the bargain basket did I realise that I must have nicked a bottle of Australian Chardonnay, a Chapel Hill at that, Gabriella's favourite tipple, which was almost worse than undrinkable. Going down on Suze would be preferable, even in the state I imagined she'd be in by now. And approaching the counter and the completely vacant sales assistant – hello, anybody in, I thought of saying – I noticed a small black camera lens protruding from the corner of the ceiling, and worse, a TV screen on the back wall, almost directly behind the chip and PIN machine. It was relaying real time and I could see myself waiting to pay, for the one bottle. Wow I was bald, my forehead looking ludicrously large and white and shiny, and my face appeared to be all spectacles and bruises and my chin, there was my pointy chin sticking out like a sore thumb. And I used to think I was good-looking. At least enough women had led me to believe that, in various direct and indirect ways. Perhaps they'd been joking – just so they could get inside my pants.

Somehow I managed to pay, piling all my loose change on the counter and avoiding even a casual glance at the screen. I definitely didn't want to see anymore of me and stepping outside, leaving Beyoncé to bang on and on, and the hope-less excuse of a sales assistant to resume his auto-manicure, I didn't even care whether there was a tape in the machine and the images were being recorded. In a way I hoped they were. Someone as ugly as me deserved to be caught, and made an example of.

EIGHT

Private Sector Recapitalisation

'What happened to your face?'

'Why does everyone keep asking? It doesn't look that bad, does it?'

'It doesn't look great.'

I could have said at least my face is not fat and saggy and glistening with sweat. But I didn't, there was too much at stake, even though I was revolted by the way fat people always sweated so much, Roger being no exception whatsoever. It wasn't even hot, despite the fact we were sitting at what they called the bar, which directly overlooked the kitchen. Of course it wasn't a bar bar. You couldn't just have a drink here, even a really expensive one, you had to eat, while observing the chefs, or artistes at work. I'm sure that's what the maître d' had actually said as she'd showed us to our places. 'Enjoy the artistes at work.' Her English was heavily accented. She was short, a little dumpy, fair, very French, and strikingly unsexy. She wasn't going to be much of a distraction.

'So what happened?' Roger couldn't stop looking around the place, at the plush dark red and black decor and the waterfall of green leaves against the far wall, and the impeccably dressed waiters and waitresses and even chefs, or fucking food artistes, all in black, with the neat L'Atelier logo in that particular red on their chests. He was eying too the other lunchtime diners, an extraordinary crowd of suits and expensively dressed late middle-aged women attempting to look at least twenty years younger. There was a smattering of youngish men with unnaturally blond hair in last season's smart casual attire, or the season's before that — when was smart casual ever fashionable and in season? — and giggly, fawning tit jobs in absurdly revealing blouses and too-tight jeans.

It was a huge disappointment. The fact that these people still had credit, that this sort of place continued to cater for them, with such confidence. The fact that Roger was still clearly so impressed by it all. But I knew he would be — the *Evening Standard*'s restaurant of the year, for the fourth year running, every VIP's favourite hangout, a heady cocktail to beat the recessionary blues, so I'd read somewhere, in the *Standard* I supposed, a glitzy blast from the past, another line I'd read, or imagined I'd read somewhere — he wasn't going to miss out. He was so predictable. Momentarily I was annoyed for being part of it, for perpetuating the show. Yet so keen was I to impress him, I'd obviously resorted to one of the oldest tricks in the book. Bribery. I even felt embarrassed to recall how lucky I'd regarded myself when I'd secured the reservation that morning. Not only that, but how I had this very strong feeling that it was a sign my fortune was about to change, for the better. Good things were going to come at last. I hadn't run out of luck. Far from it.

Supposedly I'd phoned immediately after someone had cancelled, and I hadn't even used a false name to gain attention. 'Normally we're fully booked for at least three months ahead,' the woman had said. What lies. The place was already struggling to fill seats, with cheaply dressed commoners, let alone celebrities. I recognised no one. The lunch was going to be a total disaster, a chronic faux pas, but that wasn't the point and fortunately Roger appeared to be almost beside himself with excitement. He wouldn't notice how naff it had become. Naff people never did.

'Come on,' he said, 'you can't sit here looking such a mess without telling me what happened. Or am I to presume you got yourself into yet another ridiculous tangle and someone thumped you, because, quite honestly, that's what it looks like. Not that you probably didn't deserve it.'

Despite his pathetic enthusiasm for the venue Roger wasn't quite being his normal friendly self, at least not with me. He'd been decidedly short on the phone when I'd offered to take him to lunch – with me paying not him, I'd stressed – and it wasn't until I mentioned L'Atelier that he actually agreed to come. If I hadn't then secured the reservation I was stumped.

'I can't believe we're seeing so much of each other,' he'd said while we were waiting to be shown to our little stretch of the bar. 'Months go by without a word, then suddenly it's twice in a week.'

'I thought you might need cheering up, with Emily being away.'

'She hasn't gone yet. Besides, it's not like you to be considerate and think of other people. What do you really have in mind? You want something, don't you?'

'Just your company, over a fantastic meal,' I'd said. 'I more than owe you, for all the times you've taken me out in the past. Plus I'm celebrating. Now Bobbie's gone, you're the only person I could think of to help me. And I know how you like your food.'

On the phone I'd briefly told him that not only had the North Korean deal definitely come off, and that I was flying to Pyongyang as soon as I had my visa, which was being rushed through the embassy of the People's Republic of North Korea, the commercial division, but it was looking more than possible that I was going to strike a similar deal with an Iranian outfit. He'd said something about how only I could do business with such unsavoury regimes. I let it ride. Roger was never going to get the appeal of North Korea. I hadn't yet processed what I felt about Iran, the upsides.

'No one thumped me,' I said, beginning to get my head around the vast menu, which came in various folders. The wine list was another great tome. What were they really suggesting by providing such choice, such temptation – the sheer extravagance? 'And I didn't walk into a lamp post, or trip over the kerb. It was even more stupid.'

'I can imagine.'

'We have these rubbish chutes, in the block, and the one nearest my flat has always been a bit stiff. Anyway I was trying to dump some rubbish down – they are brilliant things, when they work properly, because all you have to do is step out of your front door, walk a few yards to the chute, open it up and whoosh goes the stuff right into a huge bin at the bottom.'

'Must make living there all the more pleasant.'

What was his problem? 'But the other day, on Saturday, I was struggling with a bin bag that I suppose was a little too full – my fault admittedly – and was beginning to split. And the bloody chute flap wouldn't open, so I crouched down to see if there was anything obstructing it – sometimes people don't push their rubbish in properly and it can jam – and as I was doing that and tugging really hard at the handle, while trying to stop my rubbish from exploding all over the place with my other hand, the thing flew open and hit me in the face. It fucking hurt, I can tell you, and of course the rubbish did end up everywhere. What a fucking mess. It took me ages to tidy it up.'

'Shall we order?' said Roger. 'I'm a bit pushed for time.'

'Sure.' Except, I still had no idea how to decipher the menu. Or rather menus. There was something called the *Menu Découverte*, or two of them at £80 and £55 per head, and there was the *Menu Club* at £30 and pages of *La Carte* menu and then the *Les Plats En Petites Portions Dégustation*, which was subtitled *Small tasting dishes*. But I wasn't going to play the rookie in front of Roger. Or the small army of waiters and waitresses who were wafting around as if they were working in some Bruton Street boutique – Stella McCartney's, or more likely Matthew Williamson's. Not my favourite breed of sales assistant.

Quite possibly the most precious specimen duly appeared. He was tall, thin, with dark eyes, a light olive complexion and short black hair, glistening with gel. What was it with all this gel nowadays? What was I missing? He also had very feminine lips. Maybe it was the light, though he looked like he was wearing a touch of foundation and a smear of lip gloss. 'Are you familiar with our menus, or can I explain the philosophy of dining at L'Atelier?' he said.

'Please,' said Roger.

'We're fine,' I said. 'Just give us another couple of minutes.'

'Certainly, sir. Can I get you an aperitif?'

'I'm sticking to water, sparkling,' said Roger.

'Really? I'm going to have a glass of champagne. Why don't you join me and we could make it a bottle?'

'No. I don't want to drink. I have too much work to do this afternoon.'

'I can't say I can exactly take it easy. Come on, Roger, I'm celebrating.'

'No. Sorry.'

The waiter was still hovering by my shoulder, a little too

closely. 'A glass of champagne please, house will do and a bottle of sparkling mineral water, is that right, Roger?'

'We don't have a house champagne,' the waiter said. 'But I can recommend the Bruno Paillard, Première Cuvée.'

'Never heard of it. Do you have a Dom Pérignon?'

'We have a 1998, but not by the glass.'

'Get me the Bruno whatever it is, just a glass.' There were rip-offs and rip-offs, plus this could have gone on forever. Indeed, I had a sudden feeling that the lunch was going to go on forever, even though Roger was supposedly pushed for time, the ungrateful fucker.

'So, Bobbie's definitely no longer an item then?' Roger asked, while keeping his eyes firmly on the menu. He could barely look at me. 'Have you even seen her?'

'No, not since I last saw you. And as far as I'm aware it's still curtains. Why are you so suddenly interested in Bobbie anyway? You've never been that interested in the others, except perhaps Fran. But that was a little different, wasn't it?'

'The other day you didn't seem so certain it was curtains.'

'Who's ever completely certain of anything? But with Bobbie, well, as I said before, it's probably the age thing, and that's not going to change. She was pretty fucked up too.'

'Yeah? How?' Roger looked at me this time.

I couldn't hold his gaze. What was this, *Question Time*? One of the chefs, or artistes, was slicing what appeared to be sautéed foie gras. I couldn't understand how he could cut into it so precisely without the foie gras collapsing. In another life, I used to think, I'd have liked to be a chef. I appreciated the feeling for food, the sense of taste, the innovation, the timing and presentation serious chefs exhibited, though now catering jobs seemed more determined by hairstyles and muscle tone, make-up and obsequiousness. It wasn't for me. I was too bald. One way or another I was stuck with marketing. A shuffle sideways was probably as much as I was ever going to manage – into what? Sales? Is that where all paths now led? 'She's got this weird, dysfunctional family background,' I said. 'She doesn't really get on with her parents and her sister died not so long ago and I don't think she's quite come to terms with it.'

'I'm not surprised.'

The waiter, again getting a little too close to me – what was it with Mediterranean men? – placed my half full, at the very most, champagne flute in front of me and poured each of us a glass of sparkling mineral water, before setting the bottle in between Roger and me. I didn't recognise the minimalist labelling etched onto the smoked glass. I didn't want a glass of water either. 'You're not surprised about what?'

'That Bobbie hasn't got over the death of her sister.'

'Yeah, but it's not as simple as that. It's not like she was grieving in a normal way, if there is such a thing, though there probably is because people tend to react in pretty similar, predictable ways, certainly to such emotive issues, don't they? So I've always believed anyway. But not Bobbie. Her reaction was, well it's sort of hard to explain. In a way she had turned her sister into an icon. Out of all proportion to who she was, or what she could have meant. There's been a certain amount of shrine building – if you understand what I'm saying. In this Agent Provocateur shoebox of all things. She'd filled it full of the oddest stuff.'

'Again, I'm not surprised, Matt. Some of us do have very strong feelings for others, you know. Especially close relatives, and when something tragic like that happens, a death. It all seems quite natural to me.'

'Yeah, but by all accounts they didn't have the best relationship. In fact they used to hate each other. Siblings don't always get on, you know. I can't stand my brother. We have absolutely nothing in common.'

'You can't stand a lot of people, Matt.'

'What's got into you today?'

'Have you chosen? I'm having a problem with this menu. I'd have the *Menu Découverte*' — unsurprisingly Roger's French pronunciation was appalling — 'the eighty quid one, if I had more time. Maybe I'll just have the club menu. But it does seem a shame to come somewhere like here and not experience it fully. Especially as you're paying. Had a windfall? Someone die?'

'I told you, I got the North Korean deal and then there's this other thing in Iran, and you know I went on that trip to Dubai recently?'

'No.'

'Well that's come off too. Finally it looks as if my business is gathering momentum, against all the odds. I bet you wish you'd invested that money all those months ago, when you had the chance. You'd have stood to make a sizeable return, almost already. Certainly by the end of this financial year. What other stock would do that for you now? If I can make it in the harshest economic climate for a generation, if not a century, I must be onto something. Though you know what, Rodge, because you're an old mate, my best mate in fact, I can always make an exception. It's not too late for you, Rodge. You could still put in a bit if you wanted. A couple of thousand say, for five per cent?'

'Where's that waiter?' Roger was sweating even more than usual. 'We need to get on with this lunch. That's the problem with places like this. It's all such a bloody performance.'

'All right, ten per cent. I thought you enjoyed eating out in swanky restaurants. Do you know how hard it was to get a reservation? Perhaps we should have just stuck with the Giraffe.'

Roger began waving his arm around, looking for a waiter to summon. Normally he was far too concerned about not being demanding. 'I don't have the money right now.'

Oh yes he did. Not everyone was broke. I'd have to try another tack. 'What would you rather,' I said, 'have your tongue brushing some stripper's arse, or your slobbery gob wrapped around a langoustine fritter with basil pistou?' That was the first dish that really intrigued me from the small tasting dishes menu. But just how small were those so-called tasting dishes? I didn't want to have yet another meal where I was left still feeling hungry and dissatisfied at the end, without, this time, even having been served by an alluring albeit austere babe in a pair of tight black slacks. Aside from the fact that most of the staff here were male, despite wearing copious amounts of make-up, the women were peculiarly un-French.

Looking up from the menu and catching sight of a bright orange flame suddenly smothering a frying pan and almost as quickly dying away when the chef – I couldn't think of anyone as a food artiste – took the pan off the heat and flipped the small wedge of meat, possibly a quail's breast, I had this very scary thought about the women I'd be encountering in North Korea. Would they all be dog ugly, for the obvious reasons? How my mind worked, sometimes it troubled even me. 'Perhaps it would taste much the same,' I said.

'What?'

'Langoustine or arse.' I needed that cash.

'Matt, do you have to? We're about to eat.'

If guilt, shock and embarrassment weren't working, was Roger simply incapable of sticking up for old mates? Was he immune to such concepts as loyalty, fidelity even? Of course he was. When Emily was concerned anyway. But at least I should have been thankful that I didn't have continually to lie to and betray someone like Emily. That I didn't have to eat shepherd's pie every night and support a couple of kids with attention deficit disorders. I should have been feeling so much happier, sitting here at L'Atelier, celebrating. I was Matt Freeman, slim, trim, still with a twinkle in my bespectacled eye – only just the wrong side of thirty. Stylish, successful, currently single – to boot. Who could resist me? 'Langoustine or arse? It's a serious question. Food or sex?'

'Matt, let's order, should we?'

'Food it is then? Not what I was expecting. I thought, Rodge, that sex, even the slightest hint of any paid-for action, such as a fifteen-quid dance, as is the way with the truly desperate, came first. You always seemed happier to discuss my sex life, than any fancy food we might have been eating. Or for that matter my business, when do we ever discuss that? You're not interested because all you're bothered about is arse. Come on, Roger, you're the most sexually repressed guy I know. For years you've been getting off by either quizzing me or popping into the Giraffe.' I wasn't at all sure of my ground. Of course Roger was more interested in food. You just had to look at his chosen life partner. You just had to look at the sweaty size of him, stuffed into a black Boss suit two sizes too small. Sex was an afterthought. And maybe it was simply his way of trying to connect with me. 'For some shaved muff,' I said, crossly.

'Keep your voice down, Matt, please. I might know people here.' He was frantically looking around again – for people he knew, in here? I doubted it.

'And I might not?'

'No, probably not. These people, this scene, it's not exactly your world, is it? Or at least it's not something you can usually afford. And, you're right, we don't normally discuss your business because there's nothing to say. It's a joke, or would be if it weren't so tragic. A few absurd marketing ideas, for which you're not even qualified. It's never going anywhere.'

'Yes it is. You wait. You'll see.'

'You live in a fantasy world, Matt. You're so divorced from reality I don't know how you've survived so long without something really unpleasant happening to you. You've been asking for trouble for years.'

'Thanks. I said I was paying, didn't I?'

'Would I be here if you weren't?'

'It's come to that has it? What more do you want from me, Roger?'

'The truth maybe? Or something remotely resembling it. I'm sick of your bullshit.'

'So says the adman.'

'What really happened with Bobbie, Matt? Let's start there.'

'Bobbie? I don't know, not for sure, but there was something pretty suspicious about it. She was there, when she died, just the two of them — and you want to know how her sister died?'

'I'm not talking about that. I'm not interested in her damn sister, whether she's dead or not. Or how she died.'

'Feelings, Roger, feelings.'

'You know what I'm talking about.'

'But it all ties up. That's the whole point. That's what I'm trying to get to. If you'll give me a chance.'

'Oh Jesus. I'm too hungry to deal with this. You are always so evasive.'

'Fine, then why don't we order? I had wanted to enjoy myself too. Where's that waiter? Made up your mind?'

'I don't have a problem in that department, thanks. I can always make up my mind. If it's one thing I am it's decisive.'

'The trouble is, Roger, you make a decision and then you're stuck with it. Look at your marriage.'

'Bobbie, Matt? Don't change the subject. What happened?'

Was this ever going to end? 'So, unlike you I consider all my options carefully, and don't rush into things. I don't see that that's a particularly rash way of operating. Here he is. Our waiter.' Was I meant to laugh or cry?

'I don't seem to remember you taking your time with Fran. You were engaged almost within days. And whom had you persuaded to be your best man, before, as I understand it, you'd even asked her to marry you? Me. I must have been insane to agree to that. Thank God I never had to make my speech. What on earth would I have said?'

'What a great guy I was. How lucky Fran was. Chuck in a few laughs. The usual stuff, except that that would have been beyond you, wouldn't it? You're not the generous type. Fat people seldom are. They're too greedy.'

'How many lunches have I bought you, over the years?'

'Who's paying today?' Was a smile creeping onto his face? Was the old Roger still there, lurking behind the lard? 'I'm ordering.' The waiter was standing to my right, far too close for comfort again – I could even smell the nicotine on his breath – though he'd obviously deduced that I was the one who was in charge, despite my bruised face and somewhat casual attire, casual for me anyway, and the fact that Roger was in a suit. But what a suit. I could never understand Hugo Boss. His jackets were always too boxy, his trousers too roomy. But having the oversized, underpaid corporate German as the target market probably explained it. Maybe the waiter was more discerning than I'd first thought. I was wearing my Margaret Howells, a pale blue Paul Smith shirt, a little frayed on the cuffs – prematurely, if you asked me – and an old Nicole Farhi dark blue corduroy jacket – two-button, double vented, slightly 1970s. Not the most aspiring attire I know, but it was at least comfortable, and what was more, I felt like me in these clothes, rather than me putting on some sort of sad, executive show. And clearly, though not surprisingly, I still exuded considerably more confidence, and an air of solvent sophistication, than lame, sweaty Roger.

'Right,' I couldn't help focusing on the waiter's unnaturally smooth complexion, 'we're ready to order, I think. Roger?'

'Yeah, you know what, I'm going to have the *Menu Découverte*. This one here, the £80 one.' He held up that particular menu, pointing to the top, where it said *Menu Découverte £80*. He obviously realised how appalling his pronunciation was.

'Great. I'll have the same.' I'd been thinking of having the *Menu Découverte* anyway. Why the hell not? It was my celebration, my party, my shots to be called. 'But we'd also like a couple of portions of the langoustine fritter with the basil pistou, on the side, and what the hell, the crispy frog's legs with the garlic mash also, thanks.' I didn't bother looking at Roger for confirmation that he was also up for a few extra dishes to add to the nine, which were now already coming. Of course he'd be up for them. I doubted he'd ever turned away food in his life. 'Maybe,' I added – gosh, I hated the smell of stale nicotine on someone's breath, and a waiter's too; he should have known so much better – 'you could bring those after the Saint-Jacques and before the foie gras.'

'As you wish. I'll tell chef.'

I thought it was meant to be food artiste. What a shower. And as for the as you wish – he didn't mean it in the slightest. Would he even tell the chef? We'd see.

'And will you be having wine?'

My champagne glass was empty. How had that happened? Clearly the non-vintage Bruno Paillard, despite being a première cuvée, was entirely forgettable. I looked at him, thinking, does the bear shit in the woods? 'Can you send over the sommelier?'

'I'll be taking the wine order.'

'Oh, what about the sommelier?' I so didn't want this man hovering over me.

'We don't have a dedicated sommelier, as such. We are all trained.'

'Yeah? Classy joint.'

'Matt, let me order the wine.' Roger turned to the waiter. 'Sorry.'

I'd seen that look before. It was the please excuse my friend look, because he doesn't know how to behave. Was I embarrassing Roger? *Sorry*, honestly. How dare he undermine me. I knew fully well how to behave, and exactly what to expect where – such as a sommelier. Manners were second nature to me. It wasn't my fault everyone else was incapable of behaving decently. Roger was the one with the revolting habits, the person who didn't have a clue about civilised and considerate ways of doing things. You just had to look at him to tell that. All that bulk, what an affront, what a drain, on the world's precious resources. Did I used to care about the environment? I did now, all right. Why were people like Roger allowed to exist? I'd have to do something about it. 'It's my treat,' I said, sharply. 'I'll pick the wine for once, thanks.'

There was no way I was going to ask the waiter for his recommendations either. *We are all trained*, sure. Ordering the champagne had very nearly been a disaster. Except there were forty-eight pages of the wine menu. Were they trying to confuse you into making a rash purchase? The classic sales assistant tactic? 'Give me a couple of minutes,' I said. All I wanted was a decent Bordeaux, a St-Emilion, and preferably a Cheval Blanc Premier Grand Cru Classé, 1996

– seeing as I was celebrating. If they didn't have it, it would be yet another sign of what a pumped-up, second-rate joint this was. How did the *Evening Standard* choose their restaurants of the year? Time and again? Would I even be able to find the Cheval Blanc if it was listed? The menu was italicised and in tiny script.

'I wonder what Fran's up to now,' Roger said. 'Any idea?'

'Roger, I'm trying to order the wine.' Did I need to change my prescription already? Would my new glasses, both pairs, be redundant before I'd even had the chance of wearing them? 'What the hell are you talking about? Fran? I don't want to go there. Not today. Not ever again, frankly.'

'Maybe you should. It can't be good keeping all those feelings bottled up.'

'All what feelings? I don't have any feelings for her. She's history.' I hated using such expressions, such clichés, though I found that when I was with Roger they slipped out.

'I don't believe you.'

'Fine. But I'm not going there. This lunch was meant to be a celebration. It was meant to be fun.'

'I always thought you could have hung onto her, had you not been quite so unpleasant.'

'She was having an affair, Roger, for fuck's sake. As was Bobbie, if you must know.'

'What? Bobbie was having an affair? You never told me.'

'Do you think it's something I'm proud of?'

'How did you find this out?'

'Things she said. Things she did. I finally put two and two together,' here I went again, 'and confronted her. She denied it at first of course, but most women are terrible liars. As you probably know. And then she gets this bloke who she's having this thing with to threaten me. Can you believe that? This guy actually threatens me.'

'What do you mean threatens you?'

Roger was looking at me so intently with his beady little eyes – which were far too close together and my mother always used to tell me never to trust someone if their eyes were too close together – I had to look away. Except the chefs, the artistes weren't exactly providing much alternative entertainment. Where were the tears and the tantrums, when you needed them? This immaculate lot were so quietly, so robotically going about their business, I wondered whether they were for real, and not just models putting on a slick show, while the proper work was being done out of sight in some dingy basement.

And watching this charade suddenly, shockingly made me think that perhaps Roger had another agenda too. He was fishing for information, and not just about the nitty-gritty of my extraordinarily explosive sex life. On quick reflection he'd been asking all manner of leading questions. Was he wearing a wire? Had I walked into a trap? A sting?

'This guy keeps calling me and leaving nasty messages,' I said. Did Roger suddenly look sheepish? Guilty even? Just what did he know? But he couldn't trap me. I was in control. I knew exactly what to say and do, as ever. Plus I'd asked Roger to lunch. It was my treat. He couldn't have got himself wired up so quickly, unless they'd been onto him on the off chance I'd call and things were already pretty much in place. Or possibly he'd originally contacted them, voicing his totally ill-founded suspicions about me. Maybe it was a bit of both. I supposed it often was in such cases. Certainly, in my experience, the police needed every bit of help they could get. They were never going to solve anything off their own back.

'What sort of nasty messages?'

'You know, stuff like, leave her alone, and I've run out of luck, and that my life is going to be made extremely uncomfortable.' Worryingly I couldn't gauge Roger's expression.

'You don't recognise his voice, right? Does he leave a name?' he said quickly. 'Does he use your name? And what about his number, his caller ID? Can you ring him back? Do you have any way of identifying him?'

'He doesn't leave a name and the number is always withheld. I'm not that stupid.'

'Is he any more specific? Does he mention why he's going to get you, or exactly what he's going to do with you when he does?'

When he does? 'What do you mean when he does?'

'Sorry, if he does?'

'I'm not sure that makes it sound much better. But no, he's not very specific.'

'Are you sure the calls are definitely related to Bobbie, and not just somebody after something you owe them, like a bailiff maybe, coming on a bit heavy?'

'What about this "leave her alone" stuff?'

'Diverting tactics? OK, unlikely, but it could be a concerned friend, not a lover? Or someone teasing you about something else entirely? I don't know, you and your women, Matt.' He laughed, though coming from his great jowly gob it sounded more like a splutter.

'You're not taking this very seriously, are you?'

'Well, have you been to the police?'

'Don't be ridiculous. They're not going to be interested. Besides, with my record, how do you think they are going to react? Anyway I don't want them, or anyone else for that matter, rooting around in my affairs.'

'No, I'm sure you don't.'

Feeling something brush against my shoulder I swung round on my ludicrously padded stool. In fact it was more of an elevated mini-armchair. It was the waiter, back already. Though, looking at the space on my wrist where I used to wear my prestigious timepieces, I realised he probably

173

should have returned sooner. We'd been left gasping for ages.

'Have you decided on the wine, sir?'

'Yes.' I hadn't of course and flicking back through the massive menu it occurred to me that the waiter could be in league with Roger, that he was part of the sting. Hence the way he kept rubbing up against me. And that maybe Roger's mike was on the blink and that this guy's wire was all the exterior surveillance team had to go on. When I quietly slipped away, and I wasn't planning on sticking around until dessert – to be nabbed – I'd have to check the nearby streets for any of those telltale vans with blanked-out windows and weird aerials. I could just imagine all these geeky eavesdroppers, crammed in there with their cold lattes and soggy Pret A Manger sandwiches, poring over everything I uttered. Would they be feeling jealous about those extra portions I'd ordered? The wine I was about to ask for? Would they be salivating, in their stuffy van, parked up on, say, West Street, as they heard me enjoying the *amuse bouche*? Or, to follow, the pan-fried girolle mushroom with Iberico de Bellota ham shavings? I knew all about jealousy.

NINE

Proper Safeguards

Nail scissors. That was what I was going to arm myself with. A neat little pair, possibly gold-plated – why not solid gold, 9 carat would do, given the secure investment potential? – complete with a fancy case. I'd need that to keep them from accidentally piercing the lining of my pockets, or stabbing me as I bent over to retie my shoelaces – they were always coming undone, especially the laces on my dark brown Oxford's, which at one point were possibly my favourite footwear of all time, though I wasn't going to ruin the elegance of these timeless, bench-made, nearly bespoke shoes by tying a double bow. No matter that the soles were badly worn and in urgent need of repair, plus much of the welting was coming loose, which was why I'd been so desperate to visit a Church's for ages, though unusually still hadn't got it together to actually make the trip. This was yet another indicator of just how busy and preoccupied I'd been. Nothing normally got in the way of preserving and amending my wardrobe.

Things would have to change. I'd have to start prioritising again. Though was it still possible to buy such items? Gold,

fully working nail scissors with properly sharp blades —
though these would probably have to be made of steel.
Japanese steel at that. They'd come in a real, hand-stitched,
soft leather case, rather than leatherette. Bond Street
was my best bet. Bond Street, or just off Bond Street was
always my best bet when shopping, unless the object of
my current desire had anything to do with Prada, which of
course this didn't — though a pair of nail scissors would have
come in very handy during that particular exchange. Aside
from being able to undo that shoddy stitching and reveal
just how ill-conceived the alteration was, nothing would
have given me greater pleasure than to have driven those
little blades into that sales assistant's smug face, and scarred
him for life.

A pair of nail scissors suddenly seemed like the essential, everyday accessory. How come I'd gone for so long
without acquiring the perfect pair? There were so many
things that I didn't realise I needed until it was almost too
late.

As it was this woman, this girl, whatever age she was,
though she was fat, very fat — along with just about everyone
else these days — hadn't just wedged herself beside me, she
was nodding her enormous, perspiring head to an almost
deafening gangsta thud, which seemed to be pouring the
wrong way out of her iPod earpieces. Plus, she didn't just
look like the end of the world, nodding moronically away,
with her braided, mousy hair, greasy pale skin, and colla-
gened lips smothered in an almost luminous pink gloss, she
also stank of Burger King — probably the one on the corner
of Tottenham Court Road and New Oxford Street.

I would have moved, but there were no other free seats
on the bendy bus. There was no standing room either — that
space being taken by numerous pushchairs and an aged, male
tramp with dried vomit all down his holey black jumper.

And it didn't look as if he was wearing anything underneath. But worse, however, far worse was the noise and stink coming from the poor creature next to me. I could have tapped her on the shoulder and asked her to turn it down. I could have yanked the tiny, but surprisingly effective speakers out of her ears and ripped the iPod from wherever it was tucked within her fat body, and thrown it out of the window, had there been an open window, rather than a sea of condensation. Though what I suddenly wanted to do more than anything was snip that thin white cord, and render the thing useless. She wouldn't have noticed me do it, no chance, and I'd wonder how long it would take her to realise that no sound was blasting into her brain, so mashed it must have been by a lifetime, albeit possibly a rather short one so far, of bad music, bad food and bad blood.

After lunch in the *Standard*'s restaurant of the year, still the very place to be and be seen, full of buzz and bonhomie, exquisite food and spectacular wine, not to mention impeccable service, this was all I needed. The contrast was simply too much to bear. But wasn't that London all over? I had been enmeshed in this environment, this polarity, or, as they would have you believe, this vibrant diversity, for as long as I could remember. What did I expect? Norway, with its prosperous and sustainable welfare state? Or the North Korean version of wealth distribution? I didn't know, but I wasn't too happy about where I was right now, and how I fitted in. The brutality. Why had I taken fucking public transport?

I could perhaps understand why people chose to plug those mini headphones into their ears, and shut themselves off from humanity. But I couldn't understand why they had to do it so loudly, why they invariably thought that their particular sounds were more important than anyone else's. Unless they had no idea. Unless they were so disengaged, so unconcerned, so selfish, the only thing that mattered was their own dismal entertainment – now there was a word.

This woman, this girl reeking of saturated fat shouldn't have been sitting there nodding her great head, while she could have been observing London, one of the greatest cities in the world, crawl by – had she been able to see out. She could even have been conversing genially with a stranger, with someone like me. She had no idea who she was sitting next to. Having been around a bit, I could have told her a thing or two. What a waste, what a missed opportunity for her, and maybe I'd have learned something also. But, hey, here was a thought, maybe I could follow her off the bus, see where she was headed, see if I could intervene somehow, see if it wasn't too late. Though that iPod, those mini headphones, the aggression of the rapper, was so disturbing me I wasn't sure I'd be able to control myself. No doubt I'd end up making things so much worse.

The simple fact was I hated iPods, and iPhones, almost as much as I coveted BlackBerrys. When Roger produced his new BlackBerry Bold at lunch, on the pretext that he was expecting an important email, I knew it was time to scarper. We'd just finished the calf's sweetbread with sprig of fresh laurel, which was the one dish I most definitely wanted to taste, and I had to hand it to L'Atelier, those artistes, it didn't disappoint, so leaving Roger smugly and rudely to play with his sleek new phone, I indicated I was slipping to the toilet.

What a lousy friend he'd turned out to be. Unwilling to support my business – it wasn't as if I was asking him to lend me a few quid for my personal use – unhappy about celebrating my good news, unsure whether to have another bottle of St-Emilion's finest, unable to stop banging on about my ex-fiancée, and my most recent ex-girlfriend. No wonder I'd told him I was off on a mini-break to Mallorca, for some much-needed R&R. I had to think of something pleasant, I had to have something to brag about, I had to throw the eaves-droppers way off course, though once having mentioned Mallorca my mind was suddenly filled with a host of very unpleasant thoughts and images, quite unconnected with lush mountains and the sparkling Mediterranean.

I didn't think Roger had even heard anything I'd been saying, but somewhat surprisingly he said, 'You can't go away, surely, with everything that's happening right now. You're not really planning on leaving the country in the next day or so, for a holiday, are you? With this North Korean thing about to take off? And Iran?' Had he stifled a chuckle? Before adding, 'That seems a bit irresponsible to me.' Irresponsible. I didn't know how I was meant to reply to that. So I didn't and got stuck into the quail, which came on a slice of sautéed foie gras. It was after the next dish that he produced the Bold.

When was I ever going to get up to speed? No wonder my business was suffering. At least, I hoped, I wouldn't feel ill-equipped in North Korea. I doubted very much that mobile and Internet technology was as advanced or as accessible there as it was in the UK. BlackBerrys would be unheard of on the streets of Pyongyang.

Leaving L'Atelier, without acknowledging the maître d' or the rather more striking female on reception, not that she would have noticed me anyway so busy was she picking her nails — why did everyone have to pick their nails in public? Look what they were missing — I did a quick once-round-the-block, cutting across a damp and darkening St Martin's Lane, along Shelton Street, up Mercer, round Seven Dials, and onto Earlham Street until I was safely on Shaftesbury Avenue, looking back down West Street, though failed to notice any suspicious-looking vans. Had the Met's surveillance operations become more sophisticated? Perhaps I wasn't giving them enough credit. Before I knew it I'd found myself squeezing onto the 38 primarily to avoid the crowds and the drizzle. Silly me.

From my cramped perch on the bus, it was hard to tell where we'd now got to. Was that Theobald's Road? A dim, greasy splodge? Without my beloved Jaeger adorning my wrist – not that that particular antique had ever been much help, and to think how easily the lugs gave way – I wasn't sure of how long I'd been stuck on board. Obviously I couldn't stand it a second longer, yet we were between stops and I was trapped. Next to me the din continued.

I supposed I could retrieve the time from my mobile, a very sad old Sony Ericsson it was too, with a host of outdated functions I'd never mastered and would never need, presuming it had ever been set correctly. However, that would mean switching it on, and though it was handily in the side pocket of my jacket, I'd left it firmly switched off since yesterday evening, except for the brief call I'd made to Roger this morning and then the one to L'Atelier. I would have rung him from the landline, except my landline was no longer working. I don't know how many people had been trying to reach me on either the landline or the mobile, but while first ringing Roger numerous beeps informed me of missed calls and incoming messages. They'd clearly been piling up, yet I found that I just didn't want to be reminded of how in demand I was. There was so much else to do and think about. Why I thought I wanted a BlackBerry so much I didn't know – because everyone else had one? – and thank God I didn't possess a shiny new Bold, because I might have felt less inclined to ditch it right now.

The tragedy next to me wasn't shouldering a bag of any description, though she was wearing one of those long puffa jackets, which might once have been white. How ashamed I suddenly was of my Prada puffa – though black, and of an entirely different cut and quality, and cost, despite its dodgy zip, there were similarities. With a stop slowly approaching, at least there had to be one soon, and deducing that she wouldn't be disembarking – there was no way I could stay on the sweaty, stinking bus until it reached her destination. Hackney? Clapton? Leyton? To then do what? – I retrieved my cheap, crappy mobile from my very favourite corduroy jacket – an item of clothing entirely devoid of gangsta connotations – and noticing how the exterior pockets of her puffa weren't poppered shut, plopped the phone in the nearest. She wouldn't have felt a thing.

Long after I'd exited the bus – and that was no easy feat, having to get past the tramp and the pushchairs, and a couple, work colleagues quite possibly, who appeared to have engaged in some heavy petting right by the doors – and was striding towards the junction of Clerkenwell Road and Goswell Road, it occurred to me how even these kids were invariably armed with the latest electronic gadgets. They might not have cared especially about the food they ate or the quality of the clothes they wore, yet they wouldn't accept anything less than the latest iPod, or iPhone, or Beretta 90two. If cash flow or waiting lists were a problem, they just stole them. Naturally, I loathed thieves, and I had a special dislike of pickpockets. Who didn't? That infringement of personal space and security. That shadow of violence, and the years of trauma and stress, which victims were then left to deal with. I really hoped that girl would be caught. All she'd have to do would be to turn on my phone – I should have done it for her. They could track these things nowadays, couldn't they, locate the signal, and thus the criminal? And even if they couldn't I'd be able to give the police a pretty clear description, and tell them exactly where she'd been heading. I wasn't the only person to have noticed her, surely. Perhaps others had been robbed, too. The Met'd have plenty to go on.

*   *   *

'You,' he shouted. 'Stop. Police.'

There were two of them outside my door, in uniform. I didn't know how long they'd been waiting. Not long I imagined, because they'd both been facing the door, as if they'd recently knocked and were still awaiting the possibility that someone might answer. Of course I should have seen this coming and been a little more prepared, but, more than ever, I'd been trying to act normally. So what if my world was collapsing around me? However, with my heart beginning to thump in my chest – why did I always feel so guilty whenever I saw a copper? – I'd simply glanced at them as they turned towards me and carried on walking past, through the fire doors and out onto the emergency stairwell, which is when I heard one of them shout and I began taking the unforgiving, damp concrete steps two at a time.

Maybe I had a three- or four-seconds lead, and maybe they would presume I'd head down, and not up, which would give me a few more seconds at least, though despite my trim frame I was chronically unfit. After two floors and four flights of stairs I was gasping for breath. Had they gone down?

'Stop,' I heard one of them shout again, but faintly. 'Police. Give yourself up.' Give yourself up? Had they really said that?

Did they have these stairs covered at the bottom, by the bins? Was backup ready and waiting? Fortunately I'd never have to find out as the fire door on the thirteenth floor was slightly ajar – honestly, the security on this block – and I slipped back inside, closing it properly behind me. It was impossible to open these doors from the outside. I was thankful for the barrier, but as ever not impressed by the doors themselves. They clearly weren't original, and ruined the sense of light and air I was sure Chamberlin, Powell and Bon had intended for the communal corridors.

Hurtling along the thirteenth floor, I weighed up my options. Break into an empty flat and hide out for a while.

Take an occupant hostage, preferably someone very old, or young, and negotiate safe passage to North Korea. Take one of the lifts to the basement and escape via the underground car park. Climb down the emergency stairs on the far side of the building, hoping that wasn't covered, and make my way quickly to Barbican Tube, where I'd have to leap the barrier as that hideous bus journey had sucked up the last of my loose change – though why I had bothered to pre-purchase a ticket for a bendy bus I had no idea, except perhaps that I hadn't been expecting a bendy bus as I'd come on a double-decker, and there wasn't a lot else to do while waiting in the queue.

Or, I thought, I could quietly and swiftly return to my flat when no one would be looking, let myself in, make a cup of tea, and gather my thoughts before, indeed if they eventually returned. Was there anything else I needed to hide or get rid of? The second and last options appeared the most attractive. I was too exhausted already to make much of a run for it – I really would have to start working out. Did they have gyms in North Korea?

At the end of the corridor I was beginning to think that hostage-taking might be a little extreme, plus I wasn't entirely sure how that would go down with my new hosts. They might not want such a perpetrator, such a criminal, whatever the mitigating circumstances. Would that be the case, even in this era of stand-offs and showdowns, pernicious sanctions and all sorts of nuclear nonsense? Wouldn't they want to show how accommodating, how forgiving they really were? Probably not. Besides, they must have had their hands full with the ailing, possibly already dead, or good as dead Dear Leader. How exactly did succession work in a land where eternity was taken so seriously?

It was looking more and more as if I had little option but to make my way back to my flat – funny that. 'Sorry, I panicked,' I'd tell them, before I went on to explain my very legitimate problem with men, and women, in uniform. Besides, I really didn't understand what they could have on me, why they'd been knocking. I'd been extremely careful, from the start. If I'd made any serious lapses then perhaps it would be better to find out what they were and if possible rectify the situation, at least minimise the damage before it really was too late. Unless it already was too late. Heading slowly back to the central bank of lifts and pressing the grubby call button I realised it was a risk I was going to have to take.

With a sinking feeling in my stomach, not helped by the fact that I actually was descending, albeit very slowly – these lifts were truly atrocious and they had only been upgraded last year, supposedly, and at vast expense – I wondered briefly whether Roger had stayed for dessert, *Les Deux Desserts De François*, according to my memory of the menu. Who the fuck was François? Though not a pudding man myself I had a sudden, terrible craving for something sweet, and comforting. Why was it so cold and rank in this lift? Who the hell had just peed in here? Stepping onto my corridor I began to shiver. Cold, wet, hungover, I was in no state to be interrogated. Had I just made a very silly decision?

How long had it been? Twenty, thirty minutes? It was both sooner and longer than I expected. Sooner because I'd lost all respect for the authorities, and longer for the same reason. Though it might not have been anything like twenty to thirty minutes. I was having a major problem trying to estimate the time. Suddenly not having a working watch, or mobile, meant that I'd almost completely forgotten how mentally to judge time. Though, and maybe this was in my favour, time seemed to have become increasingly elastic.

It was either seemingly rushing past or taking forever, and what was more I was fast losing the ability to determine which. A haze was descending. In a way it felt like I was permanently stoned, but I hadn't smoked any weed for years. I loathed cannabis and I particularly loathed heavy cannabis users. I thought it such a backward way to get high.

Of course I could have walked over to my bed and checked the atomic clock, had I not tried to hawk that particular piece of equipment earlier today, to no avail, which only meant that I'd had to abandon it, as I was not going to turn up at L'Atelier clutching a five-year-old radio alarm – a gift, the last gift in fact that my mother ever gave me. I was so insulted. And this was one of the second-hand and antique watch and clock specialists I'd been going to for months. I'd put so much business their way recently, and they couldn't even recognise that the radio alarm, aside from still functioning perfectly, was already a design classic. Who had an atomic radio alarm nowadays?

What had my mother been thinking? What had she ever been thinking? I'd thrown the clock toward a bin, a wide open bin, but it had missed, before skidding off down the pavement, onto Clerkenwell Road, which was where I left it, as I ran unnecessarily for a bus. Was I really trying to get away from that thing, those memories? There was a huge queue at the stop – as always. This was on the way to meet Roger, and I remembered hoping that the next vehicle would completely flatten the clock, terminating its absurd radio signal to some atomic device in Germany – of all places. I couldn't believe I'd hung onto it for so long. Normally I was very particular with my things, and I never usually let sentiment get in the way of what I ditched.

On the third knock, I'd decided, I'd open up. It was the two of them again. 'I do have a bell,' I said.

'Matt Freeman?' the shorter copper asked. He looked bemused.

'Yes?'

'Why didn't you stop earlier?'

'Stop where, when?'

'In the corridor, when you walked straight past this door and out the fire exit, having been asked to stop. Which was when we gave chase. Were you not aware?'

'Me?'

'You.'

'You gave chase?' Did the police really speak like this? Now they looked a little sheepish, if not embarrassed.

'Don't try to be clever.' It was the short one again. 'We could do you for evading arrest.'

'Arrest? Why? How can I be done for evading arrest when I had no idea I was about to be arrested? I've been in the shower.' I was still wrapped in towels, which frankly could have been cleaner, but the washing machine hadn't worked for weeks. 'I didn't hear you knocking. The bell is more effective.' I thought about adding that it was a Chamberlin, Powell and Bon original, but I expected the reference would be lost on them.

'You saw us and ran,' the other copper said. Though the larger of the two, he appeared strikingly more harmless, docile even. He had a very droopy face, for someone so young, and dark circles under his dark brown eyes. Neither of them looked particularly fit. Perhaps I could have outrun them, and escaped, especially if they didn't have any backup. Things were looking up.

'I'm sorry, I'm not following.'

'Don't try to be clever. You're on shaky ground as it is.' This was the shorter one. Clearly he had his own issues to deal with.

'Can we come in?' the bigger one said. Good cop, bad cop,

I thought, how predictable, but how easy to handle, and at least they didn't have a warrant. Things could only get better. I almost burst into song.

'Of course. Sorry, I was just surprised you got here so quickly, which was why I was in the shower. I only called ten minutes or so ago, and I stressed on the phone, I didn't think it was such an emergency. Mobile phones must be stolen and go missing all the time. Though I suppose I do have a good description of the attacker, and time is of the essence and all that. To be honest I'm impressed.'

They looked at each other and the shorter one, whose name badge, I could finally see, revealed he was called Ferris, said, 'We were warned about you. You have quite a record.'

'Are you being prejudicial?' I wondered what his first name was. Nigel? Norman? Napoleon? The badge also revealed they were City of London police, and not from the Met. I didn't know whether that was good or bad news. The docile chap, meanwhile, was scouting my pad, even sticking his neck around the divide into my sleeping quarters. 'Are you looking for anything in particular?'

'Don't try to be clever,' the short one said, again.

Why were the police always so paranoid about people being clever? Because they were so thick was the logical answer, though it also occurred to me that perhaps they said it when they were stalling for time, and simply couldn't think of anything else to say, but that of course would imply that they were thick also.

'A bottle of wine,' the big one said, maybe realising he had to assert himself occasionally. His name, according to his badge, was Austen. All I could think his first name might be was Jane.

'You want a drink, while on duty? I thought you were here to follow up an incident I only just reported.' The little one moved quickly towards me, with some aggression.

'Mr Freeman,' he was shouting almost, right under my chin, 'don't play games. There was an incident on this estate yesterday afternoon, a serious incident, as I'm sure you're aware, and yesterday evening, at six thirty-two, you walked into Threshers on Goswell Road and stole a bottle of wine. A bottle of Chapel Hill Chardonnay. You were captured on the shop's CCTV. We've been checking all the CCTV in the area in relation to the first incident. We're not saying the two incidents are linked, but we're investigating all avenues. Unfortunately it's not up to us whether Threshers want to press charges for the shoplifting, even if as the sales assistant led us to believe, you are one of their best customers and it might have been a lapse. We can't arrest you for that, not right now – but it was no lapse, was it, Matt?'

I didn't say anything. I didn't have time.

'Though,' he continued, 'what we really want are some answers to a few questions we have, because, having stumbled upon you – really, Matt, if you want to go shoplifting don't do it in your own backyard, not when the sales assistants know you – we've checked you out and found that you have quite a record, as I implied earlier. Don't even try to be clever again with me, Matt. And then, spotting us outside your door waiting for you, you decided to do a little runner, didn't you? What was that all about? You wouldn't have got very far, mate, there are police crawling all over this estate, though lucky for you we didn't have to call for backup, because had someone else nabbed you, they might not have been quite so nice. You could say we're all a bit on edge.'

Had Nigel ever said so much in one go? He sat down on my dark chocolate Robin Day sofa, under the sparkling white wall, without asking, as if it were some bench back at the station. How disrespectful. 'I'm not really sure what you are implying,' I said. 'If you are referring to something that happened a long time ago, when my fiancée decided to be vindictive, well as you know from your records, if you'd read them properly, it never even went to court.'

'You were cautioned,' Jane Austen said.

Was there more to him than met the eye? 'I was under the impression that after a certain amount of time these cautions are written off. By my reckoning I should no longer have a record, of any description.'

'Your maths is out.' Jane again.

'Yes? Well it was never my best subject. But besides, I don't see what this has got to do with anything. It was a domestic dispute, which got a little out of hand. Have you any idea what she put me through?'

'You assaulted her, caused considerable damage to her property and a restraining order was placed on you.' This was Nigel, or Napoleon, whatever the fuck his name was.

'Which shows what you are capable of,' said Austen. He was becoming less girlie by the minute.

'This is ridiculous. I can't even believe you're bringing it up. I invite you into my apartment, to inform you in detail about the person who robbed me, and you do nothing but insult and threaten me. I'm the victim here.'

'What happened to your face?' asked Ferris.

Was he a PC or a DS? I couldn't see the appropriate marking on his uniform. He couldn't have been a DCI. I laughed. 'You want me to show you?'

'Sure,' said Ferris.

Stepping towards the front door I felt a hand on my shoulder, pulling me back once more. 'Hey, what the hell are you doing?' I said, turning to face Austen. I think I would have preferred to be floored by a full-on rugby tackle. I was sick of all this hand on the shoulder stuff.

'Where are you going?'

'To show you what happened to my face.'

'Not out there.'

'But that's where it happened.'

'How?' said Ferris, closing in.

'It's a bit complicated.'

'Nothing I'm sure you couldn't explain.'

'It would be easier if I showed you.' Though I was wearing my boxers under my towel, there was no way I was going to make another run for it. I did have some dignity left. 'So what, am I under arrest now?'

'Just explain to us what happened, please, simply and clearly,' said Austen.

'That's what I was trying to do, OK?' I gestured to my closed front door and space beyond it. 'For some ridiculous reason my neighbour across the corridor – he's this very old man, deaf as a plank – has put a coffee table outside his front door, with a chair too. There's a very sad rubber plant on the table, and a couple of antique *Radio Times*. You probably noticed it all. Who knows what he's trying to do there, expand his flat by creating another room? Fortunately he never sits out there. He's pretty gross, if you know what I mean. Aside from being old and fat, and deaf, which means I can hear his TV from inside here, he smells. Absolutely rank, as if he's slowly rotting away from the inside out.'

'Get to the point,' said Ferris.

'I came back the other night, and OK maybe I'd had a couple too many, but the corridor lights weren't working, not my end of the corridor anyway – I've complained and complained about it to the maintenance people, but nothing is ever done – and anyway that bloody coffee table was right in my path. Some of the kids who live on this estate, I tell you, they're feral. They are always antagonising this poor man and mucking about with his exterior sitting room – if I can call it that. One time they placed a shop mannequin in the chair, I promise you. A female mannequin, which they'd drawn on and arranged in a very compromising position. I bet you can imagine. And if it wasn't these kids, it was the cleaners, who very occasionally turn up. They're not too keen on his extension either.'

'So you're saying you tripped, right?' Austen said.

'Yes. But not just that, on my way down I somehow hit my face on the fire extinguisher. They are placed at the ends of every corridor. I hit it with such force it came clean off its brackets, obviously making a complete mess of my face, too. I can't say my girlfriend was very sympathetic.'

'When was this?' Ferris asked.

'The other day. Where are we now? Monday? It was on Saturday, no late Friday night.' For a moment I thought I'd blown it. My mind had gone blank and then I said the first thing that had come into my head. Obviously it couldn't have been Saturday night because I'd told that patrolman the other morning a very different account of both how I got my facial injuries and of my whereabouts on Saturday night. It was possible he might be of use sometime soon, as it was also possible, just, that I could have had the accident with my neighbour's furniture one night and then walked into a lamp post the next, before getting in a fight with an old girlfriend's cats.

At least I hadn't mentioned the rubbish chute. I didn't want to alert them to its existence unnecessarily and for them then to go rooting around down there. Their colleagues probably had anyway, though perhaps not, knowing the incompetence of the force. However, the less said about it the better. I couldn't remember on what day the rubbish was collected, not that I was sure I'd ever known.

The truth was, this was all becoming rather absurd and long-winded. I was getting myself deeper into a tangle over something that could so easily have been avoided. Me and my big mouth. 'Look, I really need to get dressed. I have to leave shortly for a business meeting. I'm negotiating a big

Spanish deal, a Balearic thing.' Why Spain was on my mind so much I had no idea, unless it was something to do with Suze, or thinking about it, Bobbie's sister. That was where she'd died. Falling from a hotel balcony. Apparently.

'At this time?' said Austen.

Both of them were still crowding me out by my front door. I was feeling increasingly claustrophobic, cold and vulnerable. 'What time is it?'

'Five thirty-five,' he said.

'Yes. What's strange about that?'

'Don't people usually finish work around this time?' added Ferris. 'Those who still have a job.' He chuckled, I'm sure.

'Not in my line of business. Christ, I'm dealing with international executives, diplomats and statesmen – people who represent their corporations and in some cases communities and whole nations. These are people who travel the world continually. They don't clock off at five, and neither do I.'

They were looking at each other and Austen was actually smirking, the prick. I didn't care whether they believed me or not. I was suddenly so much more concerned with my business and not having my schedule disrupted by a couple of idiots investigating an incident – a crime? – that clearly had nothing to do with me. 'So,' I said, 'I forgot to pay for a bottle of wine from Threshers. Who hasn't? But they know me there.' Actually weren't they the few sales assistants I was still on nodding terms with, when they could be bothered to look me in the eye? 'Of course they knew I'd settle up on my next visit. It was an oversight, sorry.'

I didn't add that I was sure it was one I'd fallen prey to before, nor that I would have made a point of going back sooner, with my Switch card, had the wine been remotely drinkable. Indeed, after the wine Roger had so kindly and extravagantly bought me for lunch, it was going to be extremely hard to quaff anything for a while. Though not impossible.

'Get ready for your meeting, by all means,' said Ferris, 'but we haven't quite finished yet.'

'Neither have I,' I said, pushing through them on my way towards the far side of the main room, where hopefully I'd find my one remaining pair of clean trousers hanging in my wardrobe, and a half-decent shirt. Did I have a spare jacket anywhere? A sports jacket, at least something that could look smart enough for a relaxed business supper? The Prada tweed jacket that I had all the problems with would have been just the thing. Why did I have such bad luck? 'I want to talk about my phone, which was stolen this afternoon, as you should know. I want to know what you are going to do about that.' I was raising my voice, emphasising my distress at its loss, and the seemingly blithe response I was getting from the law. 'No wonder crime's so rife in this fucking city. If people like you are in charge of tackling it. I can give you a good description of my attacker. OK, strictly speaking she might not have attacked me, but she snatched the phone from my pocket.' I was well on the other side of the sliding partition. I couldn't see them and was sure they couldn't see me.

However, it was a question of whether I'd be able to shift the wardrobe to access the emergency fire exit, without drawing too much attention to what I was doing, and then open the exit without it creaking. Maybe. And maybe Chamberlin, Powell and Bon's insightful incorporation of such an escape route was going to save the day. 'Where are my trousers?' I began shouting. 'This wardrobe is a complete mess. That's women for you. Totally incapable of being tidy. You have the same problem, either of you two?'

'Just get on with it,' Ferris said. Though neither sounded as if they had come any closer.

'I'm trying but it's not easy. I mean, why can't they ever take responsibility for their own property? Instead they casually dump it wherever they feel like it, messing up your own stuff. Underwear, outerwear, hair extensions and clips and bands and hairdryer attachments, and all these half-used beauty products leaking gunge everywhere. Not to mention their complete lack of common sense or money, and then all that emotional baggage. The neediness. Sometimes I really hate women. Hey guys, don't you?'

There was no answer, not even a grunt, so I continued. 'They are a bit like seals, aren't they? Can be pretty and cute and all that, but nobody actually needs seals.' I don't know why seals sprang into my mind. Could they really be pretty? Cute, I supposed, the baby ones, but I had always loathed seals and loathed the way people were obsessed with protecting seal pups. From what I understood seals were a complete menace, devouring oceans of prime cod and haddock and John Dory. If I were an Inuit, I'd happily club them to death. Being British I'd happily club them to death also. 'You're not into animal rights, either of you, are you?'

'I thought you had an urgent meeting.' It was Austen.

'Too right.' While banging the insides of the wardrobe I was also trying to shift the flimsy structure sideways, without much luck, and get dressed in the few unsoiled items I had left. The point was suddenly losing me.

TEN

Self-regulation

Which was it – warm, cold, night or day yet? Certainly the concourse was dripping with dim, yellowed light. The forensics' brilliant spots either having been removed or switched off for the night, leaving the estate's aged illuminations to mark safe passage and provide good cheer. What a joke. They were showing nothing that was fun or exciting, only a horridly still, empty scene. Where once I had loved to look out of my large though somewhat grimy – the maintenance being what it was – mid-century modern windows, believing the view uplifting in a hotel complex/cruise-liner sort of way, now I couldn't help feeling even more alienated.

Damp concrete, vacant walkways, curtained apartments, graffiti, litter, blocked drains, busted railings, smashed windows, shredded police tape. How Chamberlin, Powell and Bon would have wept. Their vision of communal, utilitarian living gone to pot. They'd have been better off practising in Pyongyang. Those sorts of notions always required a respectful audience and a firm hand. What was the point in executing such social experiments, on such a grand scale, without respect, without discipline? Discipline had to be the key. Usually was.

There wasn't even any sign of Mia, in her tight Lycra bottoms and sporty vest, stretching and bending and generally showing the world exactly what she was made of. Just when I needed her too. With Jeanette, both Jeanettes I supposed, out of the way, now in my nocturnal restlessness I couldn't stop thinking about the athleticism, the exoticism, the full and frank eroticism of my other neighbour. Her apartment, so near, was sadly sheathed with blinds and gloom. Had she been disturbed by recent events and temporarily vacated her premises? Or was she carrying on as normal? How I would like to pay her a visit right now, presuming of course that her gormless bloke was out. At a web designers' conference in San Francisco, hopefully. Or, more likely, a computer games fair in Las Vegas. There he'd be, this boyish bloke with his fledgling facial hair, his low-slung Diesels, his scuffed Birks, who couldn't stop chewing his saliva-hardened sweatshirt cuffs and poring over Manga images, when he should have been taking care of a body to die for.

Mia, where were you? Tucked up – dreaming; dreaming of a man, a proper, manly man, complete with fresh facial wounds, and with a trim physique and a snappy, albeit currently somewhat limited, though definitely grown-up wardrobe – as for wardrobe wardrobes, mine, surprisingly, had remained in place and standing, despite coming from IKEA, or some other flat-pack emporium – tapping on your door, at whatever time it was. Five? Five thirty? Would my glasses add a nice finishing touch, a sophisticated, intellectual air? Even, or rather especially as they weren't ridiculously oversized and sartorially up to the minute – another terrible joke – and had been through the wars, so to speak. That left arm was never going to be right.

'Hi,' she'd say, somewhat sleepily, in, I'm afraid, a jumbo T-shirt bearing a crass logo – his – and silky white camiknickers – hers. They'd be camiknickers, or French knickers, whatever the correct term was, because she was that sort of girl – a wearer of tasteful underwear. And I'd follow her not to her bedroom, where of course she would have entwined so lamely and regrettably too often with her hopelessly inept boyfriend – and never was a prefix so apt – but her exercise room. That place with mats and machines, that place of limitless opportunity for sexual expression, experimentation and fulfilment. Oh yes, I was really building up an urge.

Would my Mia be wet already, inside those strangely modest, yet thoroughly exciting knickers? But hang on, I was spoiling it far too quickly, again. I didn't want instant gratification. I didn't want immediate exposure to all the goods, however ready and waiting they were.

Would I ever forget that bloody story sneaked from one of my mother's – yes my mother's – *Forum*s, and quite probably made up anyway? Sex, real sex was nothing like that. It was never so casual, so free, so thrilling. There was always a price, and I wasn't talking money. I understood that, yet I couldn't stop my mind wandering. Why had I let Roger drag me to the Giraffe time and time again, exposing me to those extraordinary poses, to such provocation? Not anymore, regardless of our most recent spat. That man was a disgrace. What I wanted, what I craved, I was beginning to realise, was some subtlety, some shading around the edges. Even red, crocheted knickers with dodgy, elasticated trim would probably have been too much for me now. I wanted modesty, naturalism, real flesh, blood and hair, and not some image I'd conjured far too many times. And certainly not porn star-style manoeuvres and bald plasticity. I wanted reality. I wanted authenticity. Just like everyone else, I wanted love and comfort. I wanted long-term security – a girlfriend, a fiancée, a wife; I wasn't bothered about the technicalities. I wanted a soul mate.

Though right there across the dim concourse, through the yellowed light, through the dank early morning air, and the muted rumble of sparse traffic and distant sirens, the whine of rubbish trucks lifting vast containers of spent glass and the shrill of decelerating jet engines as jumbos lined up for Heathrow, was Mia, and Mia, I was beginning to think, could save the day. She really could. She seemed to have purpose, as well, obviously, as poise. She appeared level-headed, in control, happy. And quietly stylish, which was not at all like Bobbie, who was always obsessed with making a statement and being noticed. Bobbie wasn't simply addicted to *I'm A Celebrity . . . Get Me Out Of Here!*, she wanted to be on the show. She wanted to be known, famous, a celebrity herself. Who knew what for – though maybe I'd be able to help her after all.

Clearly and refreshingly, Mia was cool with who she was, even if she were to become famous, inadvertently too. There was even a sereneness to her. And I was sure a solvency, despite the humble abode on not much more than a sink estate. But, hey, across there, across that dank void, the apartments were so much larger than those in my block, being maisonettes or duplexes – depending on who you were talking to – with two or three bedrooms, some even had four bedrooms – triplexes, so I'd heard – and many were privately owned and designer-ed up or impeccably restored to their mid-century modern roots, by young, fashionable people keen on that sort of thing and who had just been starting out on the property ladder, before it had collapsed, and had thought they'd spotted both a bargain and an opportunity, and wanted their living space to be as much of a statement as their carefree but ultimately meticulously managed careers and lifestyles and wardrobes. Oh how everything was working out brilliantly for them now, wasn't it just – because they were talented and good-looking and young.

We were all losers, but it didn't feel so – it felt personal. That concourse still seemed like a massive cultural, economic and social divide to me. And one I used to think I was on the right side of. Those who had it all, and those who didn't. Where had I gone wrong? But clever me for spotting her, all those months ago, from up here, from my eyrie. Though nothing ever escaped me. Did it. I hadn't lost the knack. I'd never lose that particular talent. Would I. However, what was beginning to worry me was the possibility that she, that Mia, that my little Mia, might not have noticed me. Was that possible, with all the peering and peeping – peeping? – I'd done? Or if she had, and maybe she'd caught me looking her way, when strictly it probably wasn't the best thing for me to have been doing, at least not for so long and so often – but could any full-blooded male have resisted? – she might not have quite the same feelings and urges and needs, as I had. You only had to look at whom she was hooked up with to realise there might be a problem when it came to compatibility, when it came to sexual attraction no less. I mean, how could she be with that jerk and also fancy me?

'Hi,' I'd say on her doorstep, 'this might seem a bit forward' – and there lay one of my biggest problems, never having been forward enough – 'but you know me, don't you? I'm Matt, from across the way, from the block, the tenth floor, the apartment with the ill-fitting blinds, you must have seen me peering down, at least I couldn't help noticing you, out and about on the estate and of course doing your exercises at home. Yoga, is it? No? Pilates? Well, it's not as if you seem to mind people watching. Do you? You do? Really? I thought you knew you had an audience. You're pretending you don't like to be watched, when in fact it turns you on right, doesn't it? Does it turn you on? Mia? Does it make you wet? The crotch of those tight black cycling shorts?'

What was wrong with me? Was this really what being abandoned, being betrayed did to you? Though I knew I wouldn't be able to stop myself. I never could, when I'd started, on such a particular train of thought and with a particular person or target in sight.

'Does it make you want to touch yourself? Do you get the urge to run into your bedroom and strip off those tight, damp shorts and plant your hands, your right hand probably, on your pubic mound, and rub yourself, with increasing pressure, and in a circular motion, going faster and faster until you hear yourself panting, stifling a moan even, and would you be fantasising about me at this point, about someone like me?

'A person with a roughly shaved head, and bent glasses — because he wouldn't have had time to get them replaced, though he was working on that, that was next on his agenda — and pale blue eyes behind the cheap lenses — which of course were going to be replaced by top of the range polycarbonate lenses when he'd made that return trip to David Clulow — and bags under those pale blue eyes — about me paying you a visit, unexpectedly, though when you happened to be in the mood, and accommodating them, accommodating me in fact, it was always going to be me, inside you? Would you?

'Would you be thinking about me just a little bit? When you were doing it, on your own. Or would you be thinking about him, this scruffy adolescent you had set up home with, were maybe even engaged to, or married to for God's sake, would he be playing on your mind? You utter fool.'

In the dimness of my freezing room I looked down at my hands, my suddenly cold, sticky hands and at my now limp cock hanging out of my worn, stripy cotton M&S pyjamas —

so, I once went there for underwear and nightwear just like everyone else – and I could see it shrivel, before my very eyes, with the shock. I was so embarrassed. I was so ashamed. I didn't deserve to be left standing here in this damp, empty flat all on my own, my hands covered in wasted ejaculate. I didn't deserve to be ignored and frozen out by the very people I loved. I so didn't deserve this, this isolation from what made life worth living. Being connected, being secure, being in love, it was the very essence of existence, if you asked me. And if Mia, like Bobbie before her and Fran before her, those two especially, didn't feel the same way, well, well I'd have to make her. I'd have to knock some bloody sense into her. Finally.

Not that she couldn't have seen it coming. Not that she was entirely blameless. The temptress, the tease. My new plaything. Ha. Or was it simply Chamberlin, Powell and Bon's fault for providing the platform? Why did I have to justify everything? Why was I always looking for answers? As I caught my reflection in the hopelessly large, cold, dark, grimy window – prominent forehead, beaky nose, pointy chin and the glint of those crappy lenses – I wondered, once more, what was left but force, if I was ever to get my way. What a leveller. 'Quick,' I was being told. 'Quick, quick. Little bird.' Oh, not again.

The postwoman didn't come at this time, and anyway she put the post in the purpose-built mailbox, to the left of the front door, and which I could access internally. Certainly this was a blameless, faultless design quirk, and one that was still appreciated, by me anyway, with the mail, what little I received, always being nicely out of the way and secure, and never littering up my hall and conceivably advertising the fact, to petty criminals in particular, that no one was home. Even if the postwoman had been running ridiculously early, stuffed into her regulation dark blue slacks and red fleece, there was no way she would have been able to bend down that far.

How long had it been there? Here I was, all togged up and anxious to depart, and lying on the floor, just by the front door, was something very suspicious. A folded piece of paper? It couldn't have been there long, surely, as I would have noticed it walking through to the kitchenette or the bathroom, especially of course as the hall was usually utterly free from clutter. And yet I hadn't heard anyone outside in the corridor, let alone someone sliding something under the door. What had I been doing these last few hours? I hadn't been asleep, that was for sure. Most definitely I would have been aware of people approaching my property. After that laughable business with Ferris and Austen I was not taking any more chances – I was so not going to be bullied and humiliated, and ultimately threatened again, not that those idiots ever had a leg to stand on, and they knew it. So what was this piece of paper?

I stooped to pick it up, feeling a pain in my side – my liver? My kidneys? It took a moment or two to get my focus back. When was this intimidation going to stop?

Give to live, was what it said, in blue – biro? Or was it photocopied or indeed printed – one of those fonts designed to look like handwriting? There was no punctuation, neither a full stop, nor an exclamation mark, which I thought might have been more appropriate. And only the G was in upper case. I didn't recognise the writing, had it been by a real hand. I couldn't tell – these old lenses were so badly letting me down, though not quite enough for me to decide that whoever was behind this note was obviously ill-educated, which I supposed only widened the field of suspects, considerably. I screwed it up, as tightly as possible, and took a couple of steps through to the kitchen where I flipped open the built-in bin and dropped the crumpled ball inside. There was a sudden, shocking whiff of spent ground coffee and old fish. Why it smelt of fish I had no idea. 'Fuck you,' I said, loudly, addressing myself as much as anyone else. 'Fuck you, arsehole.' I could have lashed out. I could have headbutted the wall.

How had I got myself into this position? Sure, I had found myself in a few tight corners before, but nothing like this. And I'd thought that once I'd got rid of those two coppers I was in the clear. How naive was that?

At one point I was convinced they were on the verge of marching me off to the station, not so much because they suspected me of having anything to do with whatever they were investigating across the way, but for insubordination. Was there really a law against that? Or was insubordination more of a personal, moral judgement, a point of view, in fact a freedom of speech? Anyway, they kept banging on about Threshers, which I deemed more than pathetic. Threshers didn't have a problem with me. Threshers hadn't even noticed anything was missing, despite their security measures.

Clearly, so I eventually managed to convince Ferris and Austen, I would not have committed some violent, sexually motivated crime – if that was what they were implying had taken place on the estate – and then sauntered off to Threshers to lift a bottle of Chapel Hill – in full view of a CCTV camera, of endless CCTV cameras, which, because I was a local, I would obviously have been fully aware of. I, with my degrees and numerous business qualifications and accolades, and not to mention a highly observant nature, was hardly going to slip up on some minor oversight like that. And even forgetting the fucking CCTV cameras, what was I doing wanting to snatch a bottle of Chapel Hill? If I was going out of my way, against such hopeless odds, to steal some wine, I would have at least taken a serious bottle or two, say the Château Siaurac 2005, which, extraordinarily, Threshers was currently stocking. It simply didn't stack up – as I said to those increasingly hostile buffoons. Though not much else did either.

All the phone calls, the note – *Give to live*, what? – that scuffle on the way to Suze's? I was at a loss piecing it together. Racking my sorely taxed brain, in the tight confines of my kitchen, or kitchenette, not that I was certain when a kitchen became a kitchenette, or rather the other way round, because surely it always had to be that way round, with it being so much easier to expand a space rather than constrict it – no? – I couldn't help thinking back to Jeanette, or, and I know I was immediately contradicting myself, that actually you could very easily constrict and confine something, which had previously been rather expansive. Take my life. Where I lived and worked, yes worked, and socialised and holidayed. And, more importantly, who I was attached to, who I loved.

It was nearly all gone – lost, wasted, or taken away. Jeanette, yes Jeanette, was she all to blame? Is that when it started to go wrong? How, as the years went by, I'd thought of paying her a visit. I wanted to know the truth. I wanted to know just where I stood.

'What a lovely surprise, Matt,' she says. I could hear her all right, too clearly, even though her voice was a little thinner, and despite that absurd faux posh accent.

'I was passing,' I say. Though of course I was not passing. Hardly anyone ever did simply pass the isolated, mock Georgian, or was it Palladian mansion, at the end of a half-mile drive, on the edge of a small East Anglian town. 'I didn't know you'd still be living here, after all this time.'

'It's not that long,' she replies. Just who was she kidding?

'No I suppose not. You're looking well.' More lies.

'You look well too, Matt. Keeping fit, obviously. Tea, a drink? Do please come in.'

'Is Richard here? I'd love to see him too.'

'No, he's away.' On she shrills. 'When's he not? He's travelling, as much as ever. I hardly ever see him. I forget where he is right now. Dubai maybe? Somewhere in the Middle East. Or is he in Africa? Asia? Wherever. He's not due back for a couple of weeks. You know what he's like, always working on a new project or chasing a contract, or coming up with some outlandish scheme. I'd have thought with modern communications being what they are, he wouldn't need to do all that travelling, especially to some of those places. He should retire. But he still likes to get away. From me probably.' Does she laugh, or is there a sudden hint of a despondent, resigned tone?

'Stephen?'

'He's still in America. The company's based just outside Chicago. He's doing extremely well for himself.' As if I didn't know. 'It's just me, I'm afraid. With plenty of time on my hands.'

Of course her husband was away. He was always away, making even more money, not that I'd ever understood what he did. It was a different story every time you spoke to him. Same, I imagined now, as with her son. And of course she had plenty of time on her hands — the idle, the pampered rich, who always needed assisting, in one way or another. And look who could have been on the spot.

What is Jeanette wearing, as I follow her, across the vast hall, with its depressingly low ceiling and chintz everywhere, and through to the massive open-plan kitchen with islands and breakfast bars — what would Chamberlin, Powell and Bon have made of it? — and which leads onto a huge conservatory, full of firmly shut plastic windows, making it unbearably hot and sweaty? One of her short, simple, white dresses? At her age? What age is she? Does it matter?

Maybe we forget the tea and a catch-up in the conservatory and head straight upstairs, to her plush boudoir, which reeks of expensive but ultimately inadequate perfumes and powders. The things old women use and do to mask their decline. Don't, Matt, don't go there.

Yes, there I am, young, handsome, already successful, and popular, with a string of gorgeous girlfriends, though not yet engaged, following Stephen's mum – it's finally come to this. With each step I take I feel a growing tightness within my chest, and crotch, while I contemplate the best method of execution. And the best way to cover my tracks – I'm ridden with guilt. And shame. Now I've got this far. I don't want to just fuck her. I want to fuck her over. I'm just a kid, for God's sake.

I had to pull back, before the details became too overwhelming. The nitty-gritty, I'd always thought, was for the prurient, for people like Roger, and the Ferrises and Austens of this world, and, for that matter, those patrolmen who stopped me on Lavender Hill, and, too, the TV licence people from the other day. And, why not, that woman from David Clulow, and that man from Prada, the Bond Street branch – I couldn't forget him – and the countless other small-minded sales assistants trying to exert what control, what power they had. Though maybe I'd make an exception for the gormless guy from Threshers. He'd stuck up for me, sort of, hadn't he? I loved Threshers. Far superior to Wine Rack.

I seemed to be back by my front door, all set to depart once more. Yet, I couldn't help glancing over my shoulder and into the main room and spying my hopelessly empty desk, and aged laptop containing that fucking proposal, the latest anyway, and endless business plans also, few barely started. Had I even properly formatted a first page? Fuck knows how Richard had done it. But I was never going to fill in all the facts, the minutiae, every fucking detail, and pull into presentable shape a proposition or argument that might have aided my business. I was no assistant, sales or personal. I was the boss, after all, good for grand gestures and state-ments. I needed to be looked up to, to be admired and respected, and loved, if you wanted. I was the one with vision, with determination, with purpose, fuck it.

I opened the door, checked the corridor left and right, and tried not to inhale too deeply. However, it was no good. I was quickly overwhelmed by the rank odour emanating from my neighbour's appalling existence – stale urine, burnt grease, rotting flesh. How dare he soil not just my space but Chamberlin, Powell and Bon's too. He should have been removed by social services years ago. Where was the care in this community?

ELEVEN

Real Economy

'There's been another problem,' I said, at the counter, addressing my foxy friend. She was right there of course. Waiting for trouble, if not causing it.

'Excuse me,' a woman's voice, down to my left, suddenly said.

'Sorry?' I hadn't noticed her, unsurprisingly. Apart from being a midget, she was no oil painting, unless by El Greco. Oh dear. Her too-long – for her stature anyway – mousey hair was swept off her face by an Alice band, of all things. She had a piggy snout, sunken cheeks, crocked, stained teeth and was wearing a very cheap-looking pair of tiny, metal-rimmed glasses, circa 1993. Or were they meant to be retro? No wonder she was where she was. But would a new frame sort out all her problems? I could have laughed. Perhaps she was already wearing her new pair – well it wasn't as if she were ever going to pick anything remotely fashionable – and was in the shop for some other matter. Though I couldn't think what. A job? Was she applying to be a sales assistant? Yeah, I could see that. She was the type.

'I was here before you,' she said.

She had an oddly deep voice, with possibly something of a northern, or north-eastern accent. Though I supposed it could just as easily have been an East Midlands accent. I wasn't great on regional or especially northern accents, having rarely left the south-east, having rarely left London. I could see the appeal of places like Kent and Hampshire and Sussex, and straying further west, Wiltshire and Gloucestershire and Somerset, to a certain type of person, a certain mentality, but the north of England? With all that unemployment and decay, poverty and crime, short skirts, bare legs and fried food? 'Yes? Where?'

'In the queue.'

'I wasn't aware there was a queue. This counter seems rather long to me, with plenty of people on hand behind it.' It wasn't really a counter — more an extended, high desk, with a translucent glass top in a horrible shade of green, probably made worse by the powerful halogens angled onto it. Why these places always had to be quite so bright I had no idea. And so full of mirrors, too. I was becoming overly aware of my grazed and bruised face. 'This place is teeming with staff, twiddling their thumbs,' I added.

'The others are busy, aren't they.'

It wasn't a question. 'Busy trying to look busy, if you ask me.' My friend behind the desk was completely expressionless, which was exactly what I'd have expected of her. She wasn't going to intervene. Place her anywhere near a confrontation and she'd run a mile. Place her on her back and she'd be as limp and lifeless as a cheap plastic doll — so I could just imagine. Nevertheless I'd like to give her the chance to prove me wrong, and maybe I would, sooner rather than later. Later, much later, wasn't a concept I was contemplating at the moment.

I returned my gaze to my little tormentor. 'Go on, take my place. I'm sure you're as rushed as I am. Where have you got to get to by one thirty? London City? After you've had a meeting with your finance director, on the thirty-eighth floor of One Canada Square? Or will you next be ambling along to Waitrose? Or rather Tesco Metro? To resume your position by a checkout?'

Surely David Clulow wouldn't be interested in employing someone quite so inadequate and rude. Besides she wouldn't be able to stand behind the counter, let alone look a customer in the eye and say, 'Yes, these frames suit you rather well, sir.' How would she be able to adjust a pair of spectacles and slip them back on an innocent person's face? Apart from anything else she'd have no idea what suited whom. I doubted whether even Tesco, up in the twilight zone of the first floor where Cabot Place East met Cabot Place West, would employ her. She wasn't Waitrose material, which was where I'd been thinking I might pop along myself after I'd finished with David Clulow. Shoplifting from a supermarket, especially an upmarket supermarket, in a prime location – where security, though tight, was not on the lookout for conservatively dressed petty criminals, but terrorists – was always going to be infinitely easier than swiping some wine from a tiny branch of Threshers. And that, of course, wasn't difficult, and would have gone happily unnoticed had it not been for an unrelated, but obviously deadly serious incident. What misfortune.

'Wanker.'

'Sorry?'

'You heard.'

I couldn't quite believe I was being thus insulted, in David Clulow, opticians to stars – no? 'Are all your customers so polite?' I asked my blank, hopeless friend, and ignoring the midget.

'I want to book an eye test,' the midget said.

Who didn't need an eye test? 'I think that's a very good idea,' I said, 'because if you could see properly you wouldn't have called me a wanker.'

She looked up at me, her little face becoming red and blotchy, then in the direction of my friend behind the counter – could she even see her? – before shaking her head, turning and lightly stomping out of the shop.

'Do you get many like her?' I said.

My friend smiled, uncertainly. At last a reaction, of sorts, and possibly just the one I was looking for. 'Can I help you?' she said.

'I certainly hope so, this time.' I don't think she recognised me. Though I wasn't going to become angry and make unreasonable demands, I wasn't going to become abusive and threatening. I simply wanted attentive service. 'You have two new pairs of glasses for me. They should be ready to collect. And also a problem has developed with these ones.' I took off the bent and twisted pair I was wearing, waved them at her and replaced them. They just didn't feel right. I wondered whether they would ever feel right again.

'Let me see whether your new ones are in first. What's your name?'

'Kim Jong-il.'

'Sorry?'

'Matt Freeman.'

'Right.' Did she recognise the name? She walked away from the counter and began searching various drawers in a big, built-in cabinet which lined the back wall. This too was covered in that awful green glass.

Waiting for her to return with good news, once again I caught sight of myself in a mirror. The fact that my glasses were wonky wasn't as troubling as the fact that I should have shaved, beard and hair, and that in this light the scab on my face looked as if it were infected, while a livid, dark yellow bruise was spreading, literally as I watched, across the whole of one side of my head. All this from a minor altercation with a bus driver, I kept thinking. They were more vicious than cab drivers. Though did it depend on what route they drove, what garage they originated from? You wouldn't have thought buses travelling through the City of Westminster would have needed to be manned by thugs. Still I should have known better. But perhaps I'd become a little blasé about the threat some blokes could pose. Of course there were blokes and blokes. Take Fran's Joe. He was the sort of guy who wouldn't even retaliate after you hurled a London stock brick through his fancy sitting-room window. Trust such a weapon to be found lying discarded in Queen's Park. A valuable item like that would have been scavenged within seconds in south London.

'I'm sorry, but neither pair has come back yet. Both, it seems, require non-standard lenses.'

Sorry? Did I ever hear anything else? She was wearing those tight black jeans again, though her top was a fitted polo neck, in a bright baby blue. I'd been trying to ignore it because it was exactly the sort of style and colour of knitwear Bobbie would have worn, if indeed it wasn't the very same item as Bobbie had recently possessed and which she was even wearing the last time I saw her. Could they have known one another? Bobbie and this particular sales assistant from David Clulow? Obviously Bobbie had had an unhealthy interest in eyewear, in my eyewear anyway. Maybe she'd been tailing me, for weeks, on my forays to various stores and boutiques, from Canada Place to Bond Street, checking out exactly what I did all day, and maybe she had struck up a relationship with this woman, this girl from David Clulow, and my new friend here had admired Bobbie's rather idiosyncratic sense of style, and was now aping her somewhat.

212

Or maybe Bobbie, over days and weeks, had orchestrated, by subtle persuasion, the whole lookalike wardrobe thing, partly in a bid to spook me. Soon I'd be seeing young sales assistants all over the place resembling Bobbie. Fuck it, these bright lights, these massive, intrusive mirrors were making me increasingly anxious. What was I thinking? It was a sartorial accident. Plain and simple.

'You're sorry?' I said. 'I bet you are. You have no idea the trouble you are causing me. To begin with, at least one of the pairs should have been back yesterday, I'm certain of it, the Oliver Peoples. In fact they were the pair you'd given me because you'd cocked up before, and this pair, the pair I'm currently wearing, have also developed a fault. This arm's become bent and loose – I don't know what sort of cheap plastic was used in these frames – and the hinge is twisted. Frankly the whole thing is hanging on by a thread. Without these I can't see a thing.' Obviously I'd been wondering exactly how much I could see with them, but didn't see the point in complicating the matter. 'And they're the last working pair I have. I'll be quite helpless.'

'Maybe one of the on-site technicians can fix them, at least as a temporary measure. Would you like me to ask?'

How I hated temporary measures. 'I don't see I have any other option, unless you can make me a new pair on the spot.' Could they switch the lenses, to an identical frame, if they had one in stock? But of course that wasn't the point. I looked over my shoulder and through the shop front to the concourse and the Cabot Place East pedestrian roundabout. It was packed already and lunchtime was hours away. What were all these people doing? Why weren't they behind their desks? Maybe that was it. They didn't have any desks anymore, but continued to come to Canary Wharf out of habit. Out of hope, that somehow their jobs, their purpose in life would reassert itself.

But how hard were they used to working anyway? Most, surely, spent more time shopping, or buying snacks, wandering the malls for kicks. Wasn't that what office culture was all about – trying to avoid knuckling down? That's what I'd found, when I'd worked for various absurd corporations. OK, the last was a while ago, but I'd done virtually nothing, for years, except chat to my colleagues, or eye them up, then slink off for a break. I was never pushed, except in some mindless bureaucratic way. My real talents were barely utilised. What a waste it all was.

Perhaps the malls would be even more packed, as more and more people were laid off. Perhaps this was their sole purpose all along, their *raison d'être*, to amble from HMV to Warehouse, Cecil Gee to Fat Face, Ted Baker to Boots, LK Bennett to TM Lewin, criss-crossing between Jubilee Place and Canada Place, before finding themselves, weary and famished, in Waitrose Food & Home. There had never been much urgency or commitment to their actions, little belief. It was only people like me, with their own businesses to run, their own empires to build, who had any real purpose.

But I supposed I was lucky to have effectively a vocation, a calling, and that I was willing continually to push myself. Though of course it was a constant uphill struggle, against great waves of mediocrity and laziness, not to mention prejudice and badly misplaced regulatory overload. The concourse I was observing, the escalators ferrying people from one floor to the next, from David Clulow to Thomas Pink, from Charbonnel et Walker to Crabtree & Evelyn, and on up to Chili's, Itsu and Pizza Express, said it all. What a farce, a sham. Especially now, when easy credit was meant to have dried up. Though maybe no one was spending anything. Maybe no one ever had, except me. I suddenly felt very weary and famished. Could I be bothered to carry on? As if anyone would care. Did I really have to make my mark?

Maybe I'd be better off ambling along with this lot. Perhaps that was what I'd been doing all along. No, no, no. That hadn't been me. Never. I'd always had more style.

I handed my broken specs to my very personal sales assistant attempting to be Bobbie. 'I'll be right here,' I said. 'Obviously I'm not going anywhere, unless you want to take me for a latte while I'm waiting? How about it, it could be fun? No? I don't bite.' Did she smile, before she walked towards the rear of the shop and disappeared behind a door? I had no idea.

Though as soon as she was back, that strangely familiar, but wonky, bright and dark outline, I pressed her again. 'Actually, I think it's the least David Clulow can do, buy me a coffee, for all the hassle I've been put through.'

'Sorry,' she said – shyly. 'We can't do that. I wouldn't be able to leave the premises, anyway. We're very busy right now.'

I wasn't surprised, given the quality of their products. 'Who isn't?' I said, refusing again to rise to the bait. 'Well, what about a drink later? Something to eat? I know some great restaurants nearby.' I didn't. Maybe there were one or two. The latest *Evening Standard*'s *The Essential Party Guide* – which over the months had become something of a favourite bedtime read – seemed to suggest there were, not that that could be relied upon. But I'd never managed to lure Roger here to find out. 'Or do you want to come over to my place? I live very centrally – the Barbican? – and I'm a pretty decent cook. What do you like? Fish? Meat, shellfish? How about langoustine fritters with basil pistou to start, followed by quail, on a bed of sautéed foie gras, which I usually serve with truffled mashed potatoes. No? Not tempted? I could always come your way, and bring a takeaway. Or just a bottle of chilled Bruno Paillard, Première Cuvée. Where do you live?'

'I live with my boyfriend,' she said, not in the slightest bit amused or charmed by my offer.

'That wasn't what I asked.' I was losing my touch.

'I'm not interested, all right.' She stepped sideways, and addressed another customer who'd slipped up to the counter without my noticing. I wasn't sure whether this blob was a man or a woman. 'Can I help you?' my so-called friend asked. Maybe it was a woman. One of those women with exceptionally large behinds, and enormously chunky thighs, who insisted on wearing trousers. Or were they leggings? Leggings were never going truly to conceal such acreage of flesh and cellulite.

'Hey,' I said. 'What about me?'

'The technician is doing what he can. He'll bring them out to you shortly.'

'But what about my glasses which should have come back by now? Both pairs?'

'I'm afraid you'll have to wait a little longer. Sorry. There's nothing more I can do. They're not on the premises. As I said, your prescription is a special order. We'll call you as soon as they come in.'

How could they? 'Jesus wept.' She wasn't going to get away with this – this callous lack of concern, this shocking indifference. And to think, I'd offered to make her dinner. She didn't live with her boyfriend. She didn't look the type. Her parents maybe, but not a lover. She was too meek, too demure, too curtailed by tradition. I'd follow her home, to press my case, that's what I'd do. And if her parents were there, her moral, her religious guardians, well I'd wait until they went to the shops, until they went out to pray, before sneaking in – I believed I was getting quite adept at that sort of thing – and making my presence, my wishes very clear indeed.

Or, perhaps easier would be to tackle her on her way home,

along one of those dismal streets in Forest Gate – Leonard Road or Suffolk Street, say, a stone's throw from deserted Wanstead Flats. That was where she lived, I was suddenly certain – crammed into an airless, Edwardian terrace, with UPVC windows and cracked, municipal paving slabs running up to the smoked and patterned Plexiglas front door.

Or, easier and quicker still, maybe I'd just grab her in her lunch hour. How long was I really prepared to wait? I was not a very patient man – you didn't get anywhere in this world if you were – and surely she had a lunch hour. Everyone else did around here. And it wasn't just for one hour either. It was for hours. Forever. 'Jesus fucking wept.'

So I could see where I was going – to a degree. So the technician had patched up my hopelessly out of date spectacles, which Bobbie had done her very best to destroy. But was I happy, as I rode the packed escalator from promenade to street level?

The crowds seemed larger – and suddenly more frenetic, anxious even. Was it because we were closing in on lunchtime? Were they terrified that Pret A Manger would run out of Classic Super Club sandwiches, that EAT's great Thai butternut squash soup vats would run dry, that the queue at Birley's would be twenty minutes long? As I stepped off the escalator someone, a young man in a suit, a seemingly well-cut midnight blue suit too – he had to be a continental European, a Spaniard? An Italian? – shouldered me heavily. He might have been carrying a large box, and I might have been taking longer than was entirely necessary – for once, maybe I was suddenly beginning to enjoy my lack of urgency, knowing I had at least a short while to go – but he could have apologised. He didn't even look back, as he rushed on towards the DLR, his thick, dark brown hair flying off his collar. If I had hair, that's the sort I'd want.

Shaken, hassled, I needed instant respite – already. And there, just as I must have known it would be, was Church's – that beacon of calm and fine craftsmanship among all the uncertainty, not to mention tack and dross. So much of Canary Wharf was clearly bereft of anything like proper standards and regulations, let alone full service and accountability – no wonder I'd encountered problems, from top to bottom, from Barclays – for ages my fucking bank, which I'd hastily been forced to disown – to Clulow. And no wonder I found it impossible not to slip inside the famed shoe store and take a breather, plus I was wearing the right shoes. Or rather I was wearing the wrong shoes, because they were in a terrible state, with the left sole, of course, having become badly unstitched and the heel of the right shoe worn almost to the hollow core.

Disregarding the fact that the heels shouldn't have had a hollow core anyway – that that was not the traditional way to construct fine, English shoes, though I seemed to recall that Prada, or at least Prada's parent company, now owned Church's, which could explain a lot – I was obviously requiring instant replacements. Especially as it was not the first time I'd had to return these shoes, and also regarding the fact that I was shortly to depart these shores – my mini-break to Mallorca being just the *amuse-bouche* – as soon as I'd assembled the funds, which was part of the reason I'd had to return to Canary Wharf. Barclays aside, there'd always been a certain disregard for personal belongings among the crowds. Too distracted by the brittle halogens, the looped Beyoncé – or maybe it was Britney – and the steaming soup, bags were left unzipped, pockets stood unguarded, while new purchases – it can't have been all window-shopping, unless people hung onto their logo-ed carriers – were quickly forgotten about. Or so I'd always found. Regardless, there was no way I was leaving the country for some exclusive hideaway without being properly shod.

'Can I help you, sir?'

I looked up from observing a tan half brogue, a shoe that I'd coveted for some time. 'Yes, yes, I hope so.' He looked vaguely familiar — dark hair, pitted olive-skinned, tall but puny. Though I definitely hadn't seen him in here before. 'Can I speak to the manager?'

'I am the manager.'

'Right. OK. Are you new?' Things were looking good.

'Yes. This is my first week.'

'What a time to start.' I laughed. 'Well, I presume you know your way around already? I'd like to try a pair of these on, in size nine, in the tan, and also I have a problem with the shoes I'm wearing, which I bought from here a few months ago. In fact it's not the first time I've had to complain about them. They've gone back to the factory once already.'

'What's the problem?'

'The sole on the left shoe has come unstitched, again, and some of the side stitching is loose, see, and the heel on the right shoe has worn through almost completely, to this weird hollow bit, and I'm not sure it'll be repairable. I haven't seen a pair of shoes made quite like these before, and when I bought them I was assured that they were re-heelable. What do you reckon?' I sat on one of the chairs and began undoing the laces.

'We haven't stocked that model for a couple of years. When did you say you bought them?'

'Earlier in the year some time. March, April? I can't remember when exactly. But it was definitely this year, from this branch. I thought you were new anyway. How do you know what was stocked in the past?'

'I'm not just the manager of this branch, I'm the regional manager. It's my job to know everything about current and past models.'

'I bought these shoes from this shop earlier this year, OK?

I'm not lying. Where's what's his name, the old manager? Doddery, grey-haired chap. Both of the people who used to work here know me – the manager and his assistant. They'll verify it. Just ask them.'

'We're restaffing. It's only me today.'

'That means you're going to have to deal with it now then, I suppose.'

'Let me see if we have the half brogues in your size, first.' He slipped into the storeroom at the back of the shop. There was a certain extravagance to his stride.

It was hot in Church's and though I was surrounded by fine, bench-made shoes, all perfectly in line and spaced, I was not feeling particularly calmed. Pleased though I was that he was the only member of staff in today, plus the fact that he was a new addition to the not inconsiderable army of Canary Wharf sales assistants – would they soon outnumber the bankers? – and so wouldn't have observed my comings and goings, I couldn't stop thinking that I recognised him from somewhere else. And that it was not good news. Frankly, no one I was going to bump into right now would have been good news. For me, or them.

'You're lucky,' he said, springing from the walk-in store cupboard with a crisp, dark brown Church's shoebox under his arm, 'last pair.'

As if, I was so lucky. He went down on one knee to extract the shoes, and while he was folding back the tissue paper and releasing that tantalising whiff of new leather and beeswax, it came to me. He used to work for Prada, the Bond Street branch. He was the man I'd slapped. Gone was the Italian accent, though all I could think was that if he didn't watch himself very carefully he'd be getting another, and this time it wouldn't just be a playful warning. Things had moved on somewhat since then. The stakes had been raised. It was not a game anymore. I could only be deadly serious.

God, he spent an age lacing the shoes before asking me to remove my own footwear, so, as he said, 'we can just slip them on'. We? Was I wearing clean socks? I doubted it. Did I care? No. Did he recoil at all when I freed my stinking right foot from its worn, tatty casing that was once, it made me wince to remember, a very fine, leather-soled Church's Oxford, and struggled to slip it into the first tan half brogue? Maybe.

'How does it feel?' he asked.

'Slightly tight. I need to try the other one on.'

'Of course.'

There was more wearisome fiddling with the laces and the tongue before he allowed me to get anywhere near the left shoe. And then he insisted on tying the bow himself. Too tight too. Why did sales assistants always do that in shoe shops? Did they think we were children, incapable of tying a firm knot ourselves? Or was it because they wanted to inflict as much pain on poor, unsuspecting customers as they could get away with? What were they really saying? 'Why should I have to serve you, you arsehole? This is way beneath me.' Could I ever summon any sympathy for a sales assistant? No, probably not.

Amazingly, I was sure this particular sales assistant, this manager no less, hadn't recognised me. Was that slap I dealt him – albeit all that time ago – so unmemorable? Just how little presence did I exert in this world? I was suddenly overwhelmed by a feeling of futility, when the opposite should have been the case. I don't know how many times I walked around that tiny shop floor, commanding attention, deserving respect. Daring him to recognise me.

'How do they fit?' he eventually said.

'I'm not sure. Give me a minute.'

'Take your time.'

Wasn't he being polite. 'I will.' I always liked the way new leather soles felt on carpet. There was an almost complete lack of grip. Though I knew that once they became chewed up a bit, having been exposed to asphalt and paving slabs, stone and tarmac, whatever hard, rough surface I happened to be traversing, on whatever continent, they'd grip better than any man-made sole, plus they'd be highly breathable as well. I loved leather-soled shoes. I loved leather. How people could wear trainers I had no idea. Foul, squashy folds of polymeric amides, which lasted five minutes. Though these beautifully and traditionally made tan half brogues were, if I was being honest with myself, a little tight and already uncomfortable. Naturally I presumed that this was simply because they were new and that they would need breaking in. All decent shoes needed breaking in. I just wasn't sure whether I had the time or for that matter the inclination to go through the pain. Pain definitely wasn't my thing, as I'd implied to Suze, more than once. Not, sadly, that she had listened.

Except, catching sight of guess who coming up the escalator, I suddenly knew I had no choice. There she was, my PA, looking, well, Bobbie-like. She was mine all right, all mine. Had to be. I wasn't going to miss this opportunity. While keeping track of her every step and quickly discerning that, as I might have known, she was headed outdoors for the plaza, and quite possibly a rendezvous, an assignation at All Bar One, or Smollensky's, in her lunch hour of all times, the brazen little tart, I continued my circumnavigations of Church's. I'd let her get a good few paces ahead before I made a move.

Now, now was the time, and for once there was no little bird to chirp me on. This was all me, all my doing. I was firmly in the driving seat. I didn't see the point in saying goodbye to Church's new regional manager, especially as he'd effectively blanked me, and I didn't look over my shoulder either as I made my way around the rest of that bit of circular concourse, past News on the Wharf and Gap Kids, and through into the great, marble-clad lobby of One Canada Square. Across the shiny floor with its empty Charles Eames benches, I skipped, and out a revolving door, straight over the South Colonnade, narrowly missing a speeding cab, and down the steps to Reuters Plaza. While never breaking into a run I was certainly shifting and gaining ground, perhaps too fast. Slowing, I looked up at the walls of glass towers, reflecting a leaden sky and leaden water, and a band of stock prices being flashed around the building on an electronic noticeboard immediately to my right. Focusing that way, I caught the strap, *US Business News from Reuters*. Then, *AT&T, Bank of America, Citigroup, General Elec. Co*. The accompanying figures meant nothing, to me, but all the arrows, pointing down, did.

Fortunately the stock I was after wasn't making her way to All Bar One, which appeared overflowing with more people than usual, and some clandestine lover. Was she going the outdoor, and at this time of the day the normally less crowded, route to the Jubilee Mall? It was one thing following someone, discreetly, but quite another to be doing so while keeping track of the Dow and being chased at the same time.

However, my new shoes were coping well. I hadn't slipped once and surprisingly there was no outrageously painful chafing yet. Indeed, I felt that because they were so tight they must have been giving me more control, in the way that professional footballers always wore extremely close-fitting boots over the thinnest socks, and, so I'd heard, downhill skiers too. And more good fortune, because she suddenly veered to her left, past a news team. What were they doing? There was a cameraman, a young sound woman and a strikingly bald male presenter who looked vaguely familiar.

Waiting for me? They were preparing to shoot, but I was too quick for them, as I also sidestepped into the Tube.

A glance over my shoulder failed to help me identify whether I was being tailed and sinking into the depths of Norman Foster's cavernous, concrete ticket hall, I was left with the image of an even greyer London sky playing out on a thousand office windows. I was not going to miss Canary Wharf.

Her escalator was more crowded, though she seemed happy to stand stock-still and let the machinery do all the work – how could she be so calm? The far escalator, which I had cannily chosen, was almost empty and I was taking two steps at a time, knowing I could wait for her at the very bottom, by the platforms. I was well practised at pushing through barriers, not being an Oyster card carrier – never having had the time to fill out the form, or being prepared to pay for something so unreliable in advance. The trick was picking the right person to squeeze behind. Young men in suits were usually the best option, as they were always in a hurry and were often involved in shoving out of the way whoever was in front of them as well. Right now I was almost spoilt for choice. Bang, and I was through. I don't think the man, the lad, even noticed. Though he was grappling with a large, cardboard box. What was it with these cardboard boxes? Were they giving them to everyone nowadays, however junior? I'd never got one.

Why Transport for London persisted with these barriers made no sense. They were so easy to dodge. And their employees too, why did they persist with most of them? How unobservant, how unvigilant were they? It wasn't as if Canary Wharf Tube station was understaffed. There were numerous uniformed men and women standing around, chatting. But that was all they were doing, chatting, to each other and seemingly not paying the slightest bit of attention to what any of the passengers might be up to. Talk about soft targets, in this day and age. Was I the only person who noticed how slack it was and who actually cared about these things? There was a total lack of respect for my safety, and everyone else's.

She was heading into town, which surprised me. How long did she really have for lunch, and why wasn't she going east, towards familiar territory? Perhaps I'd completely misread her and she was much more metropolitan and savvy – she had spruced herself up after all – and was making her way to Green Park, and lunch at the Wolseley – she had long grown bored of L'Atelier – with an old boyfriend, possibly her current boyfriend, who had once been big in hedge funds, with a discreet but plush office in Mayfair, not to mention the Belgravia apartment, and who was still trying to hang onto both his bird and his job. I knew how he felt. There was no escaping the fact that she looked cracking today, in that bright top – Bobbie would have been proud of her – and she was clearly full of purpose, at least she hadn't hesitated to tell me where to leave off.

I was hovering behind one of those great, oval, concrete pillars, with built-in crumple zone, top and bottom, in case of earthquake or bomb – not something Chamberlin, Powell and Bon would have had to concern themselves with when making their mark on the capital – and I was in a good spot to make a dash for either platform, in my spanking new shoes, except of course she was waiting for the Stanmore train, which was still two minutes away. She had her back to me, and I was certain she wasn't aware of me so far. Also, I was increasingly convinced that I wasn't being followed. It was highly doubtful that the manager would have given chase and left his shop unguarded. I wondered whether he already regretted the restaffing programme he'd just instigated. Of course those shops, however small, needed two people on the premises at all times. At the worst, for me at least, he would have called the police and they'd still be on their way, if indeed they didn't have anything more important to be dealing with, like making sure that Canary Wharf was being adequately protected from serious crime, such as credit default swaps, and, of course, terrorism. The place really was fundamentally flawed, a complete joke, and I was glad that I wouldn't be exposing myself to such risks again. Goodbye Canary Wharf, you'd never exactly done me any favours anyway.

The two minutes seemed to take forever. I've always suspected that the timing on those electronic noticeboards was highly malleable. There had to be a sadistic, fat Jubilee Line controller, stuck in a drab, overheated centre, in somewhere like Neasden – yes, it would be Neasden all right – dragging out the seconds and minutes, pausing the digital – atomic maybe – clock, while the trains became more and more backed up – delayed by signal failure, or yet another body on the line – I'd often thought about jumping, out of pure frustration – or stalled at distant stations, by white trash intent on blocking the closing doors so their mates could swagger on board too, when, once all together, they'd then proceed to abuse and intimidate their fellow passengers. How I loathed public transport, how it had ruined London for me, and if it wasn't for my friend, regardless of whether I myself was possibly being pursued as well, I really don't think I'd have boarded the train, which had finally crept into the platform.

It smelt of KFC. Overwhelmingly. And no wonder. An extremely large woman, all sweat and thick black ringlets, had her nose in a Chicken Fillet Tower. She reminded me of Roger, and the tower bit, I couldn't help thinking, was rather laughingly appropriate for the location, but eating on the Tube was probably worse than eating on the bus, in my book. Certainly KFC was a notch or two above Burger

King, when it came to pungency. All that saturated fat combined with the Colonel's special recipe of herbs and spices. It was one secret that I had no interest in discovering. Give me a Whopper anytime. Where the hell had this whale boarded? Canning Town perhaps. Or West Ham. I imagined the whole of Zone 3 was KFC heartland. Much of Zone 2 as well.

My problem was that I was in the perfect spot to observe my friend, who was in the carriage immediately ahead, sitting relatively peacefully, probably because she was breathing slightly less noxious air. I'd have to stick it out until who knew where she was getting off. Green Park? That was still my bet. I scowled at the whale, but she was too interested in her scoff to look up. Maybe she'd get off soon. Next stop hopefully. But all on her own, unaided? I reckoned she'd need help to stand. Just my luck.

At Canada Water the object of my desire remained seated, as did the object of my disgust. Though I could sense much worse was in store, the second they got on — two hoodies, high on attitude, at the very least. As usual their jeans defied gravity. Fortunately the elastic on their — probably fake — black Calvin Kleins, was holding up. One of them was listening to rap on his mobile — a Sony Ericsson, not dissimilar from my old model. Perhaps it was mine. He was holding it at arm's length from his ear, enjoying the power, the disturbance, the menace. Naturally they chose to sit, or slouch in my end of the carriage, when they could quite easily have sidled up to the whale. Maybe even hoodies drew the line at KFC. They seemed to be going out of their way to avoid eye contact with me, or each other for that matter, and simply stared at their jigging, fat white trainers. This was becoming completely unbearable.

No change at Bermondsey, and checking the Tube map in the carriage, I decided that unless things did alter, I'd have no option but to make my next move. I couldn't put up with this for a moment longer. It wasn't just public transport that was insufferable, it was the public, too. Also, I wasn't entirely sure I could risk a confrontation in the West End, especially if she was on her way to meet her bloke, who though possibly struggling at work, wouldn't be in anything like the financial mess I was in, plus, I was certain he'd have a full head of dark brown hair to complement his bespoke, midnight blue, double-vented, two-button Richard James suit. So I was wearing a brand-new pair of Church's half brogues, in a catchy, light tan, but I was not feeling at my most competitive or sartorial best. I wouldn't be much of a match. I needed to act now.

Getting up and making my way to the nearest exit, as the Tube pulled into London Bridge, I couldn't help standing on a trainer-clad foot belonging to the hoodie with my blaring mobile. It wasn't my fault he'd left his Nike Air Max in the middle of my path. As it was I could feel the new inside edge of my heel dig into his ankle as I pressed down, with all my weight, and I could feel his ankle not exactly give way, but sort of crunch over. Accident or not, I was surprised by the feeling of force I'd exerted. Was that the difference between wearing a traditionally crafted, fine English-made shoe, as opposed to a piece of soft, Chinese-fabricated plastic? Had Prada sharpened the edges, refined the lines? Perhaps Church's would now have to come with a safety warning. Perhaps he'd be able to sue. However, I instantly knew that I couldn't hang around to say, 'Oops, sorry, my fault.' I squeezed through the doors before they'd fully opened and was racing for the way out not pausing to look behind me, let alone to see whether my special friend, my fledgling Bobbie, had also exited, or had remained sitting so peacefully, so calmly in her airy, quiet carriage. She'd be on there until Green Park all right. Where else would she get off, looking like that, full of distant poise? She was no fool.

Thankfully the platform was packed, as was the rest of London Bridge Tube, and I tore along corridors, up stairs and escalators – it went on forever – dodging and shoving people out of the way. I was always amazed at how leisurely so many people traversed these spaces – didn't they mind the decor, the odour, the company, or were they simply very lazy? It wasn't until I'd reached the barriers and the ticket hall, that I lost my footing and skidded into a Community Support Officer, of all people, and a chunky female one at that, though maybe her stab-proof vest was making her look particularly large. And vulnerable. It was pretty easy to see where to aim and where not to aim.

'I'm so sorry,' I said, gasping for breath and wiping my brow. Why did Tube stations always have to be so hot? 'I'm trying to catch a mainline, and I'm wearing these ridiculous new shoes. They have no grip at all.' Balancing on the edge of a barrier I tried to lift my foot to show her, but there was something not quite right with my left leg. I must have either damaged it bumping into her, or pulled a muscle charging up the escalators. I winced. 'Ow, that really hurts.'

'You should be more careful of where you're going, young man. You could do yourself a lot more damage, besides seriously hurting someone else. Think yourself lucky you ran into me.' She sighed, deeply. She might have meant it to be a chuckle. 'And think yourself lucky I'm not going to have you arrested for being a danger to the public.'

Could they do that, these Community Support Officers? 'Give me a break. I said I was sorry. It was an accident for God's sake. My leg hurts enough as it is. Really. I'm going to miss my train. Oh no.' I was patting my pockets furiously. Where were the real police when you wanted them? 'What's happened to my Oyster card? I don't believe it. It's either fallen out, or it's been lifted.' I began looking around the immediate area. I was also looking to see whether I had been followed this far. Not yet. 'It's not here. And neither is my wallet. Oh no.' I sighed heavily, and there was no mistaking the intent. 'I've been robbed. I must have been robbed. My wallet's gone, my Oyster card's gone. My phone. Shit.'

Though I was becoming hysterical the well-padded Community Support Officer was no longer paying me particular attention and had walked away. She was now chatting to a TfL employee, a small, white man with a lopsided face and a comb-over. He was guarding the disabled barrier. I hobbled over. 'Someone's stolen my Oyster card, and my wallet, and my phone, everything, and I have to get to Guy's. My girlfriend's very seriously ill and I have to be with her.'

'Do you want to report a theft?' the pretend cop said.

'I just want to get to the hospital. That's all that matters. Please, please help me. She could be dying, this very minute. She's called Bobbie and she's the best thing that has ever happened to me. It's a matter of life and death. I don't want her to die. Please God, don't let her die.'

Without saying anything, indeed barely even looking at me, the TfL chap released the thick glass barrier and it swung open. I hobbled through – my leg really was killing me. 'Thanks.' I didn't look back but I could hear her.

'Have you seen him before? Is he one of the regulars? These people should be cleared off the streets, for good.'

Hurrying, I turned left under the arched concourse, nearly catching an *Evening Standard* kiosk with my dicky leg. The headline on the paper at the top of the stack was all too visible – *Meltdown*. Beyond the kiosk sat two proper tramps, one with a mangy dog, the other with bare feet, swollen and caked in dirt. Both were quite oblivious to the world around them, and not remotely concerned with begging. Were they content, happy even, I found myself thinking as I emerged into daylight at the top end of Tooley Street? Was it warm, cold, dry or wet? Out in the open it seemed to be the same as usual – unremittingly damp and grey – yet something, everything was different. I wasn't able to sense things, clearly, coherently. My mind wouldn't analyse, wouldn't recognise the information it was being fed. Was it all that sudden exertion, and then the crash? I couldn't grasp anything, I couldn't feel anything, except the pain in my leg. I paused by some railings, a short distance before London Bridge itself, wondering which way to go, suddenly finding it terribly hard to focus – and this wasn't some minor problem with my prescription, a slight divergence of detail. I could barely see. The traffic was backed up, that much seemed obvious. Though it was a long blur stretching right across the bridge, both ways, with the river somewhere below and the City rising beyond. Tower 42, the Gherkin? Could I make them out?

And were those other three towers the Barbican? I couldn't get an angle on just how far from home I was. Or if I went back, for one last time, exactly what, or who would I find waiting for me? I wiped my eyes on the back of my hand, finding them wet, and tears – tears – having already dripped onto my sore face. But weren't there still things I needed? Clothes, a passport, cash? I would always need more things, whatever the climate. I wasn't sure why I hadn't gathered the essentials earlier, why I hadn't packed what I had, before I left for Canary Wharf. Because I hadn't quite reconciled myself to the fact that I was really off, perhaps. Because I was still hoping for some, however slight, reprieve – like an understanding, a commitment from Barclays, maybe. Because I knew my new glasses wouldn't be ready. Exactly what line of credit, what comfort, what unfinished business was holding me back? A North Korean visa? A new plan? A change of tack? My Bobbie lookalike? Mia? Bobbie herself?

Maybe, finally I'd have to recognise the fact that in my

line of work, in life itself, there was always unfinished business. Yes, I was off, but in my own time, once I'd assembled my few remaining possessions and stuffed them in that dusty Tumi. And anyway, what was the rush? Had there ever been a rush? Who did I have to answer to? Who did I have to be afraid of? For a brief moment by those railings I must have forgotten who I was, what I'd achieved and what I was still capable of. I'd forgotten to believe in myself, that I could rise above the turmoil. That it would take more than a melt-down to sink me. Indeed, it might have been just what I was waiting for.

Resolve, Matt. Purpose. Don't you ever forget. Setting forth, albeit slowly and limping heavily — these fucking shoes, they were hurting now all right, and my leg, my dicky leg — things soon began to clear, the traffic flow. Out of the smog always came clarity, a vision, opportunity, with the Thames bubbling below, the City dwindling above. It was my time, it had to be, if not my place.

TWELVE

Long Call

'What are you doing here?'

'What are you doing here? I somehow didn't expect to find you at home.'

'Why? I live here don't I?'

'If you say so. But I mean it's not like you exactly make yourself accessible. Your landline's not working. Did you know that? Your mobile goes straight to answerphone. You don't reply to emails. This is the third time I've been here today, looking for you.'

'I've been out. Plus what's the urgency? Has anything horrible happened? Is everything all right back home? The kids, your wife? Your art? I only spoke to you the other day. When was it? Saturday? It's only Tuesday.'

'Are you going to let me in?'

'Are you going to tell me why you're here?'

'Matt, you're my brother. I was concerned about you, and I'm not the only one, as you know. What's been going on? Look at your face. Look at you. You look dreadful. What the fuck has been going on?'

Sean seemed to push his way in and before I knew it he

was snooping around my main room. 'So, you've been chatting to my ex-fiancée again, have you? Getting even more intimate, hey?' He was scrutinising my desk, touching the lid of my closed laptop, fingering the odd piece of paper. What the hell was he looking for?

'No, as a matter of fact, not her. Though if you must know I did try to speak to her again. I couldn't get hold of her.'

'Who then? Roger? I bet Roger's been on the blower to you. So Roger and I had a little disagreement over lunch the other day. I can't even remember what it was about. Actually, yes I can, my business, the people, the organisations I choose to work with. He suddenly tried to sound rather ethical and PC, telling me who I could and couldn't work with, but I tell you the guy's a pig, an absolute pig. Do you know what he does every afternoon? Where he goes? That poor wife of his.'

'Does it matter who I've spoken to? What's important is that people were worried enough about you to get in touch with me − I am your closest living relative. I was worried too, frankly, after that last phone call we had. Let's get real.'

'Let's get real? What sort of expression is that? It's not the fucking 1970s. Though I suppose it might still be in Norway. The police, have they been in touch too? That's it. I bet they have, haven't they? They must have got your number from my phone. I hope they explained the situation properly, that I had my mobile stolen. I wonder where they found it, whether they caught the girl who nicked it off me. They must have rung you, noticing the surname, because they couldn't ring me. Though they could have called round, or left a note. Seems an odd way to go about returning stolen property − getting my brother to fly all the way over from Norway. How more incompetent can they be?'

'Matt, we all know what happened before.'

'Yes? Is that right?' I sat on the sofa, not willing to become heated, not wishing to rise to the bait – especially as a whole new agenda was forming in my mind, a bright new window, as Roger might have said. But my feet were seriously killing me now. I dreaded to think about the blisters, and whether they would hamper my mobility, just when I was set to be on the move, and for who knew how long, and if Sean's presence was any indication, very probably at my most swift and nimble also.

It had been further than I'd thought from London Bridge, it was always further than you thought in this city, and despite my leg injury or the shoes, I hadn't exactly been dawdling, suddenly full of purpose and renewed vigour, and an urge, like I'd never had before, to be off, to be thousands of miles away. Though as usual I'd got lost around Bank, those great walls of York stone, and then the Guildhall, when I should have stuck to thronging Cheapside. I'd taken side streets instead of main roads and thoroughfares, believing I was less likely to be spotted. Yet, although I was certain I wasn't being followed, while winding my way along and around narrow, shady Ironmonger Lane and Coleman Street and statuesque – I'd give it that – Aldermanbury Square, I was increasingly aware that I was being observed and scrutinised and quite often laughed at too. Who were these people, in their smart suits and expensive accessories, to be so judgemental? Why were they on the streets, drifting in and out of exquisite wine bars and restaurants – 1 Lombard Street even had a queue running back to Birchin Lane, though they might have just been smokers – when surely they should have been at work, shoring up what was left of their assets, reducing still their exposure, protecting the economy?

'Yes, Matt,' said Sean, 'that's right, I do know what happened.'

They were there because they knew it was too late. They were feeling sorry for themselves, drowning their misery, their failure in a sea of Bruno Paillard, believing it was the last they were going to be drinking for a while. Yet still they couldn't help taking a swipe at me. What the fuck had I done to them? I wasn't harming them in any way. I wasn't threatening them. Or maybe I was. Perhaps they knew they were looking at the future. And they didn't like what they saw, not one little bit, especially the tan brogues, being a shade or two too light, proclaiming a sartorial cheekiness — did I have Prada to thank for that? I could have got so very cross. And no one could blame me. No one could ever blame me.

'You don't know what really happened before,' I said. 'You couldn't possibly know. That was between Fran and me, no one else. And it's not the sort of thing that a so-called organic sculptor — or is it kinetic? Living? I don't know — who builds a love shack in some Norwegian backwater would have any idea about anyway.' Sean, though, was rich, relatively, certainly relative to me right now, and probably half of London, and, in his obscure world pretty successful, if not extremely successful I supposed, and I suddenly realised that I shouldn't antagonise him. He was probably my best bet for a ticket out of here, my only bet. 'Sorry, sorry, brother, I didn't mean to say that, but it was a very difficult time for me. As you know. And I don't like to be reminded of it. It's something I try not to think about. Plus, more importantly, I've moved on from there. I really have.'

Sean had walked over to the main window and was peering out at the gathering gloom, and were there more arc lights down there, in a different part of the concourse, angled on a far section of the block of maisonettes? I got up from the sofa and limped over to the window too and tried to put on an expression of troubled bemusement, but who knew what look I was conveying, being covered in war wounds, and with my hair, what hair I had now needing a serious trim, a number one no less. Plus I could have done with a shave, but my face being so sore and scabbing over, it wasn't easy, and having grown some facial hair for once I was beginning to wonder whether it suited me, in the way that men with shaved heads often looked even more macho and virile with beards. I wasn't talking about a beard beard of course, not in an orthodox, or fundamentalist sense – argh, how had I let my foxy friend from David Clulow slip away so easily, my Bobbie replacement, who probably wasn't remotely religious, and didn't live with strict guardians in Forest Gate but a struggling financier in Belgravia – why was I always looking for excuses, and making presumptions? – but simply some designer stubble. So I was jumping on a rather sad, wholly contrived bandwagon, which in reality was anything but macho. Though at least designer stubble was infinitely preferable to a goatee, or that sort of fluff that Mia's bloke sported. People like him could never be called upon to offer any help, any protection when it was most needed, could they? Poor Mia.

Also, thinking about it, having a beard, or whatever anyone wanted to call it – facial hair? – would, I presumed, considerably alter my appearance. A disguise, or at least a change of image, if not complete identity was probably no bad idea. It would go hand in hand with my new outlook, my new plan, for a bright and breezy future. And, of course, any altered appearance could help to fool distant CCTV footage, not to mention possible witnesses, or people with their own agendas, out to scupper my prospects. Who knew exactly what hurdles remained, what vendettas, what vindictiveness. But how long should I let the stubble grow, as long as Sean's? Perhaps I should start believing in God.

'What happened down there? Is that police tape?'

'Is it?' I stepped even closer to the window so my view wasn't polluted from the light in the room. At least my electricity hadn't yet been cut off.

'Looks like it to me.'

'That must mean there's been another incident.'

'Another incident? Yeah?'

Sean didn't say yeah in a lazy, Americanised way. His yeah was brief, to the point, high-pitched, peculiarly Scandinavian, more a 'yeh'. For some reason it made me think of sturdy leather shorts and camping knives. 'A woman was attacked last week, in her flat. She was raped and strangled. Apparently. It was all obviously extremely gruesome. And this is normally such a friendly estate as well. Everyone knows everyone. We're always saying hello and stopping to chat. There's never any serious trouble, not even from the kids. There's hardly any vandalism or graffiti, let alone muggings or burglary.'

'A murder? You're kidding? That's awful. Just over there? God, that sort of thing simply doesn't happen in Norway, not where I live anyway. How do you know there's been another incident?'

'Well, the police tape was not there earlier today, not by that part of the building. I'm sure. Where the first victim's flat was is further down the block. Seems to me like something's just happened in another flat.'

'Could be part of the same investigation. Maybe they've found something, a weapon, a crucial piece of evidence, or someone. A suspect. The suspect's flat? Whenever I think of murder, or rape, I always think of your friend Stephen's mum, what happened to that poor woman.' Sean paused. 'That was never solved, was it? They never found the man who did it.'

'I don't like to think about it. It's too upsetting.'

'I bet it was someone local, or someone who'd been keeping an eye on her. That's usually the way.'

Why had he mentioned Jeanette? I didn't like where this conversation appeared to be going, though who knew how

Sean's mind worked, how calculating he really was. We were very different animals. My heart was thumping, nevertheless, and my hands were suddenly clammy, though I wasn't going to put a foot wrong now. Resolve, Matt. Purpose. Keep control. And secure that ticket.

'What do you know about such things?' I said. 'I thought there wasn't any crime in Norway. Not serious stuff, at least not sexually motivated murders. Though hang about, didn't the Norwegians invent the concept of rape and pillage? Or was that the Danes? Was there a difference then? And anyway, I thought Stephen's mum was an open case. They never got to the bottom of what really happened. That woman used to pop so many pills, and knock back so much white wine, who knew what she used to get up to, and with whom.' Upsetting or not, I couldn't help commenting. 'Not of course, that I'm in any way suggesting she put herself in a compromising position. But, if you ask me they should have looked a little more closely at her husband. How did he make all that money to begin with? There was nothing honest or remotely decent about him. I dread to think what pies he had his chubby little fingers in — the sort of people he fraternised with, and influenced. The damage he must have done over the years. Anyone who wears Gucci loafers, and at that age, is deeply suspicious, if you ask me.'

'Wouldn't there be more activity,' Sean said, 'more police about or something if someone else had been attacked? There's just a bit of tape, and is that a broken window, in that flat? Hard to see from here. Maybe it was vandalism, nothing more serious than that. Whatever you say, this estate looks like quite a dump to me. Probably someone just chucked a brick through the window. One of your specialities, I seem to recall.'

'What are you accusing me of? Fucking hell, Sean, that's out of order.' He couldn't be wearing a wire, could he? He could quite easily, among the fleeces and baggy hiking trousers, full of security zips and secret pockets, which, as usual, he was wearing. He could be wired to the hilt. He could be a walking microphone. What I still couldn't understand was why he was really here. And how had he got here so quickly? From memory there was a direct flight between Trondheim and Stansted, but I couldn't remember what time of day it landed. Had he come yesterday, or some other route? Hadn't he once flown via Schiphol and London City? Or had they flown him over specially, in a private jet? I was suddenly jealous. But I was being absurd. Of course he wasn't in league with the City of London police, or the Met, any more than Roger was. He cared for me, as did Roger, which wasn't so surprising, was it? They understood me, didn't they? My ups and downs. They knew I wasn't perfect, but not all bad. And they weren't the only ones. There was Suze too, bless her. How she'd doted on me, and how nasty I'd always been to her. Sorry, Suze. When I got out of here, when I'd moved on, I would have to change my ways. New place, new person, new job. I really was going to become unrecognisable.

'Sorry. I shouldn't have said that,' said Sean, scratching his hairy chin.

No, he shouldn't – did beards itch? I bet they itched like crazy, especially in hot, humid countries – but I was prepared to let it go, for the moment anyway. 'Well, it looks serious enough to me. I think I can see people inside, in the flat. Can you? They might not be in uniform, though that just means they're the heavyweights, the detectives and chief inspectors. It has to be related. They are plain clothes, definitely, look at them. Even from here you can see how out of shape they are, and the dreadful cut of their clothes.'

'This makes you pretty excited, doesn't it? You been watching too much telly again? All those crime-scene programmes? Do they show anything else here?'

'I don't watch the box, if I can help it. I don't even have a licence. I'm just observant, curious. Who isn't?'

'I'd have thought, with what you've been through in the past, you'd back away from anything like that. Steer well clear.'

'I'm not exactly rushing down there, am I? I'm not rubber-necking on the front line, like most people in this city do, given half the chance.'

'Has anyone been here? Has anyone questioned you about that attack — that murder? — the one the other day? You do have a record.'

'So you keep reminding me. But hardly. I mean there's quite a lot of difference between a domestic dispute, and rape and murder, isn't there. And you know, I never exactly hurt Fran. Why would I have done that? I loved her. There was a bit of drunken pushing and shoving, I'm not proud of that, but she was just as much to blame. As everyone knew, she got hysterical at the drop of a hat. Sean, she meant every-thing to me, believe me. I still love her, in a way. Despite what she did. You know she made most of it up, to get shot of me, don't you, so she could pursue her thing with Joe? It was all designed so she'd appear the victim, in his eyes, so he'd be able to whisk her away to safety — or as the case was a fancy hotel in the Cotswolds. Now look at them. It was outrageous that I should have been made to suffer in the way I did, and still do, frankly. What do you think that did to my reputation? She wanted to destroy me, and she very nearly did. So a window or two got broken, and a few ornaments, but who effectively had the breakdown, me or her? Who was unable to work for months and months? Who lost almost everything? I'm still trying to get my life sorted out, all these years later.'

'Matt, I know all this. You've told me countless times, but as I've said before, and as plenty of other people have said too, including Mum – she was always saying it – you're not the easiest person to live with. You're obsessive, you get paranoid, you can have a horrible temper, made worse by drink, half the time you live in a fantasy world, and you're a snob, too. You don't help yourself, Matt. It's weird but you also have this horrible, macabre side to you – part of your overactive imagination? I don't know. You should have done something that required a little more imagination. You should have been an artist. But you do tend to think the worst of every situation, and then you try to make everyone else think the same. It's scary. I'm not surprised it didn't work out with Fran.'

'Scary? For God's sake, Sean, you're a grown man, an adult. Is this what happens when you spend too long in Norway, you start to think like the Norwegians? Scary? Is it scary when you leave Norway? Is it scary when you come to London? Grow up. This is the real world here.' I gestured towards my vast, modernist window, framing the specially lit concourse, and nearby blocks and buildings, all variously illuminated as well, and the greater glow of the City behind. It was almost pulsing. 'Good things happen and horrible things happen. That's life. Is it any better in Norway, living in a hut?' Maybe it was. Maybe only good things really did happen in Norway. The controls and regulations, the tight-knit communities and of course the endless state-run public services. A sort of North Korea, but with cash. 'I don't think the worst of everything. That's rubbish. In many ways I think the opposite. You don't know me at all.'

'You didn't answer my question. Have the police been here, have they said anything, have they questioned you recently? Something's up. Look, Matt, you have to understand I'm here for you. If that's the case, if the police are onto you, in any way, maybe I can help, with lawyers or whatever. I do have money.'

242

'Jesus fucking wept. This is getting completely out of hand, when I thought we'd got beyond all this. To begin with, right, there is no reason why they, that particular shower, should know I even live here. I got this place through a friend of a friend. It's all very casual. Cheaper that way. I don't pay council tax. Hardly any of the bills are in my name. And more importantly as far as I'm aware that record you keep referring to was more like a caution. I can't remember the exact technical term, but it's not like a proper record. You don't come up on the same databases. In another year or so it will be wiped off anyway. The slate will be clean. They don't have anything else on me.'

'That's not what I asked.'

'You want to know whether the police, what, frankly? Think I murdered that poor woman across the way?' I laughed. This was so ludicrous. Only someone with a very thin grasp on reality could reasonably head a conversation in such a direction and ask, with a straight, bearded face too, such impertinent, improper and entirely unjustified ques- tions – and he thought I had an overactive imagination. But my brother was never one for being exactly in touch. Living in that freezing Norwegian backwater had clearly unhinged him further.

'Have they questioned you? Have they questioned you recently about anything?'

'What are you trying to get me to say? That I did it? Are you trying to get me to incriminate myself somehow? To confess to something? Why does this feel like a set-up?'

'Matt, now you are being ridiculous. If the police really are swarming all over the place, surely they would have knocked on everyone's door.'

'OK, so yes, I did speak to them, at some length too, actu- ally. But about my mobile, which as I told you earlier was stolen. From my pocket, while I was on the bus. I couldn't believe it. I know who took it — she was almost brazen. I should have followed her, but by the time I realised what had happened the doors had shut and the bus had moved on. I hate those bendy buses — lethal contraptions.'

I stepped back to the sofa and sat on the arm. I didn't normally sit on the arm, as it was the one piece of decent furniture in the place and obviously being particular about fine things I'd always wanted to preserve it as best I could. 'Who knows who's been trying to get hold of me since then. You clearly. Though who knows who else. Anybody and everybody.'

'Are you limping as well?' Sean said, remaining by the window. 'You are, aren't you?' He couldn't stop looking across at Mia's, and to think what he might have been observing on any other evening. Did Norwegian women exercise so erotically? I doubted it.

'As well as what?'

'Your face. You still haven't told me what happened there.'

I thought about telling him that I'd slipped, in my new shoes, and crashed into a Tube barrier, in front of a whole concourse full of people, and not only smashed up my leg but dinged my face too. And I could have told him that I was being chased by a couple of hoodies at the time. But what was the point? To add to his fear of London? I was bored of not being dead straight — it didn't get you anywhere special. My brother deserved the truth, having come so far, and seeing as he was the one who would be bailing me out. Even though, or perhaps because I didn't like the way that he was still looking out of the window, yet was keeping a close eye on me as well. It was as if he were waiting for something — a signal perhaps — or someone.

'I'm ashamed to say I got in an argument with a bus driver. They're all thugs, worse than cabbies, if you ask me. This one the other night — I was going to see my friend Suze, in

Pimlico – decided to take exception to the fact that I was questioning his use of a mobile phone while he was driving. I didn't expect him to actually get out of his seat, and attack me on the pavement, but he did. I should have reported him, but as you know I have a pretty big distrust of the police. There were no witnesses willing to come forward and the police would never have believed me anyway – not if it was my word against that of a bus driver's. You know how these drivers are endlessly complaining about how threatened they feel and how dangerous their job is and how they need all the protection and support they can get. So I've been the victim of two horrific incidents on London buses in almost as few days. And will anything ever be done about it? This city, it's getting worse, and now with the recession hitting.'

'Come and live in Norway.' Sean laughed.

'What are you wearing on your feet?' Sean's shoes, or rather boots, were enormous great wedges of what appeared to be grey felt, with zips running up the middle – for God's sake. How had I not noticed them before?

'What do you think of them?' He lifted one off the floor and twirled it in the frigid air. 'I'm rather pleased with them. They're very comfortable and warm. A little too warm for London maybe.'

'Without doubt they are the most hideous shoes I've ever seen. Where the hell did you get them?'

'A friend of Anna's makes them. We've all got a pair. The kids love them.'

As always it took me a few moments to remember who Anna was. 'I'm not surprised. They couldn't be more Norwegian.'

'Matt, what's your problem with Norway?' At last Sean left the window and padded over to the middle of the room. There was real exasperation in his voice. 'I fly over here at a moment's notice, willing to help you in any way I can. And as ever, you just insult me and my family and where I live. For fuck's sake, Matt, you've never been to Norway. What do you know about it? What do you really and truly know about it?'

'More than enough.' As always it was impossible to have a sensible conversation with my brother. His emotions got in the way of his rationale, which I supposed was why he was the artist, if you could call him that, and I was the businessman. What did it really have to do with imagination? Except, for some extraordinary reason, he was the one with the money. And I knew I'd have to placate him somehow. I couldn't afford to blow this chance, and seeing him hunched in the centre of the room, anger and pain etched on his soft, hairy face – had he put on more weight? What were they feeding him? Elk? Whale? – and the ever-increasing darkness of the night behind him, framed in that huge, austere window, I felt a tweak of familial love. Well if not love, then kinship. I knew where he came from. I'd spent a considerable amount of my life in close proximity. We had the very same parents. 'You always take things so literally, Sean. Is that a Norwegian trait?'

'I don't know what's wrong with being straightforward, if that's what you mean. Norwegians certainly don't fuck you around like they do here. You know where you are there. Is that so objectionable?'

'You're missing my point, Sean.' Again, I could have said. Shame my mother had been so biased in her affections – she hadn't exactly been straightforward or fair – and too bad that Sean had felt her death so acutely. His literalism? But that was the small price he had to pay for all that love and attention, and money for that matter – how else could he have pursued his vocation so thoroughly? – which she'd foisted upon him. Would he be here now, in my humble home, I wondered, if he truly suspected that I'd had anything to do with her sudden demise, as, in his distress, he'd once intimated? 'It's a matter of interpretation, of subjectivity — you, of all people, should know all about that.'

'Don't tell me what I should or shouldn't know.'

I suddenly pictured my mother — Sean's mother — shortly before she died, her dark brown hair streaked with grey, falling across her damp forehead, her brown eyes, Sean's eyes, troubled and questioning, her limbs, her hands, having already gone weak, desperately trying to hang onto me, to hang onto life anyway. I could still hear that stuttering gasp as she attempted to take her final breath, but was defeated by time and a far stronger force. No one who has ever witnessed their mother dying will ever forget the bubble of foam, the snapping of a cord, and the sudden realisation that from now on it was all up to you. There was no more past. No more support or reproach. You were where the line stopped. A relief in a way, of course, as death invariably was. 'Why not? You're always telling me what to do or think. How to run my life. My business.'

'Matt, I'm losing the plot. You exhaust me. I'm fast getting to the point where I simply don't care.'

What would it be like to have no siblings either, not that I ever spent much time contemplating or worrying about the one I had. It wasn't as if he ever exactly cramped my style. But to be free of Sean, forever, and all his absurd notions of art and family, and all that straightforward smugness because he'd made so much fucking money out of it, while continually professing that he wasn't even interested in money. Well, I was. Had he left me anything in his will? He probably didn't have a will. He was the sort of person who thought they were invincible. Big, strong, full of life — a true force of nature. Though if he had a will it would be some hopelessly egalitarian or was it really totalitarian — what was the difference? — Norwegian idea of wealth distribution. I could just imagine it — a krone to the wife, a krone to the kids, and a krone to the little troll who lived down the lane. No one was invincible, of course.

'That's probably no bad thing,' I said. 'By and large people care too much. That's why nothing ever gets done. We're hampered by over-concern. By meddling.'

'That's your response? Fucking hell.'

My brother was back by the window, protected somewhat by his fleeces, multipocket trousers, and those ridiculous felt shoes. What resistance would I encounter if I took him by surprise? I hadn't had a fight with him for years, probably since we were in our early teens. I'd usually got the better of him then. He might have grown to be much bigger, but I was more calculating, more vicious. I raised myself from the arm of the sofa and stepped towards him. It was cash I needed, now, not in however many months' time, even presuming Norwegian probate law was as swift and efficient as one would expect, and that I was included in the damn will. He must have been carrying some cash. 'My response?'

Why was I so attuned to thoughts of such violent means to an end? My overactive imagination — as if. I'd been conditioned by my environment, the cut and thrust of life in the capital. He was my brother, and I was a changed man, wasn't I. A man on the up, only looking to offer some company, some security as we strolled arm in arm to the cashpoint.

'Sean, look sorry. Sorry. Why am I always saying sorry to you?' I was so close to him I could have put my hand on his shoulder and pulled him towards me and given him one of those brotherly bear hugs — I bet they did that a lot in Norway. 'I don't mean to be rude. I don't know what's wrong with me. I can't help it.' Now. I was focusing on his neck. Not the eyes. Can't let them see what you are thinking, planning. My elbow in his throat, that would be the first massive blow, and when he'd be gasping for breath and overcome by shock, that was the time to close in and apply unrelenting pressure until his limbs stopped flaying and his eyes rolled to the back of his head and his tongue lolled uselessly in his large, open mouth.

I really should turn to art, with my mind, my conditioning anyway. I heard a rustling, I heard movement behind me, I was sure. Backing away, I coughed. 'I guess I'm just jealous. Look what you've got. You've got everything. A family, a career, tons of money, and all that state healthcare, and who knows what other provisions and facilities, and practically no crime at all. The fjords and the midnight sun. It must be paradise. What possible worries could you have?'

'You, Matt. Believe it or not I'm worried about you. And, by all accounts, for good reason.'

All accounts? Not being able to bear such false sentiment, any sentiment from a fully grown man dressed as a – a Boy Scout just back from a winter wonderland adventure to the Arctic. I turned and as I think I must have suspected, something had just been pushed under the front door. I walked over to pick it up. It was a white envelope, sealed but with a message scrawled on the front.

'What is it?' said Sean, moving my way.

'Just a flyer, junk mail. I get this stuff all the time, day and night. There is no respect here, no privacy.' I crushed it in my hand, as tightly as possible, and stepped to the kitchenette and dropped it into the foul bin, amazed that someone would write such a thing, and not for the first time of course. Though that didn't mean I wasn't shocked, once more, by the money-grabbing, the spitefulness. Why should I be made to feel guilty? I was under siege – oh this country, this city, the mindset, the behaviour it seemed to foster.

I walked back into the main room. 'Why don't we get out of here, and grab something to eat? Have you been to St

John?' That idea suddenly perked me up no end. She could be there, my Bobbie-lookalike stand-in. She was every bit as frosty, yet alluring, as the one who had got away. For the keen observer there was opportunity everywhere – stick with the programme, Matt. 'I can tell you about the business,' I said hopefully.

'What is happening with your business? Any more developments since we spoke on the phone? Wow, it's not exactly the climate for expansion, is it? I was reading the *Metro* on my way here. I don't know where this is all going to end, but I'm glad I don't work in the City, or have massive debts.'

'Oddly enough, as I see it, for the canny, and with your eye on the long term – given the chance – there's still plenty of room to manoeuvre. Why do you think I'm working with the North Koreans? They're immune to these events. Though to be honest, I've been having a few communication problems. They are not the most open and straightforward people to deal with. I'm learning all the time.'

'You still haven't put me in the picture properly about Dubai. And didn't I hear you were off to Mallorca? On holiday?'

'Mallorca? Who told you that?' There could only have been one person who'd mention my mini-break to Sean. Roger. So Sean had been speaking to Roger. I should have known. Fat people could never keep their mouths shut. Who'd called who? Unless Roger really was wearing a wire and Sean had been informed of my Mallorcan plan by his own police handlers, and was detailed to probe me on this, and other delicate matters. But that was a conspiracy too far, surely. I wasn't being watched, I had simply been watching too much crap telly, with Bobbie – Sean was right. Besides, no one had anything on me, except possibly Church's. Sean was only being brotherly. I had to stop being so paranoid. This weather, this apartment, Barclays Bank, were all driving me mad.

'You did, didn't you?'

'I don't remember. Mallorca? There was a possibility of some work in Iran — yeh' — I was sounding like him already — 'I know, don't say, Roger's already had a go. But Mallorca, for a holiday? It's not the right time of year, is it? I can't think how you might have thought that. But if you want to discuss my future, or Matt Freeman Associates, let's do it over dinner. I really wouldn't mind getting out of here. It's freezing, and I'm starving.'

'It doesn't seem too cold to me.'

'Yeah, well it is London, not Norway. I'm finding it pretty damp and chilly.'

'You should wear more practical clothes.'

'Sean, I appreciate what you are saying, but the sort of gear you're kitted out in is not appropriate for what I do. I can't wear fleeces or felt shoes. Or quick-drying hiking trousers with snipped pockets all over the place.'

'You're too concerned with image, Matt. You always have been. In Norway no one bothers about image, at least not to the extent that they are uncomfortable all the time. We work with the environment, not against it. We adapt accordingly.'

I couldn't argue with him. 'Come on, let's have a nice dinner. You'll like St John, the food's simple and the waitresses are gorgeous.' Sean might have been boringly monogamous, but he wasn't averse to looking. As with Roger, it was always the men who professed undying love for their spouses who couldn't keep their eyes off fresh arse. I did put my hand on his shoulder now, trying to steer him towards the door. Time was moving forward, frighteningly so.

'No, sorry, Matt, I can't.'

'What?'

He stopped in the tiny hallway and faced me. 'I've arranged

to see some people, some artists – there are a couple of openings in Shoreditch. I'm not in London often and I thought I'd grab the chance. We always end up just arguing, and I wasn't sure you'd want to have dinner with me.'

'I don't get it. You've come all this way to help me, but you don't want to eat dinner with me?'

'Matt, I have a life too. Apart from everything else I didn't know you'd be free this evening, or that I'd even definitely find you here. I had to make alternative arrangements, just in case. They said they can put me up for the night, so I won't disturb you later.'

'But are you having dinner with these people too?'

'I don't know. I guess we might get an Indian. Is that a problem?'

'Not for me. It might be for you.' An Indian, instead of St John? Was this how artists lived, even rich ones? I couldn't believe this. Any of it. My brother had come all the way from Norway to see me, yet he wasn't even going to take me to a decent restaurant. Maybe he hadn't come all the way from Norway to see me, specifically. Maybe he felt he had to pop by because he was going to be only down the road, at a couple of openings. Why hadn't I been invited?

'For all I knew you might have made it up to this Bobbie person, and be having a cosy dinner, just the two of you. Or you could have been having supper with any of your other women. What's that woman called again? Suze? What's happened to her?'

'You don't want to know. And I haven't made it up with Bobbie. Far from it.'

'Sorry. Is she still giving you trouble?'

'I'm not going to talk about it.'

'You can tell me anything, you know, if it will help.'

'I said I don't want to talk about it.'

'It's not good to bottle everything up. Anna and I tell each other everything. In Norway people are very open.'

I could have killed him. 'Yeah, I'm sure they are.'

'Look, Matt, let's have supper tomorrow night. On me, wherever you want to go. This St John place? Does that sound all right? And we can discuss your business as well. Maybe I can help.'

Did he feel guilty? Not guilty enough. 'I might be busy. I need to check my schedule.'

'Try to keep it free. And frankly you could probably do with a bath and an early night tonight. You look dreadful.'

I looked dreadful? He could hardly talk, in all that scouting gear — and those great felt shoes. This was a perspective, an image that I thought I might never be able to embrace with much conviction. A new identity wasn't going to be easy. 'Thanks, thanks a lot.' Was this really happening? Sean was about to walk off, leaving me still broke and hungry.

'Would you mind if I got changed, and left my stuff here? I don't particularly want to cart it about. I'm seeing a couple of agents tomorrow, and have some expensive equipment. I'll pick it up in the morning.'

So even he wasn't prepared to spend a night out on the town, meeting mates, going to glamorous openings, having an Indian, dressed as a Norwegian and weighed down by a scruffy haversack. Thank God. But his real agenda was becoming more and more apparent. He didn't care about me. He was on a last-minute work trip. In fact it probably wasn't last minute. He'd have been planning it for months — in the way that rich people invariably sorted out the cheapest deals — and hadn't mentioned it on the phone the other day because he'd had no intention of seeing me. Only another call, this time from Roger and not fucking duplicitous Fran — did even Sean have doubts about her wily ways?

– had alerted him to the fact that his elder brother really was having a rough time, and needed help. 'Sure. Why not?' What could I say? 'And Sean, if you want to stay here tonight too, that's fine. There's the sofa. I've got some spare keys somewhere.'

'No,' I screamed. I couldn't believe it. All I wanted was some company, some background chatter, an air of normalcy, while I readied myself. Not *I'm A Celebrity*. It was still playing. Of course it was still playing. It was always playing. And there on my tiny, chronically outdated screen was that idiot, the one Bobbie fancied. But I thought he'd been voted off days ago. Was this some kind of trick, some new angle? Had they brought him back to fool the others? He was so pleased with himself, prancing about the camp, enjoying all the attention, the duplicity. Who were the producers on this show? Who was the audience? There was no time to switch channels, to search for more fulfilling entertainment. Enough. I pressed the off button, with the toe – toe? – of my new felt shoes. It was surprisingly effective. These things had considerable give. To attempt such a task with the Church's would quite possibly have resulted in considerable damage to the set. Besides after the agony of those brogues, the soft grey felt was blissful. I could have danced around my apartment. Instead, pulling on my brother's anorak and grabbing the haversack – it really was heavy, but surely not too heavy for normal baggage allowance, Sean would have made sure of that – I released the Yale and let myself out into the stinking corridor. Had Chamberlin, Powell and Bon reckoned on the quality of tenants when first drafting their great vision? Had they factored in enough provision for every variant and peculiarity? Maybe they had simply assumed people would be a little more considerate and neighbourly.

Fortunately there was no need to jump the barrier at

Barbican Tube. Unzipping one of my many trouser pockets, I retrieved a crisp £10 note, which I fed into the ticket machine. Though I didn't know what zone I was headed for. Three or four? I couldn't see the map. I didn't have time for this. Feeling flush, I bought a ticket that would see me through to Zone 4. Once on the platform, having located a Tube map, I began to regret the fact that I'd not taken a taxi. I had to change at Moorgate and Bank. However, a taxi would have taken forever, surely, and although I had plenty of cash it wasn't all in sterling. What was a krone worth? Who knew what the current exchange rate was. At the very least it had to be holding up well against the pound, and the euro. And the dollar. But the won? The North Koreans probably weren't foolish enough to expose their coinage to the international currency markets.

I also had Sean's credit card, for emergencies, and was more than certain what his PIN number would be – my dear, departed mother's date of birth. He was so predictable, and trusting. Fancy leaving your bum-belt on my sofa while you went into the bathroom to change. Fancy having a bum-belt in the first place. Fine, if you were embarking on a major trek across rugged, bandit country, but for a couple of days' business in London, ridiculous. He didn't think to check he had all his valuables before reslinging the thing around a more normal pair of trousers, and I was certain that he wouldn't notice he was missing some cash, cards, and his passport for that matter for ages – he was never one to get in the first shout. Or rush to pick up the tab. Despite his very considerable success and wealth.

It took me a few moments to realise that I was staring at myself, my reflection in the Tube window. The addition of Sean's pointed, woolly hat, complete with ear-warmers, on top of the well-padded anorak and the zipped hiking trousers, and of course the vast, felt shoes, made me almost unrecognisable. At least it made me look remarkably like Sean – I scratched my furry chin. Maybe not enough to fool Anna, but surely any passport control or immigration official. My stomach was churning with excitement, with anticipation – I was going to go far – and hunger. Sean would be tucking into his authentic Goan vindaloo by now – he always had to prove himself. Actually, he'd still be at an opening, playing the successful, handsome – in an all-Norwegian kind of way – artist, surrounded by acolytes. How did it feel? I'd find out, very soon. As it was, my get-up was not quite making me feel like an organic sculptor, who was at the top of his game. Patience, Matt. Resolve. You knew it was going to take some getting used to.

An *Evening Standard*, the West End final, was lying on the adjacent seat. There was no longer any mention of a melt-down on the front page, but starkly, *Serial Killer Fear*. Had my stop not have arrived, and had I not been encumbered with the haversack – there were straps everywhere – I'd have picked up the paper. Traversing the numerous steps and lengthy corridors of Bank, in increasing haste, I wasn't sure I needed to read the story. My mind was filled with grue-some images of Jeanette, and also Mia. Poor Mia, done in on her exercise mat – those Lycra shorts still wound around her broken neck. What were the chances? And, Suze, dear Suze. Was she safe, with her addiction to cruising? Her very particular likes and demands. I should ring her. I should have rung her. And Fran, Fran would be all right, cosseted in her comfy Queen's Park life. But missing a breath – this passageway was so airless – I thought of Bobbie. Of course I thought of Bobbie. My beautiful, idiosyncratic Bobbie. Was that why I hadn't heard from her? Did that explain the silence? Had she been nabbed by a psychopath?

No. Gosh I was hot. These clothes, though soft and full of give, were boiling. Sean was right. They were far too hot even for London. But I couldn't remove the hat, not now, because there was Bobbie. Incredibly. The coincidence, in this vast city – though didn't it happen all the time? But having just thought the very worst? Bobbie, really? Yes, Bobbie, my Bobbie. She was leaving the platform, walking towards me – had she just stepped off the DLR? She was looking good, she was looking great, as ever, in her way. Red jacket, orange skirt, green tights. Was the traffic-light look in? And no haversack for her, but a stylish, pale peach leather holdall – a Louis Vuitton? Could I ever have got used to the colour combinations, those startlingly blue eyes and that so very dark, lopsided hair? Or that sharp figure, which she was so casual with? She was just too much of a good thing. Her new man, the man who she was clutching the arm of, would be in for some ride.

However, he appeared more than capable, in his expensive mac – a Burberry, if not an Aquascutum – and with his all but shaved head and big black glasses – her choice, unless he'd already got there first – and tall, trim physique. As they passed, and Bobbie didn't so much as glance my way – I wasn't sure whether I was pleased or not – he reminded me a little of myself, of how I used to be, or I supposed how I could have been had I stuck to Bobbie's style dictates, her way of viewing the world, and been ten years younger. He looked solvent. He certainly didn't look like a sacked banker, or remotely corporate. He was too stylish, too confident. He oozed success – always Bobbie's weak spot. I didn't want to know exactly what he did, that had so enraptured her. The shop, the brand he no doubt worked for. Or where the hell they had just been.

Stepping aboard the DLR I vowed not to think further of him, or her, not to trouble myself with their prospects, and their brief, shady, devious past. Maybe he was in the media, or in fashion like her. Perhaps he was an artist. Resolve,

Matt. Purpose. I should have been happy that she was alive. Surely. That I was alive too, trundling out of the tunnel and up into Docklands, an illuminated Wren spire here, a dismal block of flats there. My time was coming, oh yes. Finally I'd be able to realise my full potential, unchecked, unhampered by outdated institutions and shallow convictions. Shadwell, Limehouse, Westferry. A gang of hoodies here – was one of them limping? – a vacant lot there. The glowing facades of Canary Wharf slipping away to my right – HSBC, Barclays, Credit Suisse. I was the artist now, the one with the imagination, the vision, the energy – Bank of America, KPMG, fucking Barclays – ready for any bandit country, equipped with portfolios and PowerPoint presentational material, courtesy of a smart, new MacBook Air and detailing a more organic, more honest, more sustainable way of life. I could go on and on.

There, across a black expanse of Thames, the O2 Arena, seemingly preparing for take-off, but in reality, the appearance, on stage, any minute, of Beyoncé – or Britney – so I vaguely remembered reading, in the *Standard*, or maybe it was the *Metro*, a few days ago. One of the performers was in the capital, on a sell-out tour. As always.

And far over there, to my left, sparsely lit, were the cranes at Stratford, the mechanical jungle that would become the Olympic Village. Hope for some. For plenty, if they finished of course. But not me. I was speeding, or at least still trundling to pastures new – through Canning Town, a slight jolt or three, and on past a sea of fancy newbuilds, many looking dark and vacant – waiting, forlornly, for that promised flood of first-time buyers – on to West Silvertown and the old Tate & Lyle factory, a reminder of a golden era, or the revisionist idea of one, past the ExCeL exhibition centre, the gleaming domes of the Thames Barrier and the dim, derelict Millennium Mills – an opportunity that would never be seized – and to Pontoon Dock, a great white wedge of an apartment block, an attempt at modernist architecture – would Chamberlin, Powell and Bon be pleased? – on my right, stretching to the river, and with the runway lights of London City Airport now almost straight ahead.

I didn't care where I went, as long as it was cool. Stuffed in this gear, my feet were beginning to melt. And they'd have, with open arms, and a multitude of financial incentives, to endorse contemporary artists. I had a slight inkling that North Korea might not be so appreciative of my efforts. How hard could bashing out art be? But the market would simply be too limited, too regulated, too protected. I'd probably be better off somewhere more Germanic, or Scandinavian. Perhaps I was always destined for Scandinavia, for Norway, for my brother's backyard – the security of family, and forgiveness. Was openness, as long as it was well regulated, and consensually approved, if not legally enforced, that scary?

There were more jolts leaving Pontoon Dock, and more as the train crept up the track towards the City Airport platform. 'Hurry up,' I was saying, as the lights went out and the train stopped, violently. Silence. I could see a small plane taking off, climbing rapidly and banking away into the night. What time did flights finish for the night at this airport? Surely, I wasn't going to be too late. I should have headed instead for Luton, where I was certain planes came and went all hours. Though the train was sparsely filled angry chatter soon began. There was talk of signal failure, a power cut, terrorist activity, but no official word over the Tannoy. For minutes. Perhaps they weren't able to relay the nature of the problem from mission control because there was no power with which to do so. London Electricity had pulled the plug – TfL couldn't pay the bill, their credit suddenly frozen.

I had this growing feeling that I was stuck in a dreadful loop, most certainly not of my making, and that it would be impossible to move on, however optimistic and determined I was. Was this what it felt like in North Korea, if you weren't one of Kim Jong-il's cronies? Even if you were one of his cronies. The dreams I once had.

'Hey,' the passenger next to me said, 'you going to the airport?' He was American. I couldn't tell what age because of the darkness in the carriage. Though he wasn't young.

'Yeh,' I said. 'Hopefully.'

'Does this happen a lot?'

'Yeh. All the time.'

'Some way to run a city. My flight for Zurich leaves in twenty minutes. What about yours? Where are you headed?'

'Oh, Trondheim, eventually – it's in Norway. I have to go via Amsterdam.'

'Norway, hey? You going for work?'

I really wasn't ready for this conversation. I was never ready for any conversation with a stranger on public transport. But knowing I'd soon have to extend a certain warmth to my fellow countrymen, and women, I stopped thinking about shifting down the carriage in the almost pitch black, and said, 'No, I live there.'

'You live there? Wow. Must be cold this time of the year, though you look prepared for it.'

He'd noticed my outfit before the lights ceased. 'Yeh, it's pretty cold, but you learn to live with it. You adapt.'

'What kind of work are you in?'

How many more minutes were we going to be stuck here? What else was he going to ask? 'I'm an artist. A sculptor.'

'You're kidding? I run a gallery in Zurich – Salomon Fine Art.'

'I've heard of it.'

'Is that right? What's your name? Might I have heard of you? I'm Harry Salomon.'

Was it possible to feel any hotter? On the verge of ripping off my get-up, the lights came on and the train jolted forward, and with a whine we gathered speed. He had extraordinarily blue eyes, a heavily lined face and a neatly trimmed grey beard. 'You won't have heard of me, not yet.'

Acknowledgements

Three people got me here – my editor James Gurbutt, my agent David Miller and my partner in crime Rachel Potter. You are the masters of my universe and I will be eternally grateful.